Trusting Liam

Also By Molly **McAdams**

Letting Go
Sharing You
Capturing Peace (novella)
Deceiving Lies
Needing Her (novella)
Forgiving Lies
Stealing Harper (novella)
From Ashes
Taking Chances

Trusting Liam

A Taking Chances and Forgiving Lies Novel

Molly McAdams

wm

WILLIAM MORROW

An Imprint of HarperCollins*Publishers*

F
MCA

TRUSTING LIAM. Copyright © 2015 by Molly Jester. All rights reserved. Printed in the United States of America. No part of this book may be used or reproduced in any manner whatsoever without written permission except in the case of brief quotations embodied in critical articles and reviews. For information, address Harper-Collins Publishers, 195 Broadway, New York, NY 10007.

HarperCollins books may be purchased for educational, business, or sales promotional use. For information e-mail the Special Markets Department at SPsales@harpercollins.com.

FIRST EDITION

Library of Congress Cataloging-in-Publication Data has been applied for.

ISBN 978-0-06-235843-1

15 16 17 18 19   OV/RRD   10 9 8 7 6 5 4 3 2 1

To everyone who has a love/hate relationship with me
because of Chase . . . I hope you enjoy Liam.

Note for the Readers

While you can read this novel without ever having read anything of mine, it is a continuation of stories and a combination of series. Some things will make much more sense if you've read *Taking Chances* and *Stealing Harper*, as well as *Forgiving Lies* and *Deceiving Lies*.

Trusting Liam

Prologue

May 15
Kennedy

CRACKING AN EYE open, I immediately shut it against the harsh light coming into the room and bit back a groan as I felt the pounding in my head. Making another attempt—this time with both eyes—I squinted at the unfamiliar hotel room and blinked a few times, then let my eyes open all the way as I took in my surroundings. Well, as much of them as I could without moving.

There was a heavy arm draped uncomfortably over my waist, a forehead pressed to the back of my head, a nose to the back of my neck, and an erection to my butt. What. The. Hell. I was naked; he was naked. *Why are we naked, and who is behind me?* If I wasn't seconds from screaming for someone to help me, I might have snorted. The *why* was obvious, there was a familiar ache between my legs, and my lips felt puffy from kissing and where he'd bitten down on them.

I inhaled softly. *He. Him.* Oh God.

Flashes from last night took turns assaulting me with the pounding in my head. Impromptu trip to Vegas with the girls after finals ended. Dancing. Club. Drinks. Arctic-blue eyes captivating me.

More drinks and dancing. *Him* holding me close, and not close enough. Lips against mine. Stumbling into a room. Hands searching. *His* tall, hard body pressing mine against the bed—still not close enough.

My eyes immediately went to my left hand, and I exhaled slowly in relief when I didn't find a ring there. *Thank God, the last thing I need is a marriage as result of a drunken night in Vegas.* I rolled my eyes. The last thing I needed was a man in my life, period. And if my family didn't kill me for it, I would have died from embarrassment if I had ended up with a ring on my finger after last night. Because unlike what everyone loves to believe so they can feel better about their own dirty deeds while in Sin City, what happens in Vegas doesn't always stay in Vegas.

Trying not to wake him, I slowly slid out from under his arm and off the bed to search for my clothes. Once I was dressed, I told myself to just leave, but I couldn't help it—I turned to look at him in the light. I needed to be sure I hadn't made *him* up.

The images from last night tore through my mind again when I saw the large, tattooed arm resting where my body had just been. The muscles were well defined, even when *he* was relaxed, and the face had a boyish charm now that *he* was asleep. Such a difference from the predatory stare and knowing smirk I kept seeing in my mind. Before I could stop myself, I gently ran my fingers through his dirty-blond hair that, now in the sunlight, I could see had a red tint to it. And I knew if he opened them, those arctic-blue eyes would once again captivate me.

But I couldn't risk that.

I'd already stayed too long; I'd already made a mistake with him. Drunken one-night stands weren't my thing. Drunken one-night stands with strangers in Vegas were even worse.

Straightening, I turned and walked quietly from the room.

1

May 21 . . . One year later
Kennedy

"WHY ARE YOU trying to doing this to me?" Kira yelled as she stood from where she'd been sitting on the couch.

I looked over at my identical twin to see a look of horror on her face, and waited for the freak-out that I knew was only seconds away. Shifting my attention back to our parents, I mumbled, "Told you it wouldn't go over well."

"But—you can't—Kennedy, why—Zane's in Florida," Kira sputtered out, and I rolled my eyes at the same time as my dad.

"Is that supposed to mean something to me?" Dad asked as he crossed his large tattooed arms over his chest.

Not willing to give Kira time to respond to that kind of question, I started talking over Dad before he could finish. "Did you ever think that maybe a little distance might be a good thing for the two of you? And did you *not* hear Dad? These guys are out of prison, Kira!" I shouted, punctuating the last few words in case she'd missed the memo the first time around.

"Maybe Zane will go with you," Mom offered with a sympathetic look on her face that I knew was as well practiced as it was a lie. The worry was still there in her eyes, as was the eagerness to get us away from Florida . . . and it wasn't exactly a secret that we all wanted Kira to get space from Zane.

They'd been together since we were fifteen, and the more time went on, the more Kira's world revolved around only him. It was annoying.

"And leave his job?" Kira countered.

"Well, then maybe this will be good for you, like Kennedy said. Get a break from Zane so you can see other options. You girls are only twenty-two, you just graduated from college, and you're too young to be getting serious anyway, Kira, just ask Kennedy. You'll regret not enjoying life first."

"Wow, thanks for that, Mom. What's that supposed to mean?"

Before she could respond to me, my dad's head jerked back and he sent Mom a look. "What the hell *is* that supposed to mean? You were twenty-one when we got engaged."

"Do I look like I'm not enjoying life suddenly? What did I miss?" I asked Kira as Dad spoke, but she didn't make any indication that she'd even heard me.

"Seriously, Kash?" Mom shot Dad a look that even I was impressed by. "That was different. *We* were different. She's *only* dated Zane."

"Can we get back to the more important discussion?" I cut in before Dad could respond, and looked back to Kira. "*I'm* going to California. *You're* going with me. *Zane* can deal with it."

"You can't do this! I'm not going!" Kira shrieked as the tears started.

"You act like I'm giving either of you a choice. Both of you need to start accepting this."

My eyes widened at my dad's dark tone, and I shot right back, "You act like you still have a say in our lives. You haven't for four years. And if you remember, I'm going along with what you want without complaint. So don't throw me into the same category as Kira when she's the only one fighting you on this."

One dark eyebrow rose, and I saw Kira sink back onto the couch from the look he was giving. Too bad I was just like him: hardheaded and stubborn. I might be my sister's mirror image, but I was nothing like her. I raised one eyebrow back at him, and Mom sighed.

"I don't know how I put up with you two sometimes," she groaned, rubbing her hand over her forehead. Looking at Kira, she said, "You're going to California, no more discussion. This is for your safety, why can't you see that?"

"I'm not going!" Kira sobbed. "Who cares if some guys Dad put away *years* ago are out of prison?"

I snorted, but before I could respond, Uncle Mason's deep voice sounded directly behind us. "These men do."

I turned quickly to look at him, and tried not to laugh when he gave Dad a questioning look and mouthed, "Zane?" as he gestured to Kira.

"Is there any other reason she would be freaking out like this?" I asked as I stood to go give him a hug.

"Are you both packed?" he asked.

"Packed?" Kira yelled again. "They just told us! I haven't even called Zane!"

"Oh my God, no one cares."

"Kennedy," Mom chastised, but I knew she was thinking the same thing.

As soon as Kira was out of the room, I sighed and headed to my room to pack as much as I could. Kira was already packing and sobbing into her phone when I passed her room, and I somehow managed to hold back an eye roll. Never mind that our parents had just told us that our family was being threatened by members of a gang our dad and uncle Mason had put away over twenty years ago. A gang whose members had kidnapped our mom

before we were born and held her for over a month in an attempt
to free their main members from prison. Or that a chunk of them
were getting out of prison within the next handful of months. Or
that Kira and I were the main targets of their threats. Nope . . .
none of that mattered to Kira right now. What mattered was that
we were going to be living in California for the time being—close
to our mom's side of the family—and Zane wouldn't be going with
us. No Zane meant devastation in Kira's world. She couldn't even
get dressed without telling everyone about a memory of wearing
that outfit with Zane, or that it was one of his many favorites.

Snatching a hair band off my desk, I pulled my thick, black
hair into a messy bun on the top of my head and started packing.
I didn't turn to face Kira when she came into my room ten minutes later, but I knew she was there.

"How could you do this to me?" she asked quietly, her words
breaking with emotion. "You're supposed to be on my side,
you're *always* supposed to be on my side. And you went behind
my back and planned this with Mom and Dad without even
warning me?"

I glanced over my shoulder, my eyebrows rising at her assumption. "I didn't plan shit, Kira. They told me while you were
talking to Zane right before they asked you to get off the phone.
They just wanted me to know because they thought you would
freak out and they needed me to be able to try to talk you into it
calmly—rather than hitting us both with the news at the same
time. The only difference between you and me is I have no problem with this move because I'm not stupid enough to think that
the gang won't actually make good on their threats if we stay
here. Or try to."

I went back to packing, and there was a couple minutes of
silence before she said, "I know why you're all really doing this.
Don't think for a second that I'm stupid enough not to realize
this is about Zane."

I released a heavy breath and shook my head. "Despite what you think, this has nothing to do with you and your boyfriend. But I *do* think that this is something we need to do, and I think it will be good for us."

"I won't forgive you for this. You of all people should realize how much this is going to kill me."

My breath caught, but I didn't reply. I knew I couldn't without lashing out at her. Without another word, she left my room. The only sounds were her soft cries and her feet on the hardwood as she walked away.

"SO NOW THAT you have us on a private jet—which just makes this all the more weird, by the way—do you mind telling us details about where we'll be spending the next however long?" I asked Uncle Mason a few hours later.

"Didn't your mom and dad tell you everything?"

I gave him a look that he immediately laughed at.

"Okay, tell me what you know, and I'll fill in the blanks."

"Basically, all I know is that Juarez and a handful of others from his crew are up for probation within a few months of each other starting next week. They're somehow threatening us—but more specifically, Kira and me—and Mom and Dad think it would be best if we weren't near Tampa. Since we just graduated and don't have a reason to stay up in Tallahassee anymore, the only other place to go is California, near Mom's family, and we'll be there for an undetermined amount of time."

"I wasn't told most of that," Kira muttered from where she was sulking across the aisle.

"You *were* told that," I shot back. "All of that. You just couldn't get past the California-equals-no-Zane part, and flipped while they told you the rest!"

Before we could start on another war, Uncle Mason spoke up. "You'll be just north of San Diego, near your uncle Eli. He's already been looking into places for you to live, and your parents are working something out with them for a car."

"Lovely. Sounds like everyone is already completely filled in," Kira sneered.

Uncle Mason didn't respond for a long time, he just sat there staring at Kira with a somber expression. It was so unlike him. "I don't want you two to have to do this any more than you do, trust me. Your dad and I know better than anyone what it's like to pick up and move at a moment's notice and not be able to have a say in it, so we know what you're going through."

Kira mumbled something too low for me to hear, but it was obvious in her expression that she didn't agree with him.

After a subtle shake of my head, I looked back at Uncle Mason and tapped his leg with my foot to get his attention again. "Okay, so we've heard about Juarez's gang and what happened with Mom being taken. But here's what I don't understand and am having a little bit of trouble with. Why, after so much time has passed, do you think it's them threatening us? Wouldn't they be over it by now? I mean, couldn't it just as easily be someone you've arrested recently, and you're just jumping ahead and thinking it's Juarez?"

Uncle Mason was shaking his head before I even finished asking my questions. "No. It may have been twenty-three years ago, but we haven't forgotten what happened, and we know for a fact they haven't and are still holding a grudge, because there have been letters delivered to your dad."

"What did they say?"

"It doesn't matter."

"What did they say?" I asked louder, and Kira leaned toward us in her seat to hear his response.

"I said it doesn't—"

"We deserve to know!" I snapped.

After a beat of silence, he admitted, "They said, 'Can't wait to meet the rest of your family,' or 'How are those daughters of yours?'" Uncle Mason sighed heavily and looked out the window for a few seconds.

"That's it?" I asked when he didn't continue. "I mean, that's really creepy but it doesn't prove much of anything."

"It does, because at the bottom it had the gang's symbol. A symbol your dad and I used to have tattooed on us when we were undercover. A symbol they left spray-painted on your parents' wall after kidnapping your mom."

"Oh," I breathed, and Uncle Mason sent me a look.

"Yeah. 'Oh.'"

May 27
Liam

SQUEEZING CECILY'S WAIST once, I deepened the kiss for a few seconds before pulling away. A smirk crossed my face when she tried to follow me. "I gotta go."

"Just a little longer?" she asked huskily as she pulled on my tie, bringing us closer together.

"I can't. You know I have to get to that meeting." Grabbing her slender wrist in my hand, I took my tie from her firm grip and sent her a look.

"Of course, the so-called meeting that no one else in the office seems to know about." Her full lips pouted, and I exhaled slowly at the annoying look.

"You know about it."

Cecily smacked my arm and huffed. "Only because you told me."

"That's not my problem. Besides, it might be a bad thing that I'm the only one. Who knows? You may get your wish, I might be getting fired."

She smiled wryly and wrapped her arms around my neck before pressing her mouth to mine. "Now, that definitely sounds like a meeting I want to happen," she murmured against my lips.

"Power-hungry bitch," I growled, and kissed her hard once more before backing away.

"Man-whore."

"Hasn't stopped you."

Her gaze raked over me as I backed toward the door before snapping up to my face. "No, it hasn't."

I grinned and nodded in her direction. "Are you going to leave my office?"

She slid off the desk and walked around to sit in my chair. "I don't know, maybe I'll sit in here awhile to get used to what my new office feels like."

"I haven't gotten fired yet." Not bothering to wait, I walked out of my office and left Cecily in there. I looked behind me to watch the door shut as I fixed my tie, a soft smile tugging at my lips as I thought about the girl in there.

There was no bullshit when it came to Cecily and me. I didn't like relationships, labels, or being tied down to any one girl; and she liked guys who demanded control. It was the complete opposite of who she was, but I wasn't going to question it. She wasn't shy about her need to be at the top of everything—including a company—nor was she shy about her willingness to step on any and everyone to get there.

She wanted my job, I'd known that before we started sleeping together, but she couldn't have it. And despite our current status and her greed-filled eyes, she wasn't one to sleep her way to the top—we just happened to be a nice distraction for each other at work.

I looked up just in time to stop myself from running into the man standing in the hallway. He hadn't been moving; he was just standing there with his arms crossed over his chest, one eyebrow raised as he studied me.

"Excuse me," I said, and moved to walk around him—he moved with me. My eyebrows slanted down, and I looked up at him. Yeah. Up. I was six-two. To have to look up at someone was saying something. "Can I help you?" I asked when I noticed his mirrored movement hadn't been a mistake; he was still staring down at me with a calculating expression.

The man didn't move, and he didn't say anything. With a huff, I gave him a once-over and smirked. My dad owned a boxing gym, meaning I'd grown up around some of the leanest, deadliest fighters around, as well as some of the biggest meat heads. But this fucker was massive. "If you don't mind, I have somewhere to be. And lay off the steroids, old man."

When I went to move around him this time, he let me pass; but when I looked over my shoulder, he was turned around and glaring at me with that same expression before he glanced behind him toward my office.

My footsteps faltered and I racked my brain trying to think of any mention of another guy Cecily might be seeing—one who would come looking for her at work—but I came up with nothing. And somehow I knew in the way he was glaring at me again that he wasn't looking at me like he was ready to fight. He looked like he was frustrated with what he was seeing in me.

Shaking my head as if to clear it, I looked ahead of me and continued down the halls to my boss's office. Before I got there, I stopped at his secretary's desk. "Hey, call security. There's a guy in here I've never seen before, and I don't think he's supposed to be here. Height is probably six-five. Weight is around two seventy or two eighty. The guy is solid muscle, tan, Caucasian, black hair." I watched as she jotted everything down. "Got it?"

"Yeah," she said as she grabbed the phone, but I didn't wait to hear the conversation.

Walking toward the office beside her, I knocked on the door as I opened it, and flashed a smile at my boss, Eli Jenkins.

"Hey, Liam, come in and have a seat."

I sat in one of the two chairs on the other side of his desk, and waited for whatever he had to say as he sat directly next to me. Despite what I'd told Cecily, I wasn't worried about losing my job. I knew Eli liked me and my work, and I was on the same path he'd taken in this industry. But that didn't mean he didn't know about Cecily and me, and our interoffice relationship wasn't exactly allowed.

Before he could say anything else, his eyes snapped up when the door to his office quickly opened.

"Two hundred and seventy to two hundred and eighty pounds? Hardly."

I turned quickly at the deep voice, and my eyes widened at the roided-out guy from the hall.

"Two hundred eighty-five, actually. I'm proud of those extra five pounds."

"Who the fuck are you?" I asked, standing up from the chair. Turning to look at Eli, I pointed at the guy. "I had security called on him."

"He called me 'old man,' can you believe that?" The guy snorted. "At least you were right about the height. Good one, kid." He walked around to sit in Eli's desk chair, and I looked back and forth between him and where Eli was sitting next to me.

Eli rolled his eyes. "Liam Taylor, it's not exactly a pleasure to introduce you, but this is Mason Gates. He's a close friend of my sister and her husband."

"You *still* don't like me?" Mason asked Eli. "It was twenty-three years ago."

Eli shot him a hard look. "She's my sister. No, I still don't like you." Glancing over to me, Eli explained, "He also dated my other sister."

Mason snorted a laugh at the word *dated,* but didn't say anything else to piss off Eli. Nodding in my direction, he said, "He's good. Probably dumb as shit, but he's funny, and he was pretty spot-on about me. Minus the steroids."

"I'm lost," I whispered to the room, and then looked at Mason. "What was your deal in the hall?"

"I already knew I wasn't going to like you. Any other questions?"

"Mason," Eli barked, then looked at me. "Act like he's not here. For whatever reason, he felt the need to be here when I talked with you."

"Okay . . ." I said, drawing out the word. "Talk to me about what?"

"Mason just brought my nieces to California from Florida so they could get away from a situation going on back home, and they're not exactly happy about being here. They know they need to be here, and that's all that's keeping them from going back to Florida, but they need something to do to keep them busy. A job, friends . . . anything. And I was hoping that you would be able to help with that."

I waited to see if he would add anything, and when he didn't, I shrugged. "I—sure. I mean, I don't know how much I can do to help them find friends, but if they're old enough for the gym, I know my dad is looking for a few people."

Mason cleared his throat, and Eli gave him an annoyed look before saying, "We also need to make sure that one of them, Kira, doesn't try to run back home. She has a boyfriend and is taking the separation harder than her sister. My sister and brother-in-law trust my judgment to find someone who can do that. I trust you as much as I trust my own son, and I think you and your connections will be exactly what they need to settle in here."

I laughed hesitantly and looked at both of them for a few seconds. "Are you serious? I'm not a babysitter, Eli; we work in advertising. Besides that, I'm twenty-four, what do you expect me to do with these girls that will make it seem okay for me to even act like their friend?"

"I knew I didn't like him," Mason blurted out, and stood. "Meeting over."

"Sit down," Eli ordered, but didn't look to make sure he did. "Liam, my nieces just turned twenty-two, they're close to your age. And no one is asking you to babysit them."

"You want me to make sure one of them doesn't run back to her boyfriend! That sounds like babysitting," I argued.

"Still don't like him," Mason chimed in, but Eli and I didn't bother responding to him.

"I don't need you to watch her every move, I was just hoping that you could maybe include them in whatever you and your friends are doing one or two times over the weekends. See if the girls get along with you or your friends, try to get them to have a good time so they won't focus on how much they don't want to be here. You don't have to give up your life for them, Liam. And if you aren't willing to do that, and if your dad does have space at the gym for them, that would be more than enough. I won't ask you for anything else." When I just sat there staring at him, Eli leaned closer. "Please. I'd have my son do this, but you know he's backpacking through Europe this summer with his friends."

If it had been something as simple as inviting his nieces to a party, I would've done it in a heartbeat. But with Mason there— whatever his real reasons—and with the part that still sounded like I'd be babysitting them, I knew there was something else behind this than the girls just needing to be introduced to a few people. The fact that there was a "situation" back in Florida, and that they didn't want to be here, only confirmed that thought. But Eli was my mentor. I'd interned for him in college, and he'd hired me on after the internship had ended. He'd continued help-ing me throughout the last couple years of college, always pushing me to work harder and be better, and then did the same so I would work my way up in his company after I'd graduated. He'd done more than I could've ever asked for, and this was the first thing he'd asked of me. No matter how odd it seemed, I knew I couldn't tell him no.

"Okay," I finally agreed. "I'll call my dad. I know for a fact that he needs new people for the drink station in the gym. I'll see if he can interview them and let you know when."

"Perfect," Eli said on a relieved sigh. "They've already been here a week, I know they need to get out of their condo."

I nodded and reluctantly said, "And I'll make sure whichever one you mentioned won't go running back to her boyfriend. I'm sure a bunch of us will end up at the beach this weekend, at least. I'll let you know when I do."

"Still don't like him," Mason said again. "I vote we find someone else."

I rolled my eyes and looked over at him. "Why did you even need to be here?"

"A question I've already asked a few times," Eli mumbled.

Mason's teasing tone and expression quickly disappeared, leaving him looking at me the exact way he had been in the hallway. "I'm here because someone needs to tell you that you aren't to touch either of them. Rachel and Kash may trust Eli's choice in *you* being the one to help them out, that doesn't mean I do. No one chose you so you would have another girl to fuck."

"Mason," Eli snapped, but Mason's gaze never left me.

One eyebrow rose, and a short laugh burst from my chest. "Excuse me?"

"You didn't try to hide the girl who was in your office earlier, and that already makes me not like you as much as I could. You see an opportunity in a girl, and you take it. Trust me, I get it. I was the same way when I was your age, which is why Eli still hates me. But those girls mean the world to Eli, to me, and to their parents. This is me warning you now: if you touch one of those girls, you will have all three of us on you. And their dad is the last person you want to piss off. Your job is to be their friend. Nothing more."

"Noted," I huffed as I stood to leave the office. "Anything else, Eli?"

He shook his head at Mason, and sighed when he looked back at me. "Just remind Cecily that I don't want her in your office."

The corner of my mouth tilted up and I nodded as I turned to leave. "I'll call my dad and let you know what he says."

"I appreciate it, Liam. Really," he called out as I reached the door.

Mason snorted. "Still don't like him."

The feeling was mutual.

2

May 29
Kennedy

I STOOD THERE staring at the closed door for an unknown amount of minutes after Uncle Mason left. The moment he'd walked out of the door and gotten into his rental car, I knew that was it. That this was all real. We were in the Golden State instead of the Sunshine State. A place where the beaches and air were different, and where girls said the word *like* too often.

It was easy to agree to move here when my parents told me everything. It almost seemed fun. Kira and I had left home for college, but hadn't left Florida; and now that we'd graduated, a big change seemed like something we could both use.

But then we got here and I remembered that I'd never actually liked California. That mixed with the facts that our only cousin in California was not even in the country for the next couple months, and that Kira hadn't stopped crying about Zane since Mom and Dad broke the news to her eight days ago, had me slowly but surely regretting all of this.

I felt trapped—or maybe that was just Kira's depression and anxiety rubbing off on me—my skin was drier than all get-out, and

I felt like I couldn't breathe because there wasn't one ounce of humidity here unless it was early in the morning. *And we were in motherfucking California*. My shoulders fell, and I wondered for the fiftieth time today why I'd ever thought this was going to be a good thing.

Turning around, I looked at our condo and blew out a long breath. It was nice, but only held the basics. Even being in here for over a week now, I still wasn't used to it—and I didn't know if it would ever feel like home, no matter how long we were here.

I walked over to Kira's room, but instead of knocking, I stood at the door and listened to her pained sobs before deciding against trying to talk to her again. After wandering around for another minute or two, I sank down on the couch and stared at the dark TV screen. I didn't make a move for the remote, and I didn't care that I was staring at nothing. I was afraid that if I turned on the TV, I would see commercials for things in California, and it would depress me even more.

I couldn't hold back a relieved sigh when my phone began ringing—but my happiness at the distraction was short-lived after I dug it out of my pocket and stared at the unknown *California* number.

"Motherfucking California," I muttered just before I hit the button to accept the call. "Hello?"

"Hey! Just wanted to make sure you knew how to get to the gym."

My brow scrunched in confusion. "Uncle Eli? What number are you calling from, and what gym? Do you know who you called?"

He laughed softly. "Yes, sweet niece of mine, I know who I called. This is my office phone. And what do you mean, what gym? The gym you and Kira have an interview at in less than an hour."

"What interview?"

"The one—son of a bitch," he murmured, and let out a heavy exhale. "Did Mason not tell you that you both had interviews today?"

"No, he didn't! What gym?"

Uncle Eli said something unintelligible and groaned loudly. "A friend of mine has openings at his gym for the drink station, and was kind enough to agree to interview you. But I should've known that Mason wouldn't say anything. He doesn't exactly like the guy who set this up. Can you be ready soon? The interviews are supposed to be at twelve thirty P.M."

"Seriously? I don't know! How far away is it?" I asked as I ran to Kira's room. Throwing open the door, I didn't wait for her to tell me to leave—as she had so many times this week—I just shouted, "Stop crying and get ready! We have interviews!"

"I'm not going," she said automatically, without looking at me.

"Yes, you are," I hissed. "Uncle Eli set these up for us. You'll go and thank him for it later. Get ready!"

"It's not far from you; ten, fifteen minutes tops," Uncle Eli said distractedly. "I'll text you the address, try not to be late. But I'll explain it if you are."

"Thank you! I love you!" I said quickly before hanging up and running to my bathroom to fix my makeup and hair. I didn't check on Kira again; if she ended up not getting ready and deciding not to go, then that was on her. I needed this. I needed to get out of this condo so I wouldn't continue feeling the way I had been. I needed something to look forward to that wasn't a new day of moping because I was in the wrong state.

May 29
Liam

"GIVE IT UP, old man," I said on a laugh as Dad got ready to throw the wadded-up paper from his sandwich into the trash. "You never make it anyway."

Wadding up my own wrapper, I eyed him as he stared down

the trash can for a few more seconds before carefully tossing his wrapper—and missing. I immediately tossed mine in and grinned mockingly.

"Bastard," he scoffed.

"Don't take the loss too hard, it's not the first time."

He smiled and rolled his eyes before checking his watch. "Tell me about these girls coming in. You didn't say much on the phone."

I held my arms out to the side, then dropped them. "I don't know anything about them other than they're Eli's nieces, and twenty-two. He just said he wanted them to try to find something to do here, or get some friends. Apparently they're not happy they're here."

My dad gave me a look. "Not happy they're here?" he asked, and when I nodded in confirmation, he shook his head. "If they're twenty-two and not happy here, why don't they go where they *are* happy."

"Question of the week, Dad. I have no clue. But I owe Eli, so I told him I'd arrange the interviews. You don't have to hire them, I really don't care either way . . . I know you've already had a handful of people apply; so does Eli. I think he's just hoping that if they get out once, they'll continue to do so."

"Jesus, you're making them sound even worse. I'm expecting awkward, shy girls who never leave their house."

The phone in his office beeped a second before one of the receptionists told him the girls were here for the interviews, and Dad exhaled heavily as he stood up.

"I'm sure this will go over well," he mumbled sarcastically, and slapped at my shoulder as he passed by me. "Thanks for the lunch, bud. Go see your mom soon, she's been complaining about how long you've been gone."

"Yeah, all right. At least be nice to them for Eli's sake," I called out just as he walked out the door.

He looked around the doorframe with an amused expression. "What is that supposed to mean? I *am* the nice one around here. I could always let Konrad do the interview . . ." He trailed off, and I shook my head as I laughed.

"I know you are, but you also look scary as shit. We don't want to scare them so bad that I get fired."

With a loud laugh, he turned and walked away. My dad had owned McGowan's Gym since sometime around when I was born, and he and his business partner, my uncle Konrad, had changed this place a lot over the years. It was a fighting gym, and always would be, but instead of a place for people to only work out or train for the ring, they now offered classes depending on what kind of training you wanted, and had a large bar up front for before-, during-, and after-workout drinks.

Dad had been an underground fighter in college until the doctors told him if he didn't stop, he'd risk paralysis, so McGowan's was the only way for him to stay doing what he loved without giving my mom a heart attack. That didn't mean he wasn't still built like a fighter and able to take on anyone who wanted to challenge him in the ring; it just meant he was a lot more careful. And it was because of his confident presence mixed with his large appearance that I was betting the girls wouldn't last more than a few minutes with him before leaving.

But then I remembered Mason and realized they might be more used to guys like my dad than we had given them credit for.

After cleaning up the rest of the lunch I'd brought with me as a thank-you for his agreeing to the last-minute interviews, I left the gym and was back at work within twenty minutes.

I'd been in my office for an hour when Eli came in talking to me before he even had a foot in the door. "Did you go to the gym?"

"Yeah. Talked with Dad for a bit, he was with your nieces when I left."

"So they made it?"

I looked up at him from my computer at the relief in his voice, and responded slowly, drawing each word out, "Did you think they wouldn't . . . ?"

"No, I—" He cut off quickly and turned to see who had just opened my door. "No! Go back to your desk and stay there," he demanded, pointing at Cecily, who gave a wide-eyed look as she quickly turned around and left. "Seriously, Liam?"

I suppressed a smile and went back to the e-mail I'd been responding to when he walked in. "I didn't ask her to come in here, I didn't even tell her I was back. She was probably just hoping to attempt to steal my office again."

"Bullshit," he huffed, but I could easily hear the amusement in his voice. "Do you have any plans for the weekend?"

"No," I said distractedly, then it hit me. "You asking because of the girls?"

"They need to get out, Liam."

"I know, I get it. I don't know of anything right now, but I'll let you know."

He stood there for a few seconds longer, not saying anything or looking at anything in particular. "Give them a shot. I know you'll like them; it's them liking everyone else I'm worried about. They're kind of—well, like I said, one only thinks of her boyfriend. The other has a personality somewhere between her dad and Mason, so you can imagine how often she gives new people the time of day without telling them exactly what she thinks of them."

I snorted. "I'm sure I can. I told you, though; I will get them out at least once. I'll let you know if there's anything going on this weekend, and if there's not, I'm sure next weekend will be different."

Eli grabbed for his ringing phone and started backing out of my office as he answered it. "It's been a slow week, there's no point in staying for the rest of the day, you can head out," he whispered before greeting whoever had called him.

I quickly finished the e-mail and checked the unread ones as well as my calendar before cleaning up and getting ready to go. I started texting Cecily as I shut off my lights and locked the door from the inside, but looked up when a husky, feminine laugh caught my attention, and stopped abruptly in the middle of the doorway.

This isn't fucking happening.

My eyes widened as I looked at the identical twin girls talking with Eli about the job interview they'd just come back from, and my mind raced as I tried to deny what I was seeing.

Long black hair. Dark blue eyes. Tall, slender, yet curvy bodies covered in tattoos. Smiles I'd thought of for months.

Memories from a night in Vegas a year ago flashed through my mind as I looked at her. *No, no, no. This can't be happening. That can't be her. That can't be Moon.*

But there was no denying it *was* her. The one girl who had slipped out before I'd woken up . . . the one girl I thought I'd never see again . . . was now standing a dozen feet away from me and talking to my boss—her uncle.

"This can't be happening," I murmured, and quickly stepped back and shut myself in my office before Eli or the girls could notice me.

I'd been in Vegas for one reason. Business. After the meetings were over for the week, I'd gone out with a few guys to grab some drinks since we would be heading home the next day. We'd ended up in three different clubs, gotten more drinks at each one, and had hung out and danced with a group of girls we'd met at the last one . . . but I hadn't seen Moon until we'd all started leaving.

Even as she danced between two guys, her eyes locked on mine and a teasing smile crossed her face. I'd told my group to leave without me, and had pulled her away from the men as if she'd belonged to me. Because that night, she had. It could've been the drinks, it could've been the music, but even in the club we'd been pulling each other closer and grabbing for each other like there was no one else there—I don't remember even actually dancing. And when her sister came up saying they were going back to their hotel, I hadn't stopped to think before telling her to come back with me.

I groaned and rested my forehead against the door as I remembered that night with her. Even though I'd been drunk, I could remember it with perfect clarity. Just like I could remember the feeling of disappointment when I'd woken up the next morning and she was gone.

I'd thought then that I would never see her again, and I had nothing other than the memory of her, and a tattoo of a black, crescent-shaped moon on her side, to help me find her again. I knew it would be impossible, so I hadn't tried. And now? She'd more or less fallen into my hands.

I knew I needed to tell Eli that I already knew his nieces—one better than he'd probably like to hear. But I couldn't. I didn't believe in fate, but, shit, I wasn't about to question how or why this was happening. I just knew I needed a chance to talk to her again, and if this was my chance, I would take it.

3

June 1
Liam

WE STUMBLED DOWN *the hall, stopping every few feet so I could push her back against the wall, my mouth capturing hers each time. Her hands were searching under my shirt, her fingers tracing the lines of muscles in my stomach as I grabbed at her thighs and hips. The kisses had been rough and demanding in the elevator, but as we got closer to my room, they started changing. She stopped fighting for control of the kiss and started leaning into it instead. Her back arched off the walls, and she whimpered when I bit down and tugged on her full bottom lip.*

I searched for the room key and struggled to get the door open without releasing her, and a giggle burst from her chest when we went stumbling into the room. She smiled that same teasing smile she'd flashed at me in the club before I was pushing her up against the wall and claiming her mouth again.

Grabbing the bottom of my shirt, she pulled up, and I quickly tore it off and dropped it on the floor before reaching for hers. When it joined mine, I made a trail of kisses down her throat and across her shoulder as I pulled down the straps of her bra and she unhooked it. Her breaths deepened in my ear as I moved down her chest and reached for the button on her shorts. She tossed her bra behind me as I slid her shorts down her legs and moved aside her underwear to run my fingers against her.

Her back arched off the wall and a soft whimper filled the entryway of the room, and I stilled when my fingers touched something hard on her clit. Everything since we'd gotten in the room had been rushed, but now I couldn't move. My breaths were harsh against her chest as I curled my fingers against the metal, and she moaned.

I slowly lifted my head until I was looking into her dark blue eyes, and couldn't stop the way my lips tilted up into a smirk when I asked, "What is this?"

Heat filled my veins when I rubbed my fingers over it again, and she bit down on her lips to stop another moan. "Piercing," she whispered through her heavy breaths.

Fuck. Me. "Do you know how sexy you are?"

"Do you know how badly I need you to keep moving your fingers?"

I laughed loudly and pulled her away from the wall to walk her farther into the room. Once her legs hit the bed, I pushed her gently down and grabbed her underwear to pull it off. She slid toward the middle of the bed, spreading her legs as she did, and I couldn't take my eyes off her as I knelt on the bed between her legs.

"Fuck," I murmured. Running my hand over her bare, wet lips, I played with the ends of the barbell before leaning forward and sucking it into my mouth.

She cried out and her hands flew up to grab my hair as I licked her from entrance to clit, before hardening my tongue against the piercing. I'd never known anyone with one, and had never been with a girl who kept herself bare either. Both were hot, especially on her, and I couldn't stop from sucking on her clit and the piercing again. Her fingers curled into my hair as her body began shaking and then falling apart on the bed, and her hands held my head pressed against her as I rode her through her orgasm.

She released my hair and started pulling on my arms, and I crawled up her body. And like earlier in the club, our hands started searching for each other. Pulling each other closer, touching everywhere, trying to get closer. I'd never felt like I'd needed to get closer to a girl—I'd never felt like I had to make her mine. Sex—no matter how different the position or girl—had always just been sex. But this girl? I needed all of her. And as she gave me more of herself, and slowly gave up fighting for control, my body roared with a need to make her mine—to let everyone know she belonged to me.

My head fell back against the bed when we'd gotten my jeans and boxer briefs off, and she took me in her hands. No matter how amazing her hands felt on me, I wanted more. Flipping us over so she was on her back again, I parted her legs with my knees, and kissed her slowly as I moved my cock over her piercing. She whimpered and her fingers dug into my back a few minutes later, and her eyes locked on mine as her rapid breaths became uneven. Just because I'd never been with a girl who pierced her clit, it didn't mean I hadn't heard enough about it. And from the way she'd instantly fallen apart the first time and was on the edge of another orgasm right now, it wasn't hard to see it served its purpose. I was officially in love with that fucking piercing.

"Oh God, I . . ." She moaned as her body began vibrating again, and the moan turned into a sharp cry when I quickly thrust inside her.

She gripped my back as I moved inside her, alternating between hard and fast thrusts and slow, torturous movements, taking me all the way out only to slam back into her. She breathed for me to go faster, and a shudder worked through my body as I tried to hold off on my own release. I wanted to give her what she wanted, but I knew what I was doing was driving her crazy, and I loved watching her. Throughout the entire time I would tease her clit for a few seconds before backing off it completely. By the time I dropped my head into the crook of her neck as I came inside her, she was whimpering and digging her nails into my shoulders, to the point where I had no doubt there would be marks. But I wasn't done with her yet.

I rested my body on top of hers, and kissed her gently before moving my lips down her throat and over her collarbone. Leaning back, I went down her chest to the swell of her breasts, and spent minutes torturing her nipples as I hardened inside her again. I slowly began moving my hips, and everything about this time was different. My body never moved from pinning hers to the bed. Every movement was slow and in sync as I moved one of her legs to wrap around my waist.

Cupping my cheeks in her hands, she pressed her mouth to mine as I slowly made love to her. There were no other words for what we were doing, and it was something I'd never had the desire to do before. None of this made sense, and all of it was too passionate an encounter when we didn't know each other, but I couldn't get enough of her.

As I went back enough so I could reach between our bodies, my movements never faltered as I rolled my fingers around her sensitive bud, and the force of her orgasm sent me into my own. There were no words as our bodies trembled against each other, and none as our breathing slowed and we came off the high of what had just happened.

Rolling our bodies to the side, I held her close and just stared at her for what could have been hours as my fingers trailed up and down her spine. I'd never wanted to fall asleep next to someone as much as I did her. I'd never wanted to replay a night. I'd also never stayed in bed and just stared at a girl. If the girl stayed it was because we were too drunk to get her home, or for me to leave. Once again, this girl was changing everything I'd ever known, and I still didn't even know her name.

When her eyelids started getting heavy, I brushed her hair back from her cheek and looked into her dark eyes. "Where did you come from, Moon?"

Her eyebrows pulled together, and a confused look crossed her face before relaxing when I traced the tattoo high up on the side of her ribs. There was a small, black crescent moon there, and it seemed to fit her for now. Why out of all her tattoos had I chosen that one to call her by? I don't know. But there was a part of me that was worried that this night would shatter if I knew her name at that moment. Tomorrow would be a different story—I would find out everything I could about her then.

With a soft smile, she lifted one shoulder in a shrug, and leaned forward to press a kiss to my lips and relax into my chest.

"Good night, Moon," I whispered before we fell asleep.

MY EYES SHOT open, and my arm automatically reached out beside me, looking for a girl I somehow knew wouldn't be there. But it took my mind a few seconds too long to catch up, to know that it'd been a dream—a dream I'd had every night since I saw her on Friday. Running my hands through my hair and down my face, I groaned as the memories continued to torture me.

I hadn't thought about Moon for months, but a year later, I still felt the disappointment I'd felt that next morning. I should have gotten her name, her number, something. Anything. But now she was here, and I was supposed to be her friend for her family's sake . . . and keep myself at a distance. My dick throbbed painfully, and I reached down to grab it, a moan building in my chest when I did.

The images I'd been seeing since Friday afternoon played through my mind as I moved my hand up and down, building up speed as I remembered her moans, whimpers, and the way she'd shattered around me with every orgasm. I gripped myself harder as I got closer to my release, and shut my eyes, welcoming the memories of her as I came.

Getting out of the bed, I walked into the bathroom and started the shower to clean up, hating that I still felt no relief. I was hard again by the time I stepped under the hot spray, but refused to do anything about it this time. There was a possibility that she was the twin with the boyfriend back in Florida. There was an even bigger possibility that she wouldn't remember me at all. Giving in to every memory of her would just make it harder to stay away from her if she wanted nothing to do with me now.

I continued to get more aggravated as the morning went on, and by the time I was walking into my office, I refused to acknowledge anyone I passed or who had called out my name. After locking the door behind me, I walked over and fell into my chair—letting my head drop into my hands as I tried to focus on what I needed to do.

I needed to work. I needed to tell Eli that he didn't want me to be around his nieces. I needed to stop being such a bitch and get over the fact that Moon was somewhere near me, and I needed to distance myself. I *needed* to stop thinking about her at all. I fucking needed Cecily for an hour . . . but at the same time, Cecily was the last thing I needed, seeing as I couldn't even picture her face at the moment.

Seeing Moon had messed with me all weekend. I'd holed myself up in my apartment and thought of everything I wanted to ask her—only to go through it all again the next hour and the next until I was getting frustrated over what her possible answers would be. When the hell had I turned into the kind of guy who let a single girl make him hide out for two and a half days so he could drive himself crazy thinking about her?

I'd already wasted more than an hour making this worse for myself, and had just decided to go home since I would be useless for the day when my office phone rang. I glared at it and the screen that flashed Eli's last name, and hesitantly answered it.

"Yeah?"

"My office . . . now. I don't care if you're hungover."

"I'm no—" I cut off when I heard the distinctive click, and groaned as I set the phone down.

I didn't need a pissed-off Eli right now. Not when I was driving myself crazy, and definitely not when I was afraid I would shout out that I'd fucked his niece as soon as I saw him.

I was still avoiding everyone as I walked down the halls, and knew I needed to do something soon to get out of this funk. I knew I was only making it worse, but it was damn hard to stop it. I didn't even glance at Eli's secretary as I passed her desk and walked right into his office, ready for whatever this meeting would bring.

"I'm not hungover," I said as soon as I was stepping through his door. Shutting it behind me, I walked over and fell into one of the chairs closest to me.

Eli's eyebrows rose up high and a corner of his mouth tilted up. "You sure about that?"

"Seeing as how I haven't even had a beer for a week . . . yeah, I'm fucking sure."

"Someone's having a great morning, then," he mumbled sarcastically, and came around his desk to sit in the chair near me. "I had a handful of employees stop me on my way to my office this morning, and every one of them wanted to know what had happened to you."

"Suddenly my moods are their business?"

Eli was still trying to conceal a smile, but he wasn't doing a great job. "Cecily seemed more than happy and was quick to let me know how qualified she was for your position."

"I bet she did," I said on a sigh, and leaned my head back until I was staring at the ceiling. Maybe Eli was right. I felt hungover, only without the benefit of the fun night and need for greasy food this morning.

"You know I'm not mad at you—"

"Mad at me?" I asked, cutting him off. He just kept talking.

"—I actually called you in here to thank you."

"Thank me? For what?"

"Kira and Kennedy got the jobs. Whether or not that had to do with you, I needed to thank you for at least giving them the opportunity to interview. As for this weekend, I know how much pressure I put on you when it came to them, so I don't blame you for not wanting the girls wherever you were."

Mother fucking son of a bitch. "Did they?" Eli nodded, and I continued, "No, I had nothing to do with that. I haven't talked to my dad since before their interview started, and he knew that they didn't have to get the job. As for this weekend, I'm telling you I didn't leave my apartment once, and no one else was ever there. I told you I'd call you if I was doing something, I'm not going to lie to you." *I'll just forget to mention the fact that I slept with your niece,* I thought to myself. *Whichever one she is.*

"Well, then you can thank your dad for me. And really, you've already done more than enough for them. Like I said, I put too much pressure on you, it wasn't fair. So we can just agree to have your part with them be over, no hard feelings."

A feeling close to panic began putting pressure on my chest. Eli and I both knew I would run into the girls from time to time since they were working at my dad's gym, but I still needed a reason to be near Moon more often than that. The last thing I wanted was to help them meet people, and over the weekend I'd thought of anything to get out of the situation. But now that my opportunity was there, I couldn't take it. I couldn't risk not having time with her.

"Eli, it's not a big deal. I know I didn't respond well the day you asked, but I didn't fully understand the situation then. I really have no problem introducing them to people; this past weekend just wasn't the right time."

His face lit up with surprise, and I hated that it was because he thought I was doing a favor for him, when it was really for myself. "Really? Liam, you have no idea how much I appreciate this. Thank you, man." He stood up and extended a hand, and when I followed his actions, he pulled his arm back. "But for the record, I tried to let you off the hook. 'Cause Paisley was livid when she found out what Mason and I had asked you to do."

I huffed softly and nodded. "Well, if your wife asks, I'll be sure to let her know this is on me."

"I owe you," Eli called out as I retreated to the door, and I just flashed him a smile as I left. If only he knew how backward that statement was.

4

June 3
Kennedy

"Once you remember the ingredients for each drink, it's pretty simple. All right! If you need anything, just ask Kristi. Good luck, ladies," our new boss, Brandon, said with a loud clap.

Kira and I had gotten hired on at McGowan's over the weekend, and after a crash training course with the boss and his daughter, Kristi, over the past two days, they were letting us take over the drink station. The drinks weren't hard to make, and we had cards strategically placed that had the ingredients for each one in case we forgot, so there wasn't much to worry about in that department. However, I *was* worried about the dozens upon dozens of men going in and out of the gym each day. I'm pretty sure I stared way more than I was supposed to, and I had a feeling boss man wasn't going to be thrilled that my greatest perk to working here was his customers. On the plus side, Kira had finally noticed that there were other members of the opposite sex than Zane, and her crying had diminished drastically.

"You get used to it," Kristi said offhandedly a couple hours into the shift, and I turned my head to see who she was talking to. She was staring right at me.

"The drinks?" I asked, my eyebrows rising in question. "I figured. I'm not too worried about it."

She laughed softly. "Not the drinks. I don't doubt you'll get the hang of them by the end of this week. I mean the guys." Nodding in the direction of the sweaty, muscled men in question, she sent me a wry look. "After a while you don't even notice they're there anymore."

"Somehow I doubt that. You grew up with this, so it's easier for you. Us? Not so much."

With another laugh, Kristi pushed away from the counter and began walking out of the drink section. "My mom just brought in lunch for Dad. I'm gonna see if I can go steal any of it from him. Call into his office if anything happens."

I nodded and turned back to find Kira doing her best to not look at two guys fighting in the ring off to one side of the gym, and failing. Just before I could try to ask her what she thought of the job, the location and . . . uh . . . scenery, and Kristi—who was our age and had just graduated college as well—someone cleared their throat.

I turned to take the order, and—oh, Jesus Christ. There was no way I would ever get used to all these guys. This easily topped a houseful of frat boys, and groups of more of the same at the beach. Everyone here was toned, a lot had shirts off or tight-fitting wife beaters, and a good portion were too perfect looking for their own good. Heaven. My new job was heaven.

Twenty minutes later I was in the middle of making a drink while Kira was beginning to take the latest customer's order, and the first words he spoke had goose bumps covering my arms. The words weren't anything special, just a "How are you today?" but all I wanted to do was turn and look at him. Knowing I had to concentrate on what I was putting in the drink, I forced myself to stare at the different containers, but I felt my body leaning back and turning the slightest bit when the deep timbre of his voice floated over to me again.

Finish the drink, then look at him. Finish the drink, then look at him, I chanted to myself over and over.

"Do you—I'm sorry." He huffed a short laugh. "Do you know who I am?" he asked Kira.

Who is this guy? We're from Florida, of course she doesn't know who you are. I suppressed a snort when Kira said what I'd just been thinking almost verbatim.

"Are you Moon?" he asked hesitantly, and I did snort then.

I started turning to finally look at the guy, who I'm sure was about to give Kira the worst pickup line known to man, when his question replayed through my mind. I sucked in a quick gasp, and the pitcher full of the unmixed ingredients I'd been holding slipped from my hand and fell to the floor—splashing everything up on my legs.

"Whoa! You okay there?" my customer asked, his expression and tone teasing. When I didn't respond or move, his expression fell. "No, seriously, are you okay?"

There's no way. He *can't be here, standing behind me, talking with my sister. My* identical *twin sister, and asking if* she *is Moon.* I hadn't heard that name since a night in Vegas over a year ago, but it was a name I hadn't been able to stop thinking of for months.

I finally turned then, and everything began spinning as I looked at *him.* My knees felt weak, my legs felt like they wouldn't hold me up for another minute, and I wasn't sure where my breath had gone. I was hallucinating. It had to be all the men in the gym or the smell of the protein shakes. But I was definitely hallucinating. Because *he* was standing there in slacks, a button-down shirt, and a tie. And in my memory, *he* definitely wasn't wearing that; he wasn't wearing much of anything.

His arctic-blue eyes met mine, and I knew in the confused—

yet relieved—expression on his face when he repeated my nick-name, that I wasn't hallucinating. *He* was there, standing in front of me, in a gym in motherfucking California.

"Look, guy, I don't know what you mean by 'Moon,' but if you want some—" Kira had been turning to look at me, and cut off on a gasp. "*No way!* You're—holy shit, *you're* Vegas!"

I wasn't moving again, I also didn't know if I was breathing yet—because it definitely felt like I had only seconds before I passed out. I just stood there staring into the lightest blue eyes I'd ever seen, trying to make myself do something . . . anything.

He opened his mouth to speak, but before anything came out, Kristi ran up behind him and jumped on his back—her arms wrapped around his neck as she shouted, "Liam! Where have you been all my life?"

I tore my eyes away from them, and finally looked down at the mess I'd made. Forcing myself to look up again, I glanced over at my customer instead. "I'm—I'm so sorry. Let me start again."

He looked over at Liam and Kristi, then looked at me again. "Not a problem. Are you sure you're okay?"

"Yeah!" I said a little too brightly. "Of course I am. Let me get right on that." *No, no, I am not okay. He—Liam is here and I have no idea why he's here. But I'm pretty sure I slept with my boss's daughter's boyfriend.*

This time I took my time making the drink—afraid that Liam would still be standing there with Kristi when I was finished, and even more afraid that he wouldn't be. Once I finished, I grabbed a few wet towels and crouched down to clean up the mess I had made. Seconds after, Liam was crouching down directly beside me . . . close enough that my knee touched his.

"Why did you leave that morning?" he asked softly, his tone eager, but with a hint of worry.

"I don't think you're supposed to be back here," I responded with a weak voice, and hated that his presence was enough to make me sound like a lost little girl. I wasn't this girl. I was stubborn, independent, and loved control. But Liam had had me giving up all of my control to him within minutes in Vegas—he'd been one of only two men to ever make me feel like I needed to be protected by them.

He released a short laugh. "I'm pretty sure no one will care." After a few moments of silence, with me just staring at the floor and Liam staring at my profile, he reached forward and grabbed my chin, turning my head so I was looking directly into his eyes again. "Why did you leave?"

I shook my head as much as I could with his fingers keeping my head still. "Why are you here?"

His lips tilted up before spreading into a full smile. "I've wondered the same thing about you for days."

My brow creased in confusion, but before I could ask what he meant by that, Kristi was next to us.

"God, Liam, the least you could do is help her. You're probably scaring her more than Dad has. Kir—wait, which one are you?"

Liam released my chin and I looked up to see Kristi watching me again and tilting her head to try to read my name tag that was currently hidden from her view. "I—I'm Kennedy."

"Right! Sorry. Kennedy, this is my big brother, Liam. Liam, this is Kennedy. She and her sister just started here on Monday."

Brother . . . *brother.* God, that word had never sounded more beautiful than it did in that moment.

"Right, so anyway . . . Liam, Mom wants to know if you want lunch."

Liam shook his head, but his eyes remained on my face. "No, I came to talk to Dad. Tell him I'll be in there soon." When seconds passed and Kristi didn't leave, he looked up at her. "I said to tell him I'd be in there soon."

Kristi's eyes darted back and forth between us, and just behind her, Kira was staring at Liam with wide eyes and an amused expression on her face.

When Kristi left, Kira stared at us for a while longer before shaking herself and looking around her. "I'm just . . . going to act like I'm making something."

"Tell me why you left," Liam prompted again, and my head shook slowly as I hesitantly looked back into his eyes.

"I can't."

His face fell. "But you know who I am," he stated; it wasn't a question. I don't know how it could have been after the way I'd reacted when I first saw him.

"Of course I do," I said on a hushed laugh. "You . . . your dad owns this gym?" When he nodded, I asked, "How did you know I was here? Your dad wouldn't know me."

Liam sighed heavily, and broke eye contact for a moment. "I need to talk to you about that. Kennedy, right?"

"Yes."

"I'll be here when you get off. Please let me take you to dinner so I can explain some things to you."

I moved away from him. "I don't know about—"

"Kennedy," he pleaded softly.

"She has no plans, she can go to dinner with you. And we're off at six," Kira added, and Liam smiled again.

"I'll be here," he said, and stood, bringing me with him. For long seconds, we stood there staring at each other, neither of us saying a word. With a step closer to me, he lowered his head so his lips were near my ear. "You'll always be Moon to me."

I exhaled audibly, and continued to stand there staring at where he had been after he left until Kira rushed up to me. "Can you believe he's here? Did you know he lived here? Is that why you were so okay with moving? Whoa, wait, is that why we applied at the gym? Oh my God, I just can't—"

"Kira," I hissed, interrupting her. "No to everything. And for the love of God, shut up about him before you send me into a panic attack."

"I'm sorry, but this is too crazy, you have to admit that."

I nodded and turned my head to look behind my shoulder, in the direction of the offices. "It is. Way too crazy. I'm pretty sure I'm still dreaming."

June 3
Liam

I PULLED BACK up to my dad's gym with five minutes to spare. I'd been sure that I wouldn't make it because of the traffic, and had no doubt Moon—Kennedy—would have taken the opportunity to leave. Not that I couldn't get her address from Eli, but that would freak her out more than I already had that afternoon. I'd had days to get used to the fact that she was here, within reaching distance. I'd only given her a few hours. But once I'd gotten to a point where all I could do was think about seeing her again, I hadn't been able to wait any longer. I almost hadn't been able to stop myself from talking to her again as I left Dad's office, but I'd known she needed time. I was just hoping the past few hours were enough.

Stepping out of my car, I loosened my tie and rolled up the sleeves of my shirt to my forearms as I walked into the gym. The girls were walking toward the entrance with Dad, and even though my eyes immediately went to the girl on the end, I had to bite back a relieved smile when she looked up and her eyes widened as her smiling expression faltered. It was going to be hard telling the two of them apart, but at least for the first time looking at them both straight on, I'd guessed correctly.

Dad shot me a look when they reached me, and said good-bye to the girls before turning around and leaving. I'd told him everything earlier in his office, so he knew the backstory . . . but explaining the need to be near Kennedy was going to be a little more difficult with Kristi and Mom. Mom because I refused to tell her about my sex life anyway, and Kristi because I didn't want her looking at Kennedy any differently than she already did since she had her own theories about one-night stands.

"So, can I take you girls to dinner?"

Kira smiled widely and spoke while Kennedy just stood there staring at me. "You can take *her* to dinner. I'd rather not get in the way of whatever's going to go down between the two of you."

"Kira, please," Kennedy whispered frantically, but Kira kept her eyes trained on me.

"But you make sure you actually bring her home tonight. At a normal time. We're not having a repeat of last year, you get me?"

"*Kira!*"

I laughed loudly and nodded. "Of course. Just dinner tonight."

"Well, my work here is done. Have fun, you two," she called out in a singsong voice as she walked past me and out the doors.

Kennedy was staring at her retreating figure like Kira had just betrayed her. When long seconds passed without her acknowledging that I was still standing in front of her, I cleared my throat to break the awkward tension that had formed between us.

"Just dinner. I need to—"

"I left, Liam, that's it." Her dark blue eyes finally landed on my face, and her head shook faintly. "There's no reason for it other than you were a nameless stranger who I thought I would never see again . . . and I just had to go. You won't get a different answer if you take me to dinner."

"I'm not taking you to dinner to get an answer. You told me you couldn't give me a reason this afternoon, I figured that would be the end of it. But there are still things I need to tell you."

Kennedy was mid sigh when her eyes widened and her body went rigid. "Do you—oh my God, did—" She looked around us quickly and leaned closer. "Did you give me something? Do you have diseases?"

My head jerked back and I barked out a short laugh. "I'm sorry—what? No. No, I didn't give you anything . . . I don't have anything to give you!"

She exhaled in relief, and her body seemed to sag. "Okay, I'm sorry. I just thought—never mind." With another glance around us, she nodded once. "We can go to dinner, and you can tell me whatever you need to. But other than seeing each other here, nothing will be happening between us, Liam. This isn't one of those moments when we finally find each other a year after a night of—well, the night we had—and we decide that we're meant to be."

"You're saying you don't want to fall in love with me?" I asked, my tone teasing to try to ease some of the tension, but her glare hardened at the question.

"If there was such a thing as love, I'd still say no."

I stared at her, part of me wondering why she actually looked like she believed what she just told me, the rest trying to force myself to say that I'd been joking—but nothing came out. I didn't know what to think of her words. I knew Kira was the one with the boyfriend, but that didn't mean Kennedy hadn't met someone in the last year. For all I knew, she could've been in Vegas to get over a relationship and I'd been a rebound. But that night—our unexplainable connection—there was no way for me to have that memory of her, and then piece that together with the girl standing in front of me. The girl who looked like me showing up today had been the last thing she'd ever wanted.

I took a step away from her and toward the door. "Understood. Let's get out of here. We can talk and then I'll take you home." Not waiting for her response, I turned and walked to the door, only stopping to hold it open for her. Thankfully, she had been following me rather than remaining where I'd left her.

We were seated at a little mom-and-pop Italian restaurant within fifteen minutes, and although the tension between us had been gone since we got in my car, we hadn't said a word to each other. But unlike before, she wasn't avoiding looking directly at me; she was now staring intently.

"So, we're here. Talk to me," she demanded as soon as we'd ordered.

I wanted to tell her I would after we'd finished eating, but knew I couldn't. It wasn't fair to her. Only problem was now that I had her in front of me, the speech I'd run through at least a dozen times in my mind suddenly didn't seem like the right way to tell her. *Nothing* seemed like the right way, it all sounded wrong.

"I—well, I knew—I was asked to—"

"Whatever you need to tell me, just say it. Really, I'd rather it just be out there than sitting here trying to figure it out myself."

I looked at her cautious and expectant expression, and exhaled roughly. "I've known you were here. I knew the day you interviewed with my dad."

Kennedy nodded slowly. "I figured." When I didn't go on, her eyebrows rose. "Is that really all you needed to say?"

"No. No, it's not. I'm just struggling with finding a way to tell you this without it sounding . . . how it sounds. And besides the fact that I've known for days that you were here, I'm still having trouble actually grasping that you *are* here."

"That makes two of us," she muttered. "Well, like I said, I'd rather it just be out there. So say it any way you can, and we'll figure out a way for it to sound better than however it comes out."

My mouth curved up in a smile. "I've known you were here

since Friday, but I *knew* you were here a few days before. I mean, I didn't know it was *you,* but I . . . knew."

"You're right. This is sounding bad."

I rolled my eyes at her teasing tone, and decided to just say it rather than slowly building up to it. "I work for your uncle Eli."

"No shit," she breathed in disbelief, her wide eyes growing even larger.

"He's been like a mentor to me for years, and I've worked for him since before I even graduated college. He called me into his office last week to tell me about you and Kira. There was another guy there, Mason—"

"Wait!" Kennedy sat up in the booth and leaned over the table. "*Mason* was there? *My* uncle Mason?"

"If it's the guy who looks like he takes steroids, then yes."

She stared at me for a few seconds before relaxing, but her confused expression deepened. "I'm sorry, I can sort of understand you working for Uncle Eli. I mean, it's weird; don't get me wrong. Way too coincidental given our past, but things like that happen, I guess. My uncles hate each other, though, I can't imagine them in the same room to talk to you . . . especially about Kira and me."

I laughed softly. "Yeah, the hatred was clear in the office. And trust me, you aren't the only one who finds this weird. Eli was telling me about the two of you and how you weren't happy you were here. They wanted someone to introduce you to people, they were hoping you'd make friends and enjoy California a little more." Kennedy scoffed and I sent her a look showing my agreement. "I said no at first. But Eli's never asked for anything from me, and he's helped me through a lot. I told them my dad was looking to fill a few spots at the gym, and I would try to get you two an interview, but I still wasn't happy about any of it."

"I don't blame you. We're kind of hard to handle individually. Both at the same time? I almost feel bad for you."

My lips spread into an amused grin, but I stopped myself from commenting on the fact that I'd handled her easily enough a year ago. "It wasn't that. It was the way they were talking about you two. They made you seem . . . like you didn't know how to socialize. I kept looking at it like they wanted me to babysit you."

"Hmm. How sweet of them," she said sarcastically.

"I was at the gym when you came in for the interview, but I'd been in my dad's office and left when you were still interviewing. But then you came in to work, and I walked out of my office when you were both standing there with Eli in the hall. I thought I was losing my mind when I saw you. I couldn't wrap my head around the fact that *you* were the niece that I was supposed to help meet people."

Kennedy let my words hang in the air for a few moments, then nodded once and cleared her throat. "Okay. This is still weird—too weird. But what I want to know is, if you've known I was here since Friday, why are you just now approaching me?"

A short, hesitant laugh left me, and I took my time figuring out my answer. "Because I didn't know what to do about you being here. I denied it at first, and then was in shock that after a year you were close enough to touch again. I kept wondering if you would remember me . . . that led to me again wanting to know why you left, and then I just got mad. I was mad you left, I was mad that I was being put in a position to be near you when there was a possibility you wouldn't remember me or want to be near me, *or* you would be the sister who had a boyfriend. I went back and forth between telling Eli that I knew you and that I was the wrong person to help you, but eventually I decided that I couldn't have you this close and not try to talk to you again. After that, it took a few days to finally figure out *how* to approach you without scaring you . . . but I still did it the wrong way. Obviously."

"We can't tell my uncle. There's no logical way to explain

how I could've met you before this, and there's no way in hell I'm telling him or the rest of my family the truth."

"Okay."

"And we can't tell your family," she added. "I wouldn't be able to face them again if they knew."

I looked away for a second and tried to brace myself for her reaction to what I was about to say. "My dad knows." Kennedy's eyes widened, and I said, "The truth. I told him today."

"Oh my God," she said on a breath.

"My sister won't know, neither will my mom. But I have a different relationship with my dad than most people. I tell him everything. He'd already known about you last year, and I knew there was no way he wouldn't eventually put things together."

"Your dad thinks I'm a whore, Liam!" she whispered harshly, her eyes darting around to make sure no one was listening to us. "I can't go back to that gym now."

My eyes narrowed at her assumption. Sure, my sister would automatically think something along those lines because that's just the way she was. But it was pissing me off that Kennedy would think I'd make her out to seem like a whore. Then again, we still didn't know each other.

"No, he doesn't. That's the last thing he thinks, I can assure you. And yes, you can go back to the gym. He was mad I hadn't told him before he hired you, and was worried you would both quit if I talked to you tonight. So if anything, he's on your side right now."

Kennedy shook her head slowly, her eyes on me, but not seeing me. Our food was brought to the table a couple minutes later, but neither of us made a move to touch it, and Kennedy still looked like she was somewhere else.

"Well," I said, and cleared my throat, breaking the silence between us. Her eyes finally focused, and I decided that now was the time for me to leave everything up to her. "That was what I needed to tell you. Being in the same city and being connected by your uncle was purely coincidental. You and Kira working for my dad wasn't, although my dad didn't think he would hire the two of you before you came in for the interview—so I don't want you or Kira to think you got the job because of your uncle or me. Dad really liked you both. But no matter how much I wanted to, I couldn't try to talk to you without you knowing how this all came about. Regardless of what happened between us after I approached you in the gym, I knew it wouldn't be fair to you to let you go on thinking that we had just run into each other out of pure coincidence."

"I appreciate you letting me know, and I appreciate dinner," she mumbled as her eyes became unfocused again. After a few beats of silence passed, she straightened and looked directly at me. Her next words held no emotion. "But as I said earlier, nothing will come of us. This is not that moment where everything changes and we realize we're meant to be together. That night last year was fun, but that's all it was . . . a night."

From her detached words and the way she immediately looked down at her plate and began eating, I knew there wasn't one ounce of Kennedy that even believed the bullshit she'd just given me.

5

June 3
Kennedy

As soon as dinner was over, Liam drove me back to the condo as a heavy silence fell over us. I still wasn't sure what to think about the fact that he was here . . . right next to me. Parts of that night in Vegas had been replaying in my mind since I first saw him that afternoon. And every single one of them left me wanting one thing.

More.

But I couldn't. Not wouldn't . . . *couldn't.* From what I remembered of him, and what I was already seeing in just speaking to him today, he was the kind of guy who had me letting down walls faster than I'd originally been able to build them, and had me willingly giving up every ounce of control to him. And I hated that feeling. I was the type of girl who had to be in control at all times. I was the way I was because I stayed in control. There had only ever been one other guy in my life who had made me feel the way Liam did, and it had ended in a disaster. Liam would be no different.

The second Liam had pulled the car up in front of my building, I offered him an abrupt "thanks" and stepped out. Anything more, any extra time with him, and I would start forgetting why I couldn't explore possibilities with him—for the thirtieth time in just a handful of hours.

As soon as I was in the condo, Kira was racing out of her room and up to me.

"You ditched me, traitor!"

"Seriously, 'holy shit' isn't big enough for today! Tell me what happened!"

"*You* tell *me* what happened!" I demanded as I walked over to fall into a chair at the kitchen table with Kira not far behind. "I don't even know how to begin wrapping my head around all of this!"

"Seeing as I wasn't there with you two, I can't. Just start from the beginning and I'll try to help you fill in the *hows*."

"The *how* is the easiest part," I mumbled, and rubbed a temple with my fingers. "He works for Uncle Eli—"

"No shit?"

"That's exactly what I said. But, yes, he does. Apparently he doesn't just work there . . . they're really close. Liam said that Eli's his mentor. Apparently Uncle Eli and Uncle Mason both approached him about us moving here and needing to meet people or get jobs. They wanted Liam to help—"

"So he already knew that you were here? I bet he jumped on that chance before they could get out the question!"

"Kira! Let me explain first, then you can cut me off however much you want to."

Kira sat back in her chair with her hands raised in surrender, but her face still showed how eager she was to hear everything.

I finished telling her the rest of my conversation with Liam at the restaurant, and true to Kira's personality, she didn't let me get more than two sentences out at a time without interrupting and throwing in her own assumptions about what happened next. The entire playback of Liam's explanations ended up taking about twenty minutes longer than it had when *he'd* been the one telling it.

"So that's it," I finished, and let my head fall into one hand while the other slapped down against the table.

"What?" she asked quickly, and sat up. "That can't be it. Didn't you guys talk about Vegas? Did he try to set up something to see you again? Don't leave out the best part! I need juicy details in my life."

"You don't get plenty of juiciness from your phone calls with Zane?"

Kira's eyes widened, then dropped to stare at the table. Back home we could never do anything to get her to shut up about her relationship with Zane, but I couldn't remember her talking about him once since we'd been in California—unless it was to complain about their being apart. Just before I could ask what her solemn look meant, she shook her head and glanced back up at me.

"Come on, Kennedy! You can't tell me that there was nothing else said. You talked about this guy for *months,* and suddenly he's here? There's no way you didn't make plans to see him again."

"Oh, I have no doubt I will see him again. Since we work at his dad's gym, I know he'll probably use that as a way to see me. But I told him nothing was going to happen with us. I said Vegas was just a night, and nothing more."

"What? Bullshit; no, you didn't!" She sat there staring at me in shock before stuttering out, "Ken—I don't—what do—why would you say that?"

"I said it because nothing can happen. I cannot let a man like Liam Taylor into my life."

"Well, why the hell not?"

"Speaking of Zane!," I said loudly, ready to talk about any other subject, "you haven't been talking about him much lately, and it is impossible to miss the way you've been staring down all the guys at the gym. It's your turn to spill the details."

"I have *not* been staring them down," she said defensively.

"Ha! Yeah . . . yeah, you have. And you're beyond smiley and happy when we're there. I'm also pretty sure I heard one of the guys asking for your number today. Did you give it to him?"

"Of course I didn't! I have a boyfriend, Kennedy."

"Yeah, who is on the other side of the country and who you don't talk about anymore. I agree with Mom, I think this is the perfect opportunity for you to see what other guys can be like."

"No. I don't want to know what anyone else would be like."

I exhaled heavily and gave her a look that let her know I thought she was making a mistake.

"How about this? If you date Liam—and I mean *date,* as in *relationship*—then I will spend time away from my relationship with Zane for the rest of the time we're in California to give other guys a shot."

"That is not happening! I *can't* be with someone like Liam!"

Kira shrugged and grinned victoriously. "Well then, I guess we can both stay just the way we are."

"Kira," I groaned as she stood up and walked toward her room.

"Good talk, sis!"

"I hate you too," I called back, and grumbled to myself. I'd have to tell Mom and Dad I failed at the Zane thing again.

"ARE YOU BUSY tonight?"

I glanced up at the guy currently waiting for his protein shake two days later, and gave him a coy smile before going back to acting like I was very into making his drink so I wouldn't have to give him an immediate answer. I'd seen him every day since Kira and I started work at the beginning of the week, but today was the first day he'd gotten bold in our short conversations.

They had been the typical "Hi, how are you?," which led to the rest of the necessities that made up a polite conversation with any stranger—but that had been it.

I'd known today would be different the second he'd walked up and said, "I was hoping you'd be here today." After that, our conversation had been filled with flirting on his part, and kicking up the polite factor on mine—and in his defense, he'd been damn good at his game and was nice to look at. He was never cheesy and never overeager, just always spoke with the perfect amount of I'm-interested-and-want-you-to-know. He looked like he was in his late twenties, and had dark hair that was already starting to gray at the temples. The combination was oddly fascinating, and mixed with his sure smile, it had me wondering if he'd ever had a girl turn him down. The only problem for me was I couldn't get a certain someone out of my head.

Just as I opened my mouth to give him a noncommittal answer, that certain someone answered for me.

"Actually, she is busy. But she won't be busy with you."

My jaw dropped and I sucked in a large gasp and hissed, "Liam!"

Liam looked over at Mr. Smooth Talker—I never could remember his name—and gave him a challenging stare. "The girls are here to work, not get picked up by the members of the gym."

Mr. ST didn't back down. Actually, his smile grew confident. "I'll gladly wait until she's off work to ask again, if that would make you feel better."

"I'd rather you—"

"Liam!" I hissed again. "You can't answer questions for me, and you are being beyond rude right now." Looking up to Mr. ST, I flashed him an apologetic look. "I'm sorry, just ignore him . . . I try to. What did you—"

"Are you really going to go somewhere with him? No. No, you're not, and we already have plans."

I couldn't stop my face from falling in horror over the way Liam was acting. I hadn't seen or heard from him since he dropped me off after dinner the other night, and was too shocked by the way he was taking over the conversation to actually continue trying to talk to Mr. ST.

"Are you kidding me right now?" I roughly slammed Mr. ST's drink down in front of him, but never took my eyes off Liam. "You honestly think you can just come in here and act like you have a say over my life? Did you *not* hear me on Wednesday? And why the hell would I go anywhere with you after what you just did?" I bit out, gesturing to the other guy standing in front of me.

"Wait. Has he been bothering you?" Mr. Smooth Talker asked, and Liam barked out a hard laugh.

"No, he's not bothering her," Kira chimed in. "This is just how they are. And, unfortunately, we do have plans with him tonight. Enjoy your drink!"

"Kira! Shut up!" I don't know what it was about Liam that had me talking like this, but I still hadn't stopped hissing. As much as I wanted to apologize to Mr. ST and say that I would go anywhere with him, as long as it pissed off Liam, I couldn't look away from the man who hadn't left my mind for two days. "You are really something, you know that? It's just too bad I didn't know the kind of guy you were *a year ago*!"

Liam leaned over the counter; his arctic-blue eyes glistened with amusement. "I don't think that would've stopped you, Moon."

Words failed me, and I made a really unattractive, girly screech. It was also possible that I stamped my foot, but I didn't want to think too much on the fact that I was now acting like a five-year-old throwing a fit.

"Okay, you two. Take it outside."

I turned to look at my boss at the sound of his voice, and pointed at Liam. "I hate your son!"

Brandon sighed and raised his eyebrows as he looked at Liam. "Yeah, well, he has that effect on people sometimes. Go finish telling him how much you hate him outside."

I started to say no when Liam looked directly into my eyes. "Kennedy," he said in a tone that left no room for discussion—and to my horror, I followed him outside without another look at Mr. Smooth Talker.

"What is *wrong* with you?"

"Did you have fun throwing that temper tantrum?"

My mouth popped open again as my eyes widened. "Are you fucking kidding me? Who the hell do you think you are? Liam, I haven't even spent half a day with you between last year and Wednesday, you can't just come in and act like you have any say in my life! And the fact that you think you can makes you look not only overly confident, but fucking creepy! You do. Not. Know. Me."

"I beg to differ," his deep voice rumbled. His cocky smile had vanished as soon as we'd stepped outside, but the way his eyes were boring into mine made it clear he would do the last five minutes over again if given the chance.

"What if I wanted to do something with that guy? What if I wanted to do something with *any* guy? You can't stop me! You can't just shove yourself into every conversation I have with a member of the opposite sex."

"Kira didn't seem to mind."

"Kira's delusional and wants us to be together!"

Liam stepped close—too close. I stumbled back a step, but he put his hand around my waist and pulled me close enough that our chests were touching. "Tell me honestly: Did you want to go out with him tonight?" I immediately opened my mouth to respond, but he spoke before I could. "*Honestly,* Moon."

I stood there staring into his captivating eyes for a few seconds as I tried to figure out what to say. At that moment, I couldn't even remember what he'd asked. All I could think of was the way his smell was putting me in a daze, and how familiar it felt being pressed up against him—and it shouldn't have.

"Moon," he prompted again, and I shook my head as if to clear it.

"No. I wouldn't have gone out with him."

"So I helped you, then."

Placing my hands on his chest, I put the slightest pressure there and whispered, "Please let me go."

Liam immediately released me, but I didn't move more than a couple feet from him.

When I spoke, the anger and shock were gone from my voice, and I hated that I sounded disappointed. Because although it may have come across to Liam as being disappointed in him, I knew it was because I was somewhat upset that he'd actually let go of me. "Just because I would have said no, you did not have the right to answer for me. Liam, we don't know each other. The way you acted in there . . ." I trailed off as I tried to find the right words. "It was too much . . . it was too much for me. All it did was confirm why I do not want to have anything to do with you."

Liam nodded a few times, but the intensity in his eyes never died. "I know, Kennedy."

I stared at him for a moment longer, then turned to go back inside without saying another word. I couldn't figure out how to say good-bye, or how to ask him to leave me alone when all I wanted was to be held by him again. A few feet from the door, Liam's voice had me stopping abruptly.

"He's married."

Turning around, I looked back at him with my face pinched in confusion. "What?"

"Jeff." Liam gestured to the doors behind me. "The guy who was talking to you. He's married."

My head jerked back, and I turned to look at the windowed doors like Mr. ST would be standing right there. "No, he—he doesn't wear a ring."

Liam huffed out a laugh when I was facing him again, and studied me for a few seconds before admitting, "It bothers me that you even checked, because I know that means a part of you was interested. But he is, in fact, married. I was actually there when he and his wife came in and signed up. And every weekend when I'm here sparring with my dad, they're here together—and the wedding ring is back on. He always hits on the girls working the drink station."

"You're serious?"

He shot me a sympathetic smile, which quickly fell. "Like I was on Wednesday, I'm going to be completely honest with you. If you still want me to leave after, I will. A good friend of mine is having a party this weekend, and I was coming in here to ask if you and Kira wanted to come with me. When I heard Jeff, I just . . . well, I took it too far. I know. But I don't like the guy, and didn't like the way he was looking at you. The party isn't even tonight, and before you say anything, I'm not going to ask you to go somewhere with me tonight." Liam glanced at his watch and took a step back. "I only came over here to talk to you two, but now I have to get back to work. Talk to Kira, and if you want to go, let your uncle know. He'll get ahold of me."

I just nodded and took another step toward the doors of the gym, but once again, he stopped me.

"Kennedy." When I looked back at him, I was surprised to find him looking unsure of himself. "Kira's not the only one." With that, he turned and got into his car and drove off; and I just stood there trying to figure out what he meant.

It wasn't until I was almost back to the drink station that I remembered what I'd said to Liam. *"Kira's delusional and wants us to be together!"*

As much as his parting words had my lips curving up into a smile, I knew that all they really meant was that I had to keep reminding Liam that nothing would come of us.

June 5
Liam

I'D MADE IT back to work quickly, the entire time wondering why I hadn't been able to leave Kennedy without that last confession. As if I hadn't pissed her off enough in the minutes before, I knew those last words were going to make her avoid me if I ever saw her again.

I knew I needed to tell Eli I'd tried, but doubted that the girls would go anywhere with me, though at that moment, I couldn't figure out a good enough reason for why they would've said no. Instead of heading right to his office, I stepped into mine and bit back a groan as soon as I was inside.

Leaving the door open, I took the few steps over to my desk and looked at the woman waiting for me in my chair.

"Aren't you going to shut the door?" she asked, her voice sultry as she ran a finger along the top of her low-cut shirt.

"No. Not today, Cecily."

Her eyes widened and she blinked rapidly a few times before cracking a smile and laughing. "Funny."

"I'm serious, I need you to go."

Cecily's face fell again; this time when she tried to cover it, there was worry in her eyes. "If you're having a rough day, I can always help you out. You should know that by now."

Stepping back to the door, I gestured toward the hall outside my office. "You need to go."

"What is your deal the past week?" she asked, her tone harsh as she pushed away from the desk and stood to walk over to me.

"I haven't heard from you at all, and now that I'm here waiting for you, you're just going to send me away like a damn dog?"

I didn't say anything, because there was nothing to say. Normally telling her to leave wouldn't have been an issue, but it was obvious she knew things between us had ended if she was getting mad.

After a few silent seconds of her waiting for a response, her eyebrows slanted down in frustration and she turned to leave my office.

Not more than three seconds later, Eli came walking in doing a slow clap. "That was the best thing I've heard all week."

I scoffed and walked over to my desk to sit down, and he followed. "I guess it was time I start following office rules, or something."

"Or something." Eli winked and leaned back to stretch in the chair. "So I just got a call from my nieces."

My head snapped up from where I'd been looking at my computer, and my eyebrows pulled together. "Did you?"

"Why do you sound surprised? You were just with them."

"Uh . . ." *Well, considering the conversation that just went down, I have every reason to sound surprised.* "Not surprised, more interested in what they had to say. They didn't exactly give me an answer."

"Really? She said you invited them to a party this weekend and told me to give you their numbers."

"And by 'she,' you mean . . . ?"

Eli shot me a weird look and shrugged. "Kira. Why? Can you even tell the two apart yet?"

Seeing how one of them always looked at me like she hated me, yeah, I could—but that was just another thing that Eli didn't need to know. "Only when they have their name tags on, but I'm pretty sure your other niece isn't my biggest fan."

"Ah, yeah. Kennedy's very . . . *cautious* when it comes to men, I guess you could say."

"I hadn't noticed," I responded before I could stop myself. Eli just laughed.

"Well, she definitely has her reasons. Give her a little while; she'll come around. To be honest, I have a feeling you'll connect with her more than with Kira," he said as he stood and walked toward the door. "You two are a lot alike, and she'll be good to have around you—I'm hoping she knocks your ego down a few notches."

If only he knew.

"I'll send you their numbers. Take care of them this weekend."

"Yes, sir."

I waited until he was out of my office, then leaned back in my chair and blew out a relieved breath. Kennedy might not have called him, but Kira wouldn't have known to call Eli if Kennedy hadn't told her about this weekend. Whether or not Kennedy was ready, or wanted it, I was going to chase the girl who was already consuming my mind.

6

June 11
Kennedy

"Why do I have a feeling you won't be ordering anything, and you would rather be talking to my sister than to me?"

I turned around from where I was washing a few blenders with my forehead scrunched in confusion, but my face immediately fell when I saw Liam standing on the other side of the counter from Kira. Both of them were staring at me with expectant expressions—though somehow Kira's seemed a little more hopeful.

After hanging out twice with Liam and his friends last weekend, and then meeting up with him and a few other friends at a bar on Wednesday, it was safe to say that my attempts at keeping Liam away were failing. Not just failing. "Crashing and burning a fiery death" would be a better way of describing them, because Liam still wasn't stopping his advances, which meant he wasn't getting too discouraged, if at all. And, unfortunately for me, I wanted the advances to stop just as bad as I wanted them to continue.

I was a mess.

"Kennedy?"

"What?" I asked quickly when I was brought back to the present.

Kira's lips curved up in triumph, and she gestured behind her. "Liam's inviting us to a bonfire tonight."

"Ah. That's nice. I'm tired, but thanks for asking, I'm sure Kira will have fun."

Liam's expectant expression didn't falter, and I was left wondering if he believed anything I said and did around him—as I had so many times over the last week and a half. No matter how many times I told him I didn't want to be with him, stepped away from him when he got too close, flirted with his friends, and acted as if he was nothing more than a nuisance, he seemed to always look at me with an expression that let me know it was only a matter of time until I stopped pretending.

"Oh, I'm sure I will . . . just like I'm sure you will too."

My eyes shifted to my sister and narrowed. "I'm not going."

"Yes, you are."

"No, I'm not."

Kira turned to look at Liam and flashed him a smile. "We'll be there."

Liam nodded at her, and slowly walked around the circular drink station. I knew when he stopped directly behind me, but I refused to turn and look at him until he said my name.

"Moon," his deep voice rumbled, and I shut my eyes and quickly prayed for strength.

Turning around, I kept my annoyed expression as I waited for whatever he would say. When nothing else came from him, I repeated, "I won't be going tonight."

A sly smile crossed his face as he nodded and backed away—like my one sentence had been the only thing he needed to hear from me. "See you tonight, then," he said confidently.

"Liam!" I harshly whispered when he turned. "I said I *won't*."

"Heard you the first time, Moon," he called over his shoulder, and I stood there with my mouth open as I watched him leave.

"*Why* does he do that?" I asked when Kira stepped up beside me. "Why does he act like he knows me so damn well?"

Kira sighed, but she sounded annoyed. "Probably because when it comes to Liam Taylor, you're kind of transparent."

"I am not transparent. I tell him exactly what he needs to know . . . that I don't want him or to be near him."

"You may say those words and have the body language, but nowhere in the tone of your voice or in your eyes do they agree with what your lips say. Or, at least, I think that's how Liam put it last weekend."

My head whipped to the side, and I shot her a look. "He said that? When?"

Kira still wasn't facing me, her forehead was scrunched in confusion and she was mouthing what she'd just told me. "Yeah. Yeah, that's how he said it."

"*When,* Kira?"

"On Sunday after that party at his friend's resort or whatever it was. You were your normal bitchy self when we were leaving, and I started to apologize to him, but he just laughed and said that."

"Seriously?"

Kira's only response was to raise her eyebrows in confirmation. "Besides, he knows just as well as you and I do that you will be at the bonfire tonight. No matter how much you want him to stay away from you, you can't stay away from him."

"That's not true, Kira, and I only end up going to all these places because I don't want to be left at the condo alone!"

She turned and elbowed me when someone cleared their throat near the register. "Keep telling yourself that when you're with him tonight," she said as she walked away to help the customer.

"I must say, I'm surprised you've held out this long."

I turned back to find Kristi standing in front of me, exactly where Liam had just been. "What?"

"With Liam."

My brows slanted down over my eyes, and I shook my head once. "I don't—what?"

Kristi smiled and rolled her eyes. "It's not hard to see that he has his eyes set on you. Anyone could've seen it from that first day he ran into you here. I'm going to be straight with you and tell you that for him, girls are more of a . . . when-he-wants-them type of thing. And Liam is incapable of loving anyone who isn't family."

"I don't believe in love."

"Well then, looks like the two of you would be perfect if you wanted to be with him, and if he was the kind of guy who did relationships. But I can honestly say, I haven't seen a girl turn him down since sometime in high school. Once he has his mind set on a girl, it's only a matter of seconds before he has her. It's disgusting, really. But like I said, I'm surprised you've held out this long."

Lovely. "Well, I won't be giving—"

"We've all made bets."

"I'm sorry . . . what? Who has?"

"Everyone who works here," she said matter-of-factly. Like the fact that they were bidding on my will to continue pushing away her brother was nothing more than what day of the week it was.

"Well, I hate to break it to everyone, but it won't be happening. Your brother already knows that."

Kristi drummed her hands against the countertop for a few seconds before backing away and saying in a singsong voice, "If you say so!"

As if I wasn't already having my own problems trying to stay away from him, I now had every person I knew in California wait-ing for me to give up and give in. If only they knew I was doing it to protect myself because of a past that still felt too present . . .

If only *I* could remember my reasons for needing to stay away when he was near me.

EIGHT HOURS LATER and I was at the fucking bonfire. And trust me . . . it wasn't by choice. Honestly. Kira and I had sat down and had a long talk when we'd gotten home from work about why I couldn't be with Liam—as well as why I *wouldn't* be with him. Because as I'd come to find out while talking with her, there were differences between the two.

Kira had actually seemed sympathetic once I laid it all out for her, and finally agreed to stop pushing the whole thing on me. An hour later, after more talking about work and California, she'd asked if I wanted to go out to dinner since our only other options were ordering in or going to the grocery store. We'd al-ready ordered in almost every night that week, and on a Thurs-day night, grocery shopping was the last thing I wanted to do.

Well, second to last, as I'd come to find out another thirty minutes later after we'd gotten ready and driven to the restaurant—a restaurant that at that moment was conveniently and suspiciously disguised to look like the beach with a bon-fire not far in the distance.

Unfortunately for me, Kira had immediately gotten out and taken the car keys with her.

So I was now standing there surrounded by a few people I'd met over the previous week, and many others I was almost posi-tive I'd never seen before. And what made it even better? Kira had taken off an hour before because Zane had called her, as I'd found out from Liam. Which meant that not only was I stuck at the beach until Liam gave me a ride home, I was also wonder-ing if I actually loved or hated my twin, and contemplating all the ways to shatter and destroy her beloved phone. All the while trying not to go cross-eyed from the one-sided conversation I was a part of.

"You look like you could use another one of these," a gravelly voice said in my ear, and I turned to look up at Liam. He was standing just off to my side holding a beer in his hand, and right then I wouldn't have cared if he were offering me sand. I would've taken anything from him if it meant I got a few seconds of distraction from the guy in front of me.

"Thank you. Is there another one for you?" I asked unnecessarily. One, there was only one can in his hand, and two, I already knew Liam wasn't drinking since he'd driven.

"Nah, I'm good." Liam's ice-blue eyes stayed locked on mine for a few silent seconds, and just when I was about to look away, they drifted to the side and a smile crossed his face. "And he's gone."

I looked quickly in front of me to find that the guy I'd been talking to *was* in fact gone. Well, if you could consider five feet away *gone*. But at least he was focused on someone else now. "Seriously, thank you so much!" I whispered in relief to Liam, and sank down onto the blanket I'd been standing on. Shoving the cool can of beer into the sand, I took a sip of the one I'd already had that was still completely full.

Liam sat down in front of me, but kept his eyes averted. "I figured you needed to be saved from him, and I couldn't think of a good enough reason."

My eyebrows rose once in confirmation, and I laughed softly. "He was . . . well, he's something else," I said as I glanced back at the man in question.

"I don't know why he comes to these things. He never drinks or eats, he never brings anyone with him, and he only talks to people about how his radish is going to save the world—"

"Avocado," I interrupted. "He said the radish wasn't going

to produce the right kind of energy. He's trying an avocado pit now." Liam rolled his eyes, but his smile was contagious. "How do you even know him?," I said.

"We don't! He just joined in on a party one day when we were out here, and it never fails, if we're at the beach he'll show up at some point. I don't think I even know his name, we all just try to avoid getting stuck in a conversation with him," I said.

"Howie," I answered before taking another sip. "He has an employee ID card clipped onto his shirt from some company."

"Well, you've now met *Howie*. You can consider it a rite of passage here."

"Yay me," I mumbled sarcastically.

Both Liam and I were silent for a few moments as we watched Howie go into an overly excited and detailed explanation to a girl who looked like she couldn't get away fast enough, and I laughed when her expression clearly showed she'd given up on trying to find a way out.

"I want to know more about you," Liam muttered, bringing my attention back to him.

My smile faded and I shook my head faintly. "Liam, I—why? *Why* do you keep pushing for something between us?"

"I just want to know more about you, Kennedy. Friends do that—hell, strangers do it. So why can't we?"

"Because you and I both know your real reason for wanting to know. You know just as much about me as you do about Kira, and probably more than your other friends know, at least the ones I've met. You asking for more is just—"

"It's just a request as a friend, Kennedy. Nothing more, nothing less."

I watched his expression carefully, and knew that it was anything *but* a friendly request. Before I could come up with another reason not to tell him more about myself, he leaned closer, and the movement had my dismissal getting caught in my throat.

"You already know where I went to school and what I majored in; why don't you start there for me?"

I released a heavy breath and began shaking my head again, but found myself saying, "I went to Florida State, and majored in psychology."

"*Psychology?* Really?"

I laughed, and tried to look offended. "Yes, really. Why do you look so surprised?"

Liam's eyes widened as he tried to find the words. "I just never would have guessed that about you. You don't seem like the kind of girl who'd be interested in psychology."

"And what kind of major do I look like I would be interested in?"

He huffed out a short laugh and shrugged. "How to show a guy you're not interested?"

Instead of saying something to get out of the conversation, or telling him he was pushing it again, I smirked and said, "I minored in that, actually."

"Figures." His eyes darted to mine before he was looking at the blanket again. "So what do you want to do with your degree?"

"Nothing," I admitted on a sigh. "I had to take a course for gen. ed., and I ended up loving it, so I majored in it. I guess in a way I'd grown up being fascinated by the way people are because of my dad."

Liam didn't respond, but his confused expression was enough to make me continue.

"My dad is a detective; so is Uncle Mason. I figured he would've mentioned something about that in the meeting he had with you and Uncle Eli."

"No. But somehow it makes sense. Eli said that your dad was the last person I wanted to piss off. I couldn't imagine how your dad would be worse than Mason when he looks the way he does. But if they're both detectives, I get it."

I smiled wryly and asked, "Would it make it even better for you to know that they used to do undercover work? Like, they lived with, and were part of, gangs."

Liam's face went blank for a few seconds before he started getting up. "Well, great knowing you."

I laughed and pulled him back down, and was glad to see the amusement in his eyes and smile. My dad and uncle had scared off enough guys while I was growing up, and the fact that Liam didn't seem to mind made him that much better. A jolt ran through my body when I realized exactly where my thoughts had gone.

It shouldn't have mattered if the news of Dad and Uncle Mason's job caused Liam to run or not. If anything, I should have been hoping for it to make him too scared to keep pursuing something with me. But as usual when I was in Liam's presence, my walls were falling.

Sitting back, I cleared my throat. "Anyway, growing up with them and hearing their stories about the people they encountered must have been what started it for me. We also used to watch these shows on serial killers, and I remember always being fascinated when they interviewed them and we got to hear their reasons for doing what they did."

"That's a . . . morbid thing to be fascinated by."

I laughed at the way he was looking at me—like he was concerned for my mental stability. "But like I said, I've never wanted to do anything with my degree. There was never anything in particular I wanted to be or do when I grew up, and that hasn't really changed. I feel like I'm still waiting to find what I'm meant to do."

We spent the next two hours talking about everything and nothing. And somewhere in there, we ended up moving closer and closer as we joked with each other and I told him more about myself than I'd ever intended. Thankfully, the conversation had never gotten deep. It stayed playful and had mostly been full of childhood memories and embarrassing teen and college stories.

"Here," he said as he came back to sit on the blanket after disappearing for a couple minutes.

I straightened when I saw what was in his hand, and my eyebrows rose. "S'mores? You all make s'mores at your bonfires?"

Liam's lips curved up, and he shook his head once. "Not usually; someone must've brought them, though. Do you want it or not? Because if not, I'll take one for the team and eat it by myself."

"No, no! I want it!" I grabbed for it when he started putting it near his own mouth, and pulled it toward my body like I was protecting the treat. "I've been trapped here for hours, there's no way you're denying me one of these."

With a short laugh, he put his hands up in surrender, and I took my first bite of a s'more since high school.

"Oh my God," I moaned, and licked at my lips as I handed it over to him for a bite. "Easily the best thing I've eaten in years."

We passed it back and forth a couple times, and when the last bite was between my fingers, I began handing it over, then quickly brought it back and shoved it into my mouth.

"Mm, yep. Yeah, that last bite was the best part for sure," I mumbled around the treat, and tried not to laugh at the betrayed look on his face.

"That hurt."

"I bet it did. You gonna get over it?"

"I don't think I can," he replied with false hurt. "That was low, even for you."

"Poor Liam." I pouted for his benefit. "I'll go make another one, and this time you can have the first *and* last bites." I started to stand, but stumbled when I got caught in the part of the blanket I'd pulled over my legs as the night grew colder, and fell against Liam.

His hands immediately went up to help steady me, but the force of my fall had landed me in his arms with my chest pressed to his. Liam's hold tightened around my waist, and instead of helping by pushing me back, he pulled me closer—and I didn't once try to fight him.

We stared at each other for a few tense seconds, and my breathing grew heavier as I tried to tell myself that I needed to back away, but what I wanted was much louder than what I needed at that moment.

I wasn't sure who moved first, but our mouths crashed together in a hungry kiss that was so much like our first one a year ago. My hands slid from his shoulders to his neck, and the tips of my fingers played in his hair as I moved so I was up on my knees and straddling him. His arms tightened once against my waist before dropping lower and pulling my hips toward him as he let me take control of the kiss for a moment. But like last year, it was only seconds before he was the one demanding and controlling—and not one part of me had the will to fight him on it.

I wish I could say I was having a lapse of judgment because of the beer, but I hadn't even finished my first one. Liam had kicked down my walls. He'd had me laughing more than I had laughed in years, and as always, he'd had me forgetting why I couldn't be with him. And with the scent of the fire mixed with the salty ocean breeze, and with my body pressed up against his, I was positive I'd been silently begging for his kiss, and was now begging for it not to end.

But it *had* to end. It wasn't until he whispered my name that I was able to remember why.

"Liam," I breathed against his mouth, and moved my hands down to plant them on his chest. Countless seconds passed as we both sat there breathing heavily, and I forced myself not to give in again. "Liam, I think it's time I went home."

His body hardened beneath my hands, and I knew he knew what I was saying and doing. I was stopping this before it could continue. I was pushing him back. And I was throwing up my walls again.

No words passed between us as we got ready and left, and there was only a silent good-bye as we stared at each other when he pulled up in front of my building. I fought with myself over the apology that was on the tip of my tongue, but kept it in as I opened the door and stepped out of his car. If I had voiced it, I knew my already shaky walls would quickly fall again, and I didn't think I would have the strength to get them back up.

June 12
Liam

"READY TO SPAR, old man?" I asked the next night as I walked up behind my dad and punched his shoulder.

He turned around from where he was helping a member perfect his technique, and raised an eyebrow to match the smirk on his face. "We'll see if you're still calling me that when I'm done with you. Go do something to warm up while I finish here."

I nodded and tore off my shirt as I crossed the gym. After last night, this was what I needed. I needed time to clear my head, and I needed to focus on not getting my ass handed to me by my dad instead of replaying my night with Kennedy over and over.

My eyes automatically drifted over to the drink station, but I already knew I wouldn't find the girls there. I'd waited until they'd been off work for a couple hours to show up to fight tonight instead of waiting until tomorrow like I normally did. Because ever since I'd gotten off work, it'd taken all my focus to keep myself from going to their condo to try to talk to Moon. I knew I would eventually give up and show up at her door if I didn't do something to get my mind off her soon, and the gym would do exactly that.

"You ready?" Dad asked fifteen minutes later as he pulled off his shirt and climbed into the ring.

I glanced over at him and gave him a calculating stare. "I'm not going easy on you just because you might break a hip."

He laughed. It didn't matter that he was in his forties, just like it didn't matter that he'd stopped fighting for a living over twenty years ago. He was still unbeatable, and he and I both knew he could easily take me down with just a few hits.

"You want to tell me what has you in such a bad mood?" he asked when we began.

"Kennedy." Okay, maybe the gym wouldn't get my mind off her. I took a few swings and dodged one of his, and grunted when he landed a kick to my ribs.

He blocked one of my hits. "And what about her has you showing up a day early?" After a few more swings, he took a few steps back and sent me a condescending smile. "It can't be because she turned you down, because she's been doing that for more than a week now, son."

I glared and closed the distance before I threw another hit. "Yes and no. We kissed."

He stumbled back when I kicked his calf, and bent over laughing. "You're here to fight, looking pissed off at the world, just because you two kissed?"

I straightened and threw my arms out to the side. "She fucking shut down again after. The entire night she was completely different from how she's been since I first talked to her here. It was good; everything about last night was good. And then a couple minutes in, it's like she remembered that she'd been pushing me back before, and did it again. She didn't say a word the entire ride back to her place."

One eyebrow rose, and for a second, he actually looked sorry . . .

until he spoke. "Maybe she was thinking about giving you another chance, but once she kissed you sober, she realized that last year was a fluke and decided to bolt."

"Are you serious right now? That's really what you're going to go with? That's your great fatherly advice? To try to tell me that my kissing is what had her shutting down again last night?"

"Looks like it's a possibility." He sucked air through his teeth and shook his head, but his mouth started twitching up into a smile, and soon his shoulders were shaking from the laugh he was trying so hard to hold in. When my face fell, he barked out a laugh and kicked out my legs from underneath me. Leaning over me once I was lying on my back, he grinned knowingly. "You want my honest opinion? I think she has a very real reason for trying to hold you back, one she's not ready for you to know—*if* she'll ever be ready for you to know. But from what I've seen, she's a lot like your mom. She's feisty. My bet is you just have to figure out the right buttons to push for her to completely open up to you. If I'm right, she'll be trouble . . . but she'll sure as shit be worth it."

Accepting his hand to help me up off the ground, I got ready to go again. "I'm already starting to figure that out."

Once my dad and I were done fighting and had talked awhile longer, I grabbed some food and drove over to the tattoo parlor where I got all my work done. Walking in, I headed over to Brian, a friend of my parents'. He was practically family and I'd always gone to him whenever anything happened in my life. But I hadn't seen him since I'd found out Kennedy was in California, and I knew it was only a matter of time before he somehow found out and got pissed because I'd failed to mention anything.

"What's up, Little Chachi?" Brian called out when he saw me.

I rolled my eyes but smiled at the nickname he and his wife had passed on from my father to me.

"You lookin' to get something? I'm sure I've got a good hour or so before the weekend crowd starts pouring in."

"Not today." Grabbing a burrito out of the bag I was holding, I tossed it in his direction.

"Ah, yes. Gift from the gods. How did you know I was dying of starvation?" he asked as he opened up the foil.

"Because you're always dying of starvation." I pulled a chair into his station and groaned as I ran my hands over my face.

Brian clucked his tongue. "Ah, one of *those* visits. Good thing I'm not stoned. I need to be clearheaded for this."

"Shut up, Brian."

He laughed and took a massive bite of the burrito, then nodded once and spoke around the food. "Talk at me."

"You might want to swallow the food before I tell you this."

His brow creased as he studied me, and after a few seconds, he went back to chewing. "Done," he grunted, and his eyes narrowed. "Are you in some sort of trouble?"

"No, not at all. I just have a feeling you're about to start yelling as soon as I tell you what's going on, and I'd rather not have to call an ambulance for you when you choke on the food."

"Makes me all warm and fuzzy to know you wouldn't try to save me." Brian set the burrito on his desk and crossed his arms over his chest.

"I'm sure it does," I said with a grin, but it quickly fell. With a deep breath in, I asked, "Do you—"

"You get her flowers and beg her to forgive your stupid ass."

My eyebrows rose. "What the fuck, Brian? I barely got two words out!"

"This about a girl?"

"Yeah, but—"

"Then you get some motherfucking flowers, and you go to her and beg her to forgive your dumb ass. There. Heart-to-heart done. Now I'm still starving, and this little piece of heaven is

begging me to eat it." Grabbing the burrito again, he took another bite and smiled through it.

"How did you even know it had to do with a girl?" I asked,
somewhat amazed that Brian of all people could have guessed
that.

"Because I've seen that exact same tortured face before." His
eyes darted to the side, and he swallowed thickly. With a slight
shake of his head, he mumbled, "I still can't believe how much
you look like him now."

"I know." I sighed, but couldn't even begin to imagine what
he was seeing when he looked at me. Because even though pictures helped tell a story, they would never be the same as the real
thing, and the guy he was talking about had died before I was
born.

"So what'd you do to screw up this time?"

"What did *I* do? Nothing. Nothing, unless you can count
wanting to be with her."

Brian looked at me for a second as he slowly chewed his food,
and made a sound of disapproval in his throat. "LC, man, I told
you. Once they get a restraining order, you can't keep going near
them."

Despite the aggravation I was still feeling even after sparring
with my dad, hard laughs burst from my chest. "Aw, Bri, did you
find that out firsthand?"

He shrugged. "Maybe I did, maybe I didn't. Maybe I ended
up marrying her despite it."

My eyes widened, and my mouth curved up. "Riss had a restraining order on you?"

"Fuck no. Her dad did. He got over it eventually. Anyway, I
know you didn't come in here to have me tell you about my life,
so continue."

"Okay, well, this is the part I didn't want to tell you while you
were eating. So stop." I gave him a look when he started to go

for another bite, and after a heavy sigh, he set the burrito down. Again.

"This better be fucking good," he grumbled, and pouted when he eyed the food again.

"Do you remember Moon? The girl from Vegas?"

"How am I supposed to forget her? She's the only girl you've talked to me about more than once."

I rolled my eyes at his annoyed tone, but didn't comment on it. I knew it was just because I'd told him to stop eating. "Well, she's in San Diego."

Brian sat up and sucked in a large breath. "No!" he said loudly, drawing out the word.

"And she's working in Dad's gym."

"No! No fucking way, dude! Holy shit!" His excitement died suddenly, and he pointed at me. "I forgive you for making me put the burrito down. This made up for it. But, seriously, what are the chances of this?"

"It gets better. *Her* uncle is *my* boss."

Brian stared at me for a minute with his mouth wide open. "Did you find her through him? Did you see a picture of her or something?"

"No, nothing like that." I sat back in my chair and told Brian the entire story from the meeting with Eli and Mason up through last night.

Throughout it all, as Brian finished both his burrito and mine, his shock-filled eyes never left me.

When I was done, I held my arms out to the side for a second, then let them fall. "And that's my problem. It is obvious what she wants, but every time she starts to show or act on it like last night, she just throws another wall in my face."

"Damn, LC. That is some heavy shit." Before I could agree, he asked, "When did you figure out you were in love with her?"

My head jerked back. "I'm not." Brian's expression turned

amused, and I repeated, "I'm not. Jesus Christ, Brian, I've only known her name for a little more than a week. I know I won't stop chasing her even though she's driving me crazy with how she constantly pushes me back, but that doesn't mean shit about loving her."

Instead of trying to convince me that I was in love, like I'd expected him to, he got really quiet and stared at something behind me. When the silence continued and his gaze didn't waver, I turned to look, but only saw another one of the artists bent over, outlining a tattoo.

"You know," Brian said suddenly, bringing my attention back to him. "About twenty-five years ago, my station was right over there." He nodded in the direction where he'd been staring. "I was sitting in there with Chachi, and we had a conversation a lot like this one. He was telling me all about your mom only a couple weeks after he'd met her, and how crazy she was making him. I think I'd been making fun of him because he was whipped by a girl he wasn't even with, and somewhere in his explanation of her, I realized he was in love with her. He denied it just like you're doing, but the truth was all over his face. And I swear to Christ that exact same fucking look is on your face right now— and it's taking me right back to that afternoon with your dad. I told you I've seen that tortured look before; trust me when I say, Little Chachi, you're in love with this chick."

"Brian . . . I'm not—"

"Don't worry, LC. You'll figure it out when you're ready, just the same as she will. I've seen this before. If I hadn't, you wouldn't be here today."

7

June 13
Kennedy

"ARE WE GETTING out of the car, or are you going to keep sitting here worrying over how fat your ass looks in that bikini?"

My head whipped to the side to face Kira, my mouth and eyes going wide. "Don't be a—wait! My ass looks fat in this?" My hands immediately went to where my skirt-covered butt was planted in the seat, and suddenly I *was* worried about it. "Why didn't you tell me before we left?"

Kira rolled her eyes and reached for the handle of her door. "Because it doesn't, you're just pissing me off because you won't leave the car and we've been parked here for eight minutes. But if we don't get out of here soon, I'm sure you'll be able to start worrying about having a *flat* ass."

"You're such a brat," I muttered, and looked straight ahead at the ocean again.

"Are we going or not? I'd rather sit on the couch in the condo than stay in a car that is rapidly turning into an oven." Before I could respond, she added, "You already know he's going to be here since he's the one who invited us. You spent an extra half hour getting ready for him, which is even more pathetic considering we're going to be at the beach all day."

"*For* him? Get ready *for* him? Are you fucking kidding me? I couldn't care less what he thinks of me and the way I look."

"You're still feeding yourself that line, sis? Neither Liam nor I has believed that since the beginning . . . I'm surprised that you're still trying to get *yourself* to believe it." She laughed, but it sounded more annoyed than anything. "The last time you spent so much time trying to make yourself and those around you believe you didn't care about someone, he was your—"

"I will kill you if you finish that sentence," I said, cutting her off, the warning in my tone clear.

Kira raised a challenging eyebrow. "Starting to see the resemblance in the two?"

With a shake of my head, I reached for the handle of my door and tossed the keys onto Kira's lap. I didn't exactly want to go hang out with Liam and a bunch of his friends after what happened between us the other night, but right then I would have done anything if it meant having space from my sister. "I don't know what's happening between you and Zane, but Jesus Christ, he has turned you into such a bitch."

Stepping out of the car, I shut my door and began walking toward the sand without looking back. I knew after what I said, it would take Kira a few more minutes to leave the car—if she left it at all—and for a second I felt bad about using Zane against her just then. But then I remembered who she'd been using against me, and it didn't take me long to get over it.

"Hey!"

I looked up to find Liam jogging toward me, and my body froze. Part of me wanted another taste of what he'd given me not forty-eight hours before, the rest wanted to run from him while I showed him how little he meant to me.

He stopped suddenly when he got close to me, and his eyebrows slanted down. "Whoa, are you okay? And where's Kira?"

"She's in the car."

I'd taken a step to walk around him, but he caught my arm and pulled me closer. "What's wrong?"

"Nothing is wrong." I tried yanking my arm from his grasp, but he never loosened his hold.

"You're lying to me. It's all over your face."

"Well then, it's the sun getting in my eyes." After another yank, I glared up at him and took a step back.

"Kennedy, why—"

"Will you let go of me?" I asked, my voice rising.

He immediately released my arm, but those ice-blue eyes still held me captive. "You need to tell me what I'm missing here. I know after what happened the other—"

"What happened Thursday night was a mistake."

"Mistake," he stated, his voice low and flat. "Are you—God, Kennedy, what do I need to do? Where am I going wrong, because even though you shut down again, I know damn well that 'mistake' is not even close to the way you looked after. You looked scared."

I couldn't respond to the last part, because even though he and I both knew he was right, I wasn't about to admit it. "What you need to do is stop trying to make something happen—or stop thinking that there's something happening. I told you the first day that nothing was going to happen between us. That hasn't changed." I started walking past him again, but hadn't made it more than two steps when I was pulled back. "Liam—"

"Tell me why you're doing this!" he demanded, but the harsh whisper of his tone had my automatic response dying in my throat. "Tell me what it is that has you running from me."

The way his eyes were pleading with me was almost enough

to make me crumble right there. The truth was bouncing around and around in my mind, begging to be voiced, but I couldn't allow it. Getting Liam to think that nothing could happen between us was the only way to keep my heart safe. The only mistake I made on Thursday night was that I had given in and kissed him and, in that moment, had fallen for him a little more. That moment had made all of this harder. I hated seeing the pain and confusion on his face, but I couldn't let myself fall in love with him.

Wait . . . love? That thought snapped me back to the present and to the way he was silently begging me for an honest response. That was the problem right there. Being around Liam had me entertaining the possibility of love again, and I knew better than anyone that love wasn't real. It was an idea made up for couples. I knew if I let something happen between us, I would stop remembering that, I would let myself believe in it again . . . and then my world would be ripped from me. Just like it had been years ago.

"Kennedy, please."

With a shake of my head, I pulled my arm away from him—this time there was no resistance. "I don't know what you want me to say that I haven't already said."

When I began walking again, Liam didn't try to stop me. I wanted to go back to the car and leave, but I knew doing that meant facing Kira—and I wasn't sure either of us was ready for that yet. As I got closer to Liam's friends, I continued walking straight ahead instead of joining them. I didn't know if I knew any of them anyway, and being there meant facing Liam again too soon and without the distraction of my sister. The only reason I'd even agreed to come after what went down the last time I was on this beach was because Kira had told him we'd be there. And despite my own discomfort with the situation, I would do anything if it meant getting her away from the condo.

Because the longer we were indoors, the more she fell into her Zane depression . . . not that I'd done much to help that by what I'd just said in the car.

As soon as I reached the shoreline, I walked along the hard, wet sand for ten minutes before turning around to head back. When I knew I was getting closer, I looked up to search out the group, and just in time to catch Kira as she came barreling toward me.

"I'm sorry," she whispered as she squeezed me tighter.

"*I'm* sorry. I shouldn't have used what's going on with you and Zane like that."

She shrugged and shook her head as she took a step back. "No, you were right. I've had the worst mood swings since we moved here. I really shouldn't have used . . . well, *him*. That wasn't fair, I know. It was low, and I knew it would be before I even said it."

I started to deny it, but a laugh bubbled up from my chest instead. "Yeah, that was pretty shitty. Didn't know you had it in you."

Kira smiled widely, but it fell soon after. "Tell me really, why are you pushing Liam away?" I started to respond, but she cut me off by talking over me. "And don't lie to me again. You know you can't anyway. I didn't buy any of what you told me before the bonfire."

I sighed heavily and my shoulders fell. "I just can't let him get close to me. You were right . . . about the similarities between the two of them. I hadn't realized it until I left the car, but I think I still knew before, and it scares me. I'm terrified of the way he makes me feel just by being near me."

"Just because *he* was a dick doesn't mean Liam will be too. You can't write off all relationships because of one bad one."

I raised an eyebrow. "But it was a *really* bad one," I said in an attempt to help my case.

"They won't all be."

"But where will this even go? Liam lives here, we live in Florida. Who knows how much longer we'll be here? It won't be forever, and what then? There's no point in allowing myself to get involved with him."

Kira was quiet for a minute, her brow pinched together as she thought, and I knew she couldn't deny that I had a point. "Maybe . . . maybe not. All I know is that when you let your guard down, I see a side of my sister that I haven't seen in years. I remember the way you looked that day Liam first came up to us in the gym. And I still remember the way you thought about him for months and months after only *one* night with him. So whether or not this ends badly, I think you should let yourself have fun while we're here, and while he's close to you."

"I don't think I—"

"You're already hurting both of you, Kennedy. Just think about it."

And I did. For about an hour.

I didn't let my walls completely fall like I had at the bonfire, but I was letting myself have a good time with Liam and his friends, and it was impossible to miss the way Liam was reacting to my mood. I kept catching him staring at me with a hopeful look on his face, and his smiles were never ending, but he was making sure not to get too close. I knew he was being cautious to protect himself, but I was still thankful for it. And without having to watch out for me and my bitchy mood, Kira looked like she was enjoying a day away from her Zane depression.

"See? Not so bad, is it?" Kira asked when we were grabbing drinks out of the coolers.

I tore my eyes away from where Liam had just stretched out on a towel, and looked up at my sister. "What?"

"Letting yourself go when you're near him. It's not so bad. It already looks like it's easier for you than forcing yourself to be miserable."

I bit back a smile and elbowed her side. "No one said I was changing my mind."

Kira started to laugh, but cut off abruptly and grabbed my arm. I didn't need to ask why, because I was watching it too.

A girl who had shown up only about twenty minutes before had walked over to where Liam was lying down, put a foot on either side of his hips, and sat down on his lap—like it was an action she'd done a thousand times. The second she was down, Liam pushed up so he was sitting as well, and then the next movements were so fast that it was hard to see who leaned in and reached for the other first. As soon as their mouths were pressed together, I looked away and into Kira's confused and apologetic eyes.

"Do you want to leave?" she asked softly, but I shook my head and glanced back at the pair and found Liam watching me as the girl said something to him and ran her fingers through his hair.

"No. No, I think we should stay."

After all the times he'd made me feel sorry for pushing him away, I didn't even care about the way it seemed like something was painfully squeezing my heart. If that was how he wanted to play after everything that had already happened . . . I was game.

June 13
Liam

I'D BEEN TRYING to find Kennedy and Kira for the past twenty minutes. It shouldn't have been hard, we were all in my apartment . . . but so were about thirty other people. It only took five minutes for me to regret letting everyone come back here after our day at the beach. I should have known that our group of fifteen would quickly double in number, and the last thing I wanted was to act like I was actually enjoying the night when all I wanted was a chance to talk to Kennedy alone.

A pair of arms wrapped around my waist. Fingertips found their way into the band of my shorts, and I bit back a groan. Okay, I also wanted Cecily to stop trying to maul me every chance she got . . . which was also part of the reason I needed to talk to Kennedy. I hadn't missed the way she'd been looking at me earlier after Cecily had kissed me—it'd been impossible to. Just like it had been impossible to figure out why Cecily was trying to bring back our relationship and make it public suddenly.

Sure, some people at work had known . . . but that had been it. Even if we had been at the same event or party, we stayed away from each other. That was the agreement. We only did anything in my office, or when we were alone in either of our places. Nothing more.

Grabbing her searching hands, I pushed them away and turned to look at her. Her dark eyes were pinned to me, the challenge in them clear. She wanted Kennedy to see this; she also wanted me to give in to her as much as she wanted me to publicly announce what we'd once had. I held her stare until I was sure she was listening to what I was about to say. "Cecily, you have to stop. Whatever it was we had is over—I thought I'd made that clear the other day."

Her eyes narrowed marginally at my soft tone, and when her next questions came out louder than necessary, I knew I'd been right. She wanted a public scene—and she wanted one girl in particular to get a front-row seat. "Since when, Liam? What is your deal lately? You have never *once* tried to push me away from you, and don't try to deny it. There are plenty of people who remember you pulling me into your office and the noises you had me making not long after."

I grabbed the back of her neck and brought her close to me. "You really want to start this shit? No one will look bad after this except for you, believe that if nothing else." Her eyes widened, and I knew I had her. She would do anything as long as she came out on top, and I would make sure she wouldn't this time. With a heavy sigh, I released her and took a step away. "You know why things have changed, and you know they changed awhile ago. This weekend isn't anything new. What I don't get is why you're suddenly letting someone make you act like you're some insecure girl who's been burned when there was never anything between us *to* burn."

Her expression went flat, and just when I saw her anger coming through and prepared myself for whatever she would say, she turned and pushed through the people behind her—making her way to the door.

"Whew. Talk about drama," a husky voice said next to me.

I turned and jerked back when I saw Kennedy standing directly beside me. But at second glance, my body relaxed when I realized the wrong sister was standing next to me. "Where's Kennedy?"

Kira shrugged and turned to look behind her. "Dancing . . . somewhere. I don't know, I lost her a little while ago."

"I'm gonna go look for her."

"You gonna save her from all the big and bad guys at your place, Liam?"

I smirked and gave her a questioning look. "You say that like it's a bad thing."

She held up her hands in mock surrender. "Didn't say that. You just might want to be prepared for what she throws at you after what happened at the beach. I may have heard what just went down between you and that girl, but she didn't, and I know she isn't forgetting what she saw earlier."

If Kira was warning me, I could only imagine how bad it was

about to be. Turning around, I moved slowly through the people standing around drinking and dancing. I was just about to turn around to go back to where I'd left Kira when everything in me halted, and my blood boiled. My hands clenched into fists, and I had to force myself to stay where I was instead of going over to punch a guy sitting on the arm of one of my couches.

Kennedy was practically fucking his thigh along to the music, and his hand started wandering up her skirt as I sat there watching them. I knew I needed to turn around and go someplace where I couldn't see them. I didn't have a right to make her stop what she was doing, especially after she watched me with Cecily, but that wasn't stopping me from feeling like it *was* my right.

A hand touched my arm, and when I turned, I found Kira looking at me with wide eyes—her head shaking back and forth. "She's just doing it to get a reaction out of you."

"Don't—"

"No, Liam, I *know* her. I know what she's doing! She wants to get back at you for this afternoon even if she won't admit it!"

"Well, then it's fucking working! But there's no point to try to stop it when all she has done is push me away, and now I've finally given her a reason to."

Kira's eyes widened. "There isn't?"

I ground my jaw and narrowed my eyes at her. "You and I both know she doesn't want to be saved—"

"That doesn't mean she *shouldn't* be saved by you!" she yelled, cutting me off. "Liam, don't let her continue to push you away. I know she needs you despite everything she's done so far!"

My eyes darted to the side, and my body locked up again. Kennedy's head had dropped back and the guy was leaning his head toward her chest.

Fuck this.

I moved from Kira's hand and pushed forward through the crowd as fast as I could. As soon as I was close enough, I grabbed Kennedy around the waist and yanked her back before the guy's mouth could touch her.

She was yelling at me. But with the music and my rage, I couldn't make out her words as I pulled her away. It was taking everything in me to continue walking forward rather than going back and beating the shit out of someone who had no idea that the girl in my arms belonged to me. I practically carried Kennedy out of the main room, down the hall, and into my room. As soon as the door was shut, I turned and pinned her back against it.

"What the fuck is your problem?" she screamed.

"I want to know the same damn thing, Kennedy! What was that out there?"

Her eyes widened, then narrowed in anger. "You're really going to ask me that after what I saw today?"

Leaning in close to her, I spoke low. "You have no idea what that was this afternoon, but I'll tell you it wasn't welcome."

"I'm sure," she bit out. "Because having girls climb onto your lap must be so rough on you!"

"If it's not you? Then yeah, it is. You would know that if you hadn't been avoiding me for the last few hours, and then trying to get off on some guy's leg in *my* goddamn place."

A cynical smile was plastered on her face. "What's wrong, Liam? Jealous because it wasn't you? Have you forgotten you don't have a say over who I—"

She cut off quickly when I slammed my hand against the door and put my face directly in front of hers. "You are *mine*."

"You do not know me, Liam Taylor, don't you dare act like you own me!"

"Don't I?" I challenged. Without giving her a chance to respond, I continued, "One last time, Kennedy. Why are you pushing me away when I know that's not what you want?"

"I don't know what you want me to say anymore!" she yelled.

"What do you want, Liam? Do you want me to say you're right? Okay, yes! Yes, Liam, I want you! Obviously you already know that. But I can't—"

Before she could finish, I pressed my mouth firmly to hers. An aggravated moan rose up her throat before her lips parted— and then she was grabbing me and pulling me closer. My tongue slid into her mouth, and each stroke was matched with one of hers. If I had been watching us, I wouldn't have known if we were kissing or fighting. Like the night in Vegas over a year ago, there were hands searching, I was situating myself between her legs and biting down on her lip, and she was moaning and arching away from the door—all the while we both fought to be in control of the kiss.

I knew the exact moment she gave in to it. Her body relaxed against the door, her hands began clinging to me instead of grabbing, and her moans turned into soft whimpers. But like at the bonfire, her body suddenly stiffened and she began pushing against my chest. When I looked down, her eyes were glued to her hands, her breathing ragged.

"I can't," she whispered.

"What?"

"I can't do this."

"No. No, you can't go back to that."

She pushed harder, but I held her against the door—afraid if I let go she would leave and that would be it for us. "It doesn't matter if I want you or not, I can't be with you! Don't you get that?"

"No, I don't! For so many reasons, including what just happened, I don't buy that bullshit for a fucking second!"

She shook her head, indecision and fear covering her face.

"Tell me why you're scared. Tell me why you're fighting this."

"Scared?" Kennedy gave me a puzzled look and laughed. "There you go acting like you know me again, Liam. You don't.

You don't know me, and you do not own me. You need to forget about what happened between us."

"Forget about you?" I asked softly. "You can't ask me to do that."

Her dark eyes bounced back and forth between mine for a few seconds before they dropped to the floor. "After what I saw of you and that girl this afternoon, I don't think it'll be that hard for you."

"What you saw with Cecily was her trying to make sure you would want nothing to do with me—nothing more."

She shook her head a few times and choked out, "I can't." The words came out thick, and I watched her face tighten as she fought through whatever emotion she was trying to hide from me.

"Kennedy," I whispered, and leaned close to speak into her ear. "Yes, you can. If you would give us a chance, you'd see exactly why I would be good for you. You're scared; I want to erase your fears. You're fighting something that happened long before you met me; I want to face whatever it is head-on so the pain in your eyes goes away."

She didn't say anything for long moments, but I stood there waiting for the words that would either confirm what I already knew or cause me to back off for good.

"Moon, please," I begged.

Her hands pressed against my chest again, and I held back a disappointed sigh as I took a step away. But as soon as I raised my head, her hands were curling into my shirt and she was reaching up to crush her lips to mine.

This time there was no fight. Kennedy never tried to gain control. Her body immediately relaxed between mine and the door, and she easily moved with me when I pulled her farther into the bedroom.

Our lips never parted as I laid her on the bed and followed her down until I was hovering over her. One of her knees curled

up along my side when I settled my body onto hers, and I ran
my hand up her long leg, pushing the loose material of her skirt
up her thigh until it was bunched in my hand against her hip.
Moving down her throat, my lips made soft passes against her
skin, and a frustrated whimper escaped her mouth at the teasing touches. My fingers gripped against her hip and the bed as
the need to run my hands over her grew stronger, but I knew if I
went there, I wouldn't stop—and I needed to stop. "You're done
pushing me away," I said against her skin.

"I'm done," she agreed breathily. Kennedy's hands moved
from where they'd been gripping my shirt between our chests,
and made a slow trail down. The moment they touched the skin
just above the top of my shorts, I groaned against her neck as I
fought with myself over what I knew we needed, and what we
both obviously wanted. Before she could do anything else, I
pushed away so I was hovering high above her, and stared down
into her dark blue eyes.

"We already know what we're like together, Kennedy. I'm not
making the mistake of starting this with another night like in
Vegas."

"You're saying Vegas was a mistake?" she asked huskily, but
even with the breathy sound of her voice, it was obvious she was
joking.

"Never. But sleeping with you the moment you give yourself
over to me again *would* be a mistake. You could easily disappear from me in the morning, or realize how much you don't
want this once the night is over because I rushed things with you
again. I'm not taking that chance."

She looked at me for a long moment without saying anything,
her eyes thoughtful. "And if I'm the one who wants tonight to go
a certain way?"

The corners of my mouth curled up, and I leaned closer to run
my nose down hers and kiss her quickly. "You wouldn't be the

only one who wanted it, but it wouldn't matter if you begged for it. I'm not risking it after fighting so hard for you. You finally acknowledging that you are mine is all I need tonight. I've been waiting for that moment since you fell back into my life, Kennedy Ryan." After another slower kiss, I pushed up and rolled away from her to sit on the bed.

Kennedy followed me up, but sat facing me. "That girl— what'd you say her name was?"

I looked at her with my forehead bunched together, but before I could ask who she meant, I knew the answer from the way her eyes took on that same betrayed look they'd had this afternoon on the beach. "Cecily?"

"Right, Cecily. Who is she?"

As much as I wanted to say she was nobody, I knew I couldn't. To any other girl in my life, that would have been my immediate answer . . . but not to Kennedy. "She was one of many girls who meant nothing more than the fact that she was convenient to have around. She also works for your uncle, and we'd been . . . uh, *seeing* each other for a handful of months before you moved here. Nothing ever happened outside of work or our places. If we happened to be out with the same group, we acted like we worked together and that was it. That was what I liked about her. She wasn't clingy, and she saw me simply as someone who could satisfy a need. It wasn't until I backed away and started turning her down when you moved here that she got mad. I think she wanted to make you ignore me, and have me make a big scene so it would look like she had been wronged."

Kennedy raised an eyebrow and cleared her throat. "Is this—is that what you're wanting from this?" she asked, using a finger to indicate the two of us.

I laughed and shook my head once. "Are you serious? No. If you were like them, I wouldn't have thought twice about trying to pursue you—especially after the first time you made it clear you didn't want anything to do with me."

Kennedy's eyes got bright with amusement, and the look was so welcome after the intense beginning of this conversation. "Oh, a little confident there? So many women fall at your feet that you don't have to bother yourself with something like pursuing one of them? Must be nice."

I huffed softly and stood. Grabbing her hand, I pulled her up with me and over to the door. Just before I opened it, I turned to face her and waited until her eyes were locked on mine. "No one was ever worth the chase. But you? You will be worth it every time. I will always chase you, Kennedy."

8

June 27
Kennedy

AT THE SOUND of knocking, I shot Kira a look and stood to go open the door. "I don't need dates, Liam," I said by way of a greeting.

"Yes, you do," he countered, and smiled at Kira.

"I don't *do* dates."

"Neither do I, which is exactly why *we* should." Stepping into the doorway, he laid one hand on my waist and passed his lips across my forehead. "You look beautiful."

It'd been two weeks since I finally gave up trying to fight my attraction for him, and every time we'd hung out in that time, he'd asked if he could take me on a date. I just didn't see the point in going on one when we were together all the time, and dates to me meant that there would be a small title attached to what we were—and I wasn't a fan of titles anymore. It had taken Kira agreeing for me to get to this night. But I had to admit— with his confidence, sweet observation, and nonchalant attitude toward the whole night, he was already making it easy to go through with it.

After my initial swoon at hearing his deep voice tell me I looked beautiful, I shook my head and tried to hide my smile. "This is stupid."

"I don't care, we're still doing it. I even made reservations—we're going all out tonight."

I stopped trying to fight my smile, but still raised one eyebrow. "We're going all out, and I don't even get flowers?" I asked, trying to sound hurt. I clicked my tongue and whispered, "Strike one, Mr. Taylor."

"You mean these?" He brought his other arm out from around his back, and produced a brightly colored bouquet.

"Aw, look at you being sweet."

"I tried," he said with a cheesy grin.

I took the flowers from him and started backing up to put them in a vase, but Kira was right behind me and took them out of my hand. "I've got this, you two go."

"See you later," I called out to her after she'd retreated, and followed Liam outside and to his car. My eyes widened in surprise when he opened the door for me, and I couldn't hold back my smile as I slid inside.

"Okay, fine. The first strike has been erased," I said once we were reversing out of the spot.

"Good," he huffed, and sent me a look. "Because I have no fucking clue what I'm doing."

"Ah, yes, of course. Because you're used to having girls just fall at your feet, right?"

"Exactly," he responded immediately, his eyes never leaving my face. "Until you."

We'd barely reached the street outside of the complex when a car behind us began honking repeatedly. Looking behind us, I saw the driver was waving with one arm, and his passenger was holding both her hands out and mouthing the word *stop*.

"What the hell?" Liam whispered, but pulled over to the side of the road and rolled down his window.

The car pulled up beside him, and the lady pointed to the back of the car. "Your tire is flat!"

Liam looked in his side mirror, then out the car toward the back. "Are you kidding me?"

"Nope. Sorry, man, but it is *flat* flat."

With a wave, Liam mumbled a thank-you, and sighed when the other car pulled away. When he turned to look at me, his eyes widened as he saw how hard I was trying to hold in my laughter. "This is funny?"

The laughter finally burst past my lips, but I cut it off quickly. With an amused expression, I asked, "Did you not see this?" I pointed to the huge screen on his dash. At the top was a warning about the pressure in the tires.

Liam sighed, and looked like he was kicking himself. "Wait. You saw it and you didn't say anything?"

"No, no. I saw it after those people pulled up and started talking to you." Liam was looking at me like he was trying to figure out if I was telling the truth, and I laughed. "I swear! But can we bring back strike one now?"

He rolled his eyes, but I didn't miss his smile as he got out of the car and popped the trunk. Once he'd taken the spare out and disappeared behind the rear of the car, I got out and went around to watch him.

"Stay in the car," he ordered, but his tone was gentle. "I don't want you out here in case anything happens."

"Oh no, this is a must watch. Besides," I mumbled as I took a picture of him, "Kira needs to see how the night is starting off."

Liam raised one hand to flip me off before going back to jacking up the car, and I couldn't help but laugh again.

It wasn't long before the spare was on and we were heading

toward the restaurant. The entire way there, we talked about the only other time he'd gotten a flat, and I told him about all the times Kira and I had gone out to our cars to find our dad had taken off a tire and hidden it when we were supposed to be grounded.

The second we stepped inside the restaurant, I was blasted by a distinct smell, and I looked around to try to find the name of the restaurant—since I hadn't bothered to look while we were outside. I didn't have time to find what I was looking for, but kept my mouth shut as we were led back to a booth. I just hoped like hell that there would be something on the menu that I could eat.

After quickly glancing through everything, I bit back a smile and had to hide my face from Liam for a minute before I dropped the menu to the table and looked at him.

"You already know what you want?" he asked, surprise coating his words.

"Uh, well, if you want to end this date in the ER, then I can try to find something," I offered, and my lips stretched into a wide smile when he looked at me in confusion. "Liam, I'm allergic to seafood."

"Bullshit."

I shook my head. "Not bullshit. I'm allergic to anything that comes from water, and if it's something from the bottom of the ocean, it's bye bye, Kennedy."

His face fell, and a soft laugh bubbled past my lips. "Why didn't you say anything when you saw where I was taking you?"

"I didn't know! I wasn't paying attention when we walked in. When I smelled it, I was hoping there would be something else I could eat. Coming from Tampa, there are obviously a ton of restaurants with seafood, but more often than not, there are other things on the menu as well."

His eyes widened, and he leaned over the table. "Don't touch anything! We'll get out of here, just try not to touch anything!"

I laughed at his panicked expression, but did as he said as I slid out of the booth. Our waiter was walking up as we got out, and after a short explanation from Liam, we were walking out of the restaurant.

"Strike two?"

Liam didn't seem to find this funny; he was looking at me like he was waiting for something drastic to happen. "Are you going to be okay?"

"Liam, really, I'm fine. My allergy's not so bad that I can't be in a restaurant that serves fish. If my hands touch something that has had any kind of contact with anything I'm allergic to, then my hands swell up and start itching. If *I* actually touch a food I'm allergic to, then I'll be sucking down Benadryl like it's water. But if I were to eat it, then it would be really bad." Lifting my hands for him to inspect, I wiggled my fingers for a second. "All I touched was the menu. I'm fine."

He sighed heavily and wrapped an arm around my waist to lead me back toward the parking lot. "I swear to God, this night is already a fucking disaster."

"You still have one strike left, don't write off the night yet," I teased.

Liam was mumbling about flat tires and trying to kill me when we got to the car and he abruptly stopped walking. Releasing my waist, he searched his pockets quickly before uttering a curse and trying the passenger side door. It was locked. "You've got to be fucking kidding me," he groaned.

I laughed loudly and leaned forward to look into the car. When I saw the keys in the ignition, I started giggling so hard that I snorted, which made me laugh harder and hold myself up against his car so I wouldn't fall. "How—how did—oh my God, I'm sorry. I can't," I forced out between hysterics. "How is it locked?"

Liam was looking straight ahead with an expression that

had me laughing even harder, and doing everything not to pee myself. "If the car is turned off, the doors automatically lock after a few minutes."

I was laughing so hard that no sound was coming out, and all I could do was hold up three fingers, indicating strike three.

After calling someone to come open the car, we waited for forty-five minutes in the parking lot until Liam sucked in air and whispered harshly, "Fucking son of a bitch."

"What?" I asked in alarm, and looked around us.

"Don't," he warned as he left my side and went to the driver's-side door. "Don't say a damn word." With his frustrated stare fixed on me, he pressed his fingers to the very edge of the driver's-side door, and his door unlocked.

My brow furrowed before my eyes and mouth widened, and immediately I began laughing all over again. "Fingerprint sensors?"

"I've never used it before, I forgot about it."

As soon as I heard my door unlock, I pulled it open and got inside. I wasn't laughing anymore, but I couldn't stop smiling—and that smile got even wider when I saw his face.

"This has been—" He started, but I cut him off by leaning over, grabbing his face, and pressing my lips to his.

"Tonight has been beyond perfect."

"Perfect," he said, his voice and face blank.

"I don't think it could have gone better for us. Two people who don't date can't just have a perfect date their first time. It's like when you buy a new car. As soon as you get it home, you kick it."

"Kick it," he stated, once again with no emotion.

"Yes! Because it's all shiny and new, and if you don't kick it yourself, you'll always be worried about the first time *anything* happens to it—because eventually something *will* happen to it. So, we just kicked our first date. Now we don't have to be scared for when something bad will happen on any of our dates after this. Like I said, perfect."

Grabbing the back of my neck, Liam pulled me in for another kiss. This one was longer, and slower, and like tonight—it was perfect.

"I'm taking you home so nothing else can happen tonight. Three strikes are more than enough."

"Or instead of that, I vote we go get ice cream. You can never go wrong with ice cream. Unless, wait, are you allergic?"

He huffed, but his mouth curved up into a smile. "I'm never living down this night."

"Nope," I agreed. "You're definitely not."

June 27
Liam

"SO YOU DON'T date, because you don't like the 'title' of dating?" I asked a little over thirty minutes later.

Kennedy nodded and took another bite of her ice cream. "Pretty much."

I looked at her with my brow furrowed for a minute. I could understand that to an extent. I didn't date the girls I was hooking up with, but that's because I didn't want relationships with them, and I knew dates would lead them to think something would happen between us. But I also knew that once I found a girl worth pursuing—like Kennedy—that would all change. "But eventually you'll find a guy you know you want to marry and spend the rest of your life with."

"No, no," she said quickly. "There's no chance of that happening."

"No chance of what? Marrying someone, or finding someone you want to spend the rest of your life with?"

"The whole thing," she answered, and waved her spoon in the air. "I won't get married, and the other is just basically the same, without the husband and wife part of it."

"I don't understand what's wrong with either of those things."

Kennedy sighed, but paired with her expression, I knew it was because she was trying to figure out how to explain herself. "Both of those things are something people do because they think they're in love with whoever they're with. They like the idea of love and being with only one person, and that's just not practical."

"Being with only one person for the rest of your life isn't practical?" I asked blandly.

"No. It's a lie. It's saying you want to be with someone so much that they're the only person you will ever be with again. People only do that because that's what they think love is— sharing your life with someone. And love doesn't exist."

I shook my head. No matter how much I wanted to laugh, I couldn't figure out how to because Kennedy looked completely serious. "What about your parents? Your grandparents? Eli and Paisley? They're all still together, aren't they?"

"They are."

"So you're saying none of them are in love?"

"No, I'm not. Okay, let me rephrase. Love doesn't exist *anymore*. Not in this day—not for our generation. You see how many divorces there are now? It's just people who get tired of being with their spouse because they're no longer in 'love' with them, or they 'love' someone else. If you actually loved them, that wouldn't ever go away. You'd always love them. Now? All love is, is a dream. It's something people want and pretend they find."

I studied her for a second and asked, "How could you grow up around people like your parents and come to the conclusion you have?"

"Growing up around them is the exact reason I figured all this out. I grew up around perfect couples. All of them were happy, and I remember always wanting to have that someday."

"And?" I prompted when she didn't continue.

Kennedy just shrugged. "And then I found out it didn't exist anymore."

"Just like that? One day you just randomly decided that?"

For long moments, she just sat there watching me. After a while she finally said, "I had that. I was sure I had what they had. I was positive I was in love. And then I found out how wrong I was one day. After that, I stopped looking at the world through love-clouded glasses, and started seeing relationships for what they were. They look perfect on the outside, and inside, they're just a disaster."

"Is that relationship what happened to make you push me back?"

She shook her head and rolled her eyes before scooping up another bite. "It was a long time ago. I pushed you back because it wasn't hard to see you wanted something I couldn't give you because I don't believe in it."

"And yet, here you are. On a date with me, and you talked about future dates in the car."

"Well, it's not like you and Kira gave me a choice about tonight," she said with a teasing tone. "But after everything I told you before tonight, I know you already know how I feel about an actual relationship. So I'm not worried about you waiting for this to turn into something it won't."

Looking around us, my gaze stopped on an elderly couple, and I leaned in toward Kennedy. Grabbing her hand, I nodded my head in their direction. "Look at them. The couple in the corner."

Her eyes drifted past me, and I watched as her face softened. Turning, I looked at the pair too. Both had white hair and were permanently hunched, and the man had a cane resting against the table. There was a bowl of ice cream between them, and he took turns giving his wife a bite before taking one for himself.

He was holding her hand across the table, and their fingers were curved around each other's like they'd spent the last sixty-plus years never letting go of each other.

Looking back at the girl I was holding on to, I spoke softly. "I know I want that someday; there's no way you can't want it too."

"I used to," she admitted when her dark blue eyes met mine again. "But it just doesn't exist for us anymore."

"You're twenty-two, Kennedy. You have a long time to change your mind."

AN HOUR LATER, I was walking back into the familiar tattoo shop with a bag of food in my hand. I'd just dropped Kennedy off at her condo, and even though the rest of the night had been great, I couldn't stop thinking about the beginning of our conversation at the ice cream shop.

"Little Chachi!" Brian called out from where he was wrapping someone's leg. "What'd you bring me, and why are you visiting me again on a Friday night? Don't you have better things to do than come talk at ol' Bri on nights like tonight?"

"I just dropped Kennedy off."

"Who?" he asked distractedly before telling the guy he'd been working on that he could pay up front and giving him a rundown of after-care instructions.

"Moon," I said when the guy was gone and I was in Brian's station.

"Oh, no shit! Like date night? Hell yeah! What changed since I last saw you—wait! Tell me what you brought me first."

I tossed him the bag full of hamburgers and fries, and he groaned in appreciation.

"You just knew I was starving, didn't you? That's why you're here?"

"Of course that's not why I'm here. Kennedy doesn't believe in love," I said as I took a seat on his desk.

"So what?" he mumbled around a bite. "You don't love her anyway—or do you now? I told you you would! See, LC! I know you. I know these things. I know how those faces of yours work; you were in love before you even knew it."

"Still don't love her, Brian."

He kept talking as if I hadn't spoken. "Just like with Chachi before you, I know what the fuck's up. I should be Cupid's sidekick or something."

"Brian," I barked, and kicked at his leg. "I don't love her. But I want to know what you think about what *she* said about love."

"You came to me for this, Little Chachi?" Brian made a face like he was about to cry, and wiped away an imaginary tear. "I knew it. Cupid's sidekick. I've got this love shit down."

With a weighted sigh, I decided against saying anything about the new title Brian had given himself, and told him all about my conversation with Kennedy. When I was finished, Brian sat there staring at me with a handful of fries half hanging out of his mouth.

"Again, so what? You're still acting like you don't love her."

"I *don't,* but I want to know what you think."

Brian rolled his eyes, like I was asking him to stop eating again. "*I* think that she's been hurt."

"That's obvious," I said, cutting in. "She said she had a bad relationship."

"Do you want me to tell you or not?"

I lifted an arm out and to the side. "Continue."

"Anyway! I think she's been hurt. Not just in a way people get hurt in normal everyday relationships. I think whatever happened in that relationship hurt her in a way she was never expecting to be hurt, and a way *you* probably can't understand. *So* hurt that her only way to get past it is to make herself believe that love doesn't exist anymore."

I leaned forward and rested my arms on my legs. "What could've happened that was so bad?"

"Lot of things, LC. He could've hurt her physically. You just never know."

"But she's twenty-two, and she said this happened a long time ago. How could she have been old enough to be so in love with someone that she thought she had what her parents had? And knowing her personality, there's no way she was ever the kind of girl to be in love with every relationship and boyfriend she had."

"Your mom was eighteen when she fell in love and then had her entire world ripped out from under her in ways that I can't begin to understand—and I was there with a front-row seat during it," he said like that should've been explanation enough. And I guess in a way, it was. With a shrug, Brian said, "This kind of shit happens sometimes. If you ever find out, you'll probably never be able to understand what your girl went through. But I have no doubt that it's just going to take the right guy to make her believe in all that lovey-dovey shit again."

"It's not gonna be me," I reminded him when he gave me a knowing look.

"We'll see, LC. We'll see."

9

July 11
Kennedy

"KIRA, ARE YOU really not going to go?"

I waited for Kira to turn and face me, but she never moved from the fetal position she was in on her bed.

"No," she finally grunted.

After waiting a few seconds more for her response, I walked over and sat so I was resting against her back. "Well then, I'm not going," I promised as I played with her long hair.

Last weekend she'd started staying in the condo instead of going out with Liam and the people we'd been regularly hanging out with. During the week, she'd been mostly normal at work—although more than a handful of times I found her staring at nothing with a worried look on her face. Then yesterday at work she didn't say a word the entire time we were there, and hadn't left her bedroom since we'd gotten home.

"Just go, Kennedy. I don't want to talk today."

My forehead pinched, and for a second, my hand paused in her hair. Once I started up again, I shrugged. "That's okay. We don't have to talk. But there's obviously something going on with you. I'm not going to leave you when you're like this."

"I don't want you here," she responded immediately with a monotone voice.

"That's okay too," I whispered.

"No, Kennedy, really. Please leave." This time her voice shook with her words.

I heard the front door open with a knock and looked up, waiting until I saw Liam fill the doorway to Kira's room. I shook my head slowly in response to his question-mark expression, and he just nodded.

"Hi, Liam. Bye, Kennedy and Liam," Kira mumbled, and I sighed.

Given the way she was acting, I normally wouldn't have left her. But we'd gone through a similar conversation last night, and I'd ended up backing out of dinner with Liam to stay with her—which had resulted in Kira shrieking for me to leave her alone until I finally left her room.

Kira and I could bicker like there was no tomorrow, that's just how we were and always had been. Probably because my parents were the exact same way, and while Kira was just like Mom, I was too much like our dad. But nothing that was said in this conversation could have made me pick a fight with her. I was too upset for her, and I wasn't even sure what was bothering her this time. If she and Zane were fighting, I wouldn't have known because she wouldn't talk to me about him anymore.

"Kennedy—" she began, but I cut in.

"Okay, I know. We're leaving." I stood and walked over to Liam, but called back to Kira, "Call me if you need me."

When she didn't respond, I looked up to Liam and pushed him away from the door so I could close it behind us.

"We don't have to go anywhere," he assured me.

"No, it's fine. Once I left her room last night, she never said a word to me or left her bed. I sat outside her door most of the night, and she never even cried. There's no point in staying here again. She'll call me if she needs me."

Liam didn't move toward the front door, and with a deep breath out, he asked, "Are you sure? I really don't care if we don't leave."

"I'm sure." Grabbing his hand, I started walking toward the door, but he didn't budge. "Liam," I groaned on a laugh.

He took a few steps forward, closing the distance between us, and pulled me close. "Your sister's upset. I'm not going to make you—"

Pressing my mouth to his to make him stop talking, I smiled and stood on the balls of my feet to wrap my arms around his neck when he deepened the kiss.

"Nice distraction," he murmured against my lips, and I made an affirmative noise in the back of my throat.

"Kira will be fine. I want to leave the condo, and I want to spend time with you. *Please,* can we go?" When Liam just stared at me with a torn expression, I added, "I'll text Zane."

"Fine," he conceded. "But only if you text him."

"As soon as we get in the car, I promise."

With a look back at Kira's room, Liam released me and began towing me toward the front door. As soon as we were in the car and it was turned on, he looked at me expectantly, and waited until I was done texting Zane about Kira's mood and begging him to call her. Once my phone was back in my lap, Liam leaned in for a quick kiss before backing out of the space and heading over to his friend's place.

I'd been there before, but still couldn't believe the size of it when we pulled up. This guy's house was so extravagant and large that he even hired a valet parking service for when he had parties. Kira had called his house a resort because that's pretty much what it looked like. You could easily get lost trying to find a bathroom, and I'd told Kira he should have signs up directing guests.

He had a kitchen the size of our condo—that was only for entertaining purposes and appearance—and a much larger kitchen in the back for his chefs. Outside there was a basketball court, tennis court, two pools and a hot tub, and a small golfing area—and by small, I mean it was large enough for nine holes. And that's not including the third pool and hot tub that were in the house, as well as the bowling alley. There were also menus placed near random phones in the house so you could call in a food order to the kitchen. And the best part? The part of the beach the house was on was private.

Like Kira said . . . resort.

Liam had gone to school with the owner of the house's younger brother and sister, and apparently Eli and Liam did a lot of the advertising for the man's business. Whatever his business was. I'd forgotten as soon as he'd told me just like I'd forgotten the guy's name. Kira and I had been referring to him as RB—Rich Bastard.

There were hundreds of people there. Some in the house, some outside at the pools, and a few mingling on the beach. Weaving through the bikini-wearing girls and guys without shirts were waiters delivering drinks and food.

Liam kept his arm around my waist as he talked with someone he knew, and I just tried to take everything in again. It was all super overwhelming—even more so the second time around since Kira wasn't with me.

"Well, don't you two look a little overdressed?" a loud voice boomed from behind us, and we turned to find RB standing there with a wide smile. "Liam, how are you?"

"Good, doing good. Rob, do you remember Kennedy?"

Rob . . . Rich Bastard . . . same thing. I plastered a smile on my face and extended a hand toward him. "Good to see you again!"

He took my hand quickly, then pulled his away and pointed at me. "Was I really wasted last time, or were there two of you?"

"There were two. My twin, she's not here," I explained seconds before he pulled me in for a hug.

"Good deal, I was about to worry about my alcohol intake if I'd been seeing double." He laughed and pointed at a man passing us. "Chris! This couple needs to be relieved of some clothing. Care to help them out?"

A uniform-wearing guy stepped up to us and pulled a key ring out of his pocket. After taking the key off, he handed Liam the key ring that had a gold plate with the number 103 on it. "Don't lose that, please, otherwise I won't be able to get your clothes back until everyone else has left the party. What clothes and belongings can I take for you?"

The last time we'd gone through this, Kira and I had looked at him like he'd lost his mind when he'd asked for our clothes. This time, it wasn't any less awkward, but at least I'd known to expect it. Once I had my shirt off, I handed it and my purse over to Chris, and waited while Liam shoved his keys, wallet, and phone in my purse and handed over his shirt as well.

"Do you want me to take your shorts, miss?" he asked, and I shook my head.

"No, I'm fine with them. Thank you, though." I knew every other female at the party wasn't wearing anything more than her bikini, but I found it weird to walk around some stranger's house without *some* kind of cover on. Not that my shorts covered much anyway, but it still made me feel better to have them on.

"There, much better." RB gestured toward his house and smiled. "Have fun, anything you need, just call it into the kitchen. As always, it's on the house! I have to go act like a host or something now."

After our good-byes, I looked at Liam. "That sounded like the exact same speech as last time."

Liam smiled and pulled me close. "It was, I don't think he's realized people have caught on to that—or he just doesn't care."

"The latter," I mumbled.

"Probably. Do you want anything to eat or drink, or do you want to go outside?"

"Outside, please. There's a lot of cologne and perfume clashing together in here."

With a loud laugh, Liam pulled me toward the back, and I was quick to regret begging him to take me out. While RB's house was something in itself to look at and explore, I hated how the other people attending the party had me feeling insecure.

I'd never been insecure until the last time I was here. I couldn't look at any woman and know for sure that her hair was natural, just like I couldn't look at them and find a natural chest. Mine wasn't small, never had been. But my boobs didn't stay up unnaturally high, looking surgically enhanced like all the other women's. And while I'd never had a problem with my tattoos—and still didn't—it was incredibly obvious that I did not fit in here because of them.

The only tattoos I saw on the other women were either little symbols or a word on their wrist, or something to make guys stare at their ass. And there I was with sleeves and more art and words on my chest, sides, back, and legs. I loved my tattoos; it was the other women's looks as we passed by them that made me want to curl in on myself or leave. It didn't really help that more often than not, people stopped talking when we walked by. They'd done the same when Kira was with us, but I'd been making myself believe it was because she and I were so identical looking. I'd been wrong.

"I don't fit in here, Liam," I whispered as we moved through the crowd.

"And? I don't either. I wouldn't want you if you *did*."

I sighed, and turned to face him. When he stopped walking and leaned close, I shook my head. "But I'm not them . . . I don't look like them."

Liam's eyebrows rose, and a smile crossed his face. "You don't look like them? *That's* what you're worried about? Kennedy," he mumbled as he lowered his head so his mouth was next to my ear. His hand squeezed my hip when he asked, "Have you seen yourself lately? Did you see how all the guys we passed were looking at you? You are easily the sexiest woman here, Moon. Trust me."

"I don't care about what the guys were thinking." I pushed my fist against his stomach, but he didn't move away. "But the differences between the other girls and me—"

"Are obvious, yeah," he finished for me. "And I love every fucking one of those differences. Your confidence in yourself and your looks is one of the best things about you; don't let the shallow people here make you lose that."

I sighed and leaned away so I could look in his eyes. "If you don't like them, why do you come here?"

"I've known Rob most of my life, but me being here also helps maintain the relationship between our two companies."

I nodded, and with a deep breath in, I looked around us. There was still a group of women near us staring directly at me as they spoke quietly to each other, and instead of looking away, I raised an eyebrow and waited for them to look down.

"That's the Kennedy I've come to know," Liam said in amusement. "Let's grab a drink, walk around the beach for a bit, and then we'll get out of here. Okay? Rob won't even notice we're gone."

As soon as my margarita and Liam's bottle of water were brought to us, we took off for one of the paths leading down to the sand, and I couldn't believe how much easier it was to breathe once we were away from everyone.

After a few minutes walking along the beach, Liam pulled me to a stop and looked at me in confusion. I immediately stopped laughing at what we'd just been talking about and asked, "What?"

"I just don't understand why you had to get away from all of them to be yourself. I thought you were supposed to be this tough girl who didn't take shit from anyone. Even your uncle said you couldn't be around people for long before letting them know what you thought of them."

I laughed again, and shook my head once before looking up at the mansion. "There were a lot of them, and they all looked the exact same. It was hard walking through that while they were all staring me down." Before Liam could respond, I said, "It would be like showing up to a black-tie party wearing a cow costume because you thought it was *that* kind of dressing up."

Liam laughed loudly and eyed me. "A cow costume? Really, of everything you could have said, you came up with cow costume?"

"Shut up! I used to wear one while we were in college. I'd randomly walk around campus with it on during finals week, and Kira would wear her pig one. It eased the tension on campus and made people laugh."

Liam was still laughing, but now he was bending over so his hands were on his knees. "You're comparing tonight to your cow costume at a black tie?"

"Shut up," I mumbled again, and pushed him so he stumbled backward. "It was really that awkward!"

"I'm just trying to picture you in a cow outfit. Did it have the face and everything?"

I rolled my eyes and started walking away. "Yes, it did. It even had a ribbon with a bell on it."

"Was it named Bessie?"

I laughed and pushed at his chest, but he caught my wrist and held me close.

"Come on, it's a fair question."

"No! She didn't have a name," I said through my laughter, and a look of horror crossed his face, making me laugh harder.

"How could you not name her? That's like not naming your car!"

"Because it was an outfit."

Liam raised one eyebrow in a look that clearly said he was trying to picture me in the costume, and his eyes traveled down my body for a second before he asked, "Did it have the udders too?"

"Yes, Liam, it had the udders. There was a tail too, if you were wondering."

"I was, actually. But what I really want to know is if I can call you Bessie when you wear it again."

This time when I shoved him, he stumbled back again. "No, you cannot! And I didn't even bring it to California."

"You're telling me that you're going to tell me about this, and then deprive me of seeing Bessie?"

"Yes, that is exactly what I'm saying!"

"Whoa, whoa, wait!" he said suddenly with a serious look on his face, and my laughs stopped while I waited for whatever he was about to say. "Is that why you have the crescent-moon tattoo?"

"What?"

"Because the cow jumped over the moon. You have the cow, you needed the moon to complete it."

"Oh my God, how did you even put those two things together? You're so weird!" I called out as I walked away from him.

"But it's perfect! I already call you Moon, now I get to call you Bessie too!"

"I will never speak to you again if you do!"

"Aw, come on, Bessie."

"I hate you," I said through more laughs and tears. "Seriously, this is not okay."

"It'll be fine, Bess. I'm sure of it. I promise to only say it in public if—"

His words cut off when I turned and dumped the rest of my margarita over his head, and now I wasn't breathing because of how hard I was laughing.

Liam was staring at me with wide, shock-filled eyes as the icy drink dripped down his face, and in that moment, nothing could have looked better. "Now, *that* is perfect."

With a deep breath in, he said, "That wasn't nice, Bessie."

Before I could tell him I didn't agree, he lunged forward and grabbed the back of my thighs before lifting me up over his shoulder. "Oh my God! Put me down!"

Liam didn't say a word as he began walking, and I slapped at his back.

"You are covered in icy liquid, and it is freezing! Put me down!"

"Trust me, I know just how cold it is."

I stopped slapping him when I realized what direction we were walking in, and shrieked when he started jogging into the cold water and it splashed up on my legs. "Don't you dare, Liam!"

"What?"

"You know what! Don't. Do. It—" My last word ended on a scream as he launched me away from him and into the ocean.

As soon as I came up from the water, Liam was pressing his mouth to mine and slamming us back into the water.

"I hate you so much right now!" I yelled when we both came up.

I took off for the shore and, once I reached it, had only made it a few feet before I was bear-hugged from behind and started falling toward the sand. At the last second, Liam turned so he landed on his back with me on top of him. I awkwardly rolled over on top of him so I could yell at him, but his lips were on mine again, and for a few moments, I gave in to the kiss until he started rubbing sand all over my wet skin.

A high-pitched sound rose up my throat, and I struggled to

get off him. I was running the instant my feet hit the sand again, and though I knew he was right behind me, he never made another grab for me until I made it up the first flight of stairs to the rinse-off station.

Liam's arms wrapped around me and he slammed me against his chest as he moved backward. One of his hands came up to the side of my face and turned my head so his mouth could find mine, and he grunted into my mouth when he hit a wall. Turning around, he pressed me against it and moved down to kiss my neck.

"I hate you," I whispered even as I pulled him closer, and a low, husky laugh vibrated against my skin.

"I doubt that, Moon." Liam slammed his hand against a button on the wall as he brought his mouth back to mine, and water started pouring down on us from the showerheads.

Grabbing the back of my thighs again, he lifted me up so I could wrap my legs around his waist, and then he was pressing me up against the wall again. I met his next kiss eagerly, and my fingers secured themselves in his hair as his tongue met mine with teasing strokes. I moaned into the kiss when I felt him harden against me, and let my head fall back against the wall when he pressed himself closer to me.

His lips traveled down my throat and chest, and one of his hands moved up to push my bikini top aside before his tongue and lips were torturing my nipple. I wanted to move against him, but couldn't given the way I was pinned between him and the wall, and a frustrated whimper left me.

Liam glanced up with a heated look in his eyes as he tried to catch his breath. "Let me take you back to my place," he pleaded, and it wasn't until that moment that I realized we were outside with a party going on not far above us.

I nodded and pressed my mouth to his once more before he released me and righted my top. "Let's go."

As soon as we got our things back from Chris, we were in the car and on the way back to Liam's . . . but no words passed between us as the heated tension grew. When we pulled into the complex, I checked my phone and saw nothing from Kira or Zane. With a quick text to Kira letting her know I might not be home tonight, I shoved my phone back into my purse just as Liam parked.

I reached for the handle on the door, but stopped when I realized he was just sitting there watching me.

"I need to know what you're thinking right now," he said on a deep rumble.

"What do you mean?"

"You haven't touched me or talked to me since we got in the car thirty-five minutes ago. I need to know if you've changed your mind about being here."

A small smile crept across my face, and I leaned forward to slowly press my mouth to his. "I haven't been talking because I've been anxious to get here. And now I'm wanting nothing more than for you to take me inside."

As soon as I grabbed for the handle again, Liam was opening his door and getting out. He waited for me at the front of his car, and pulled me into his arms when I got closer. Despite how I'd been envisioning this, I knew it was about to be completely different.

After the heated moments at the party, I'd been ready for us to start tearing at each other as soon as we were in his apartment. But even the walk to his apartment was slow, as I knew our movements would be inside. And once he shut the door and locked it behind us, I knew I was right.

He was looking at me with a stare that had goose bumps covering my body and my breathing deepening, and he wasn't even touching me.

After putting his stuff on the table just inside the door, he walked up to me and reached for my purse before putting it down as well. And with his eyes still on me, he grabbed my hand and walked me to his bedroom. Liam hadn't bothered with any of the lights in the apartment, and somehow the last of the setting sun's glow outside of his windows was making the moment more perfect than I could have imagined.

Stepping up to him, I slowly started lifting his shirt, then let him finish taking it off. My eyes fell down to study his upper body and all the ink covering it, and I reached out to run the tips of my fingers across his skin.

He sucked in a soft breath at my touch, causing the corners of my lips to twitch up. The dark orange glow outside lit my forearm and hand when I rested it on his chest, and my fixated stare on it had Liam glancing down and grabbing my hand to press my fingers to his lips.

Turning me around so I was facing the window, Liam pulled off my shirt before slowly trailing his fingers up my arms and across my shoulders to untie the top of my bikini. Once it, my shorts, and the rest of my outfit were on the floor with my shirt, I leaned back against his chest as his hands made light passes across my skin—and never once took my eyes off the unblocked view of the ocean and multicolored sky until one of his hands made its way between my thighs.

My mouth opened on a muted sigh when his fingers found the piercing there and moved in a slow, steady rhythm while his other arm wrapped around my hips hard enough that I couldn't move against him the way I wanted to. I had to raise a hand up to wrap around the back of his neck to keep myself from falling when the pressure increased, leaving me only seconds away from falling apart against him. I whimpered when Liam's lips met the sensitive skin behind my ear, and after a few soft kisses there, he bit down gently just as my body began shaking before completely exploding. His arm around my body tightened to keep me standing when my knees went weak; and when my orgasm ended, he easily pulled me back toward the bed and laid me down.

I grabbed at his shoulders to pull him toward me as he took off his shorts; but the second he was on top of me I released my hold on him—knowing that it wouldn't have been long before he'd remove them for me. Unlike last year, I never once tried to fight for control of what we were doing. Instead, I waited for what he would do.

This wasn't me. I liked being on top. I liked having control of any heated situation, and not being in control usually left me panicking—but not with Liam. Everything about Liam, from last year in Vegas through now, had me being someone I didn't recognize. But nothing about that bothered me now like it had before. I liked the way he silently demanded control, I liked the way he made me feel like I was someone to be cherished and protected during sex rather than just a means to an end. And I loved that he had me forgetting everything except the two of us just by kissing me.

Liam pulled one of my legs up so my knee was curved around his narrow hips and lowered himself onto me. With his arctic-blue eyes on mine, he squeezed my thigh as he pressed against me, and my breath came out in a quick rush at the feel of him pushing inside me.

"You're still on birth control?" he asked through rough breaths, and when I nodded, he whispered, "Good," just before his mouth crashed down against mine and he began moving inside me.

His grip left my thigh, and soon both of his hands were curled around mine and pinning them to the bed, where they were stretched out beside me. The way he was pressing against my piercing had me whimpering as I got closer and closer to another orgasm, but his mouth never once left mine, even when my high-pitched moan was swallowed by his kisses as I came again.

My body felt weightless and heavy at the same time when he released my hands. Pressing his forearms into the mattress on either side of my head, he dipped his face down to place it against my neck as his movements quickened, and I took the opportunity to run my hands over the muscles in his chest and torso. My arms were shaking from the aftereffects of coming again as I trailed my fingers up his back to grip his shoulders, but the way his muscles tightened and relaxed beneath my touch had my grip tightening instead of releasing him.

His hard breaths rushed against my skin as he moved harder and faster for long minutes until they stopped when his body froze above mine. My grip on his shoulders relaxed when I felt the way he was vibrating above me, and as soon as I released him, he rested his body on mine, then rolled us over so he was on his back and I was draped on top of him.

Neither of us spoke as we waited for our breathing to return to normal, and when I felt my body moving in time with Liam's steady breaths a couple minutes later, I looked up into his bright eyes just in time for him to press his lips to mine. I smiled against the kiss, and couldn't stop the giggle that bubbled up my throat when he pushed me aside only to climb over me and off the bed, and then pull me up into his arms.

He didn't break away from the kiss until we were in the bathroom and he was setting me down on my feet. "I'll use the other bathroom to clean up," he said, and turned to leave.

Liam was returning to the bedroom when I walked out of the bathroom a couple minutes later, and without giving me a chance to put any of my clothes back on, he grabbed one of my hands and towed me back to the bed. Once we were under the covers, I moved closer to him until I was pressed against his chest with his arms around me.

My body instantly relaxed against his, but it wasn't long before I realized that his felt tight—too tight. I looked up to find Liam watching me with a worried expression, but before I could ask what was wrong, I felt the smallest pressure where his hands were touching me—like he was worried I was about to disappear—and I knew.

"I'll be here in the morning," I assured him.

He nodded once, and his face instantly relaxed as he settled in against the pillow. "Good night, Moon," he whispered, and I hid my smile against his chest.

"Good night, Liam Taylor."

10

July 17
Liam

"YOUR MOM'S MAD at you."

I looked over to where my dad had just sat down in the sand, and set down my board before sitting next to him. "Mad? Why?"

"Jesus, Harper isn't the only one who is mad. Your aunt Bree wouldn't let me get ready or leave the house this morning without lecturing me the entire time about you," Uncle Konrad added as soon as he was sitting on my other side.

"Doesn't surprise me," Dad groaned, and lay back. "The two have been on the phone every time I've come home from the gym this week."

"Well, are you going to tell me why they're mad?"

Dad looked over at me with his eyebrows up high. "Seriously? You have no clue? You've been with Kennedy for how long now?"

I shook my head slowly as I tried to figure it out. "I don't know . . . a month? We're not really together. Kennedy's afraid of commitment. She says she doesn't believe in it, but I don't buy that and I can't figure out why she's scared of it."

"Doesn't matter," Uncle Konrad mumbled, and Dad nodded in agreement.

"Yep, doesn't matter. The girls see it as a relationship, and they're mad that you haven't brought her by the house to meet them."

"What do you mean? Mom sees her almost every day because she brings you lunch at the gym. And I have no doubt that Aunt Bree has been stopping by so she can spy on Kennedy." I turned to look at Uncle Konrad, and found him smiling. "Figures."

"Still doesn't matter. Your mom wants you to bring her by for dinner or lunch or something to formally meet her as your girlfriend—or some shit like that."

"Dad, Kennedy would take off running if I introduced her to my family as that. Shit, *any* girl would probably take off running after trying to introduce her to my family after only a month. But you should have seen her when I let the word 'girlfriend' slip to one of my friends—she completely froze and wouldn't say anything the rest of the night. A family dinner is not going to happen."

"Then invite both her and her sister, act like it's nothing special or uncommon for us to have people over for dinner."

"It's not," I reminded him. "But you don't invite the employees from the gym over. Whatever I come up with, she's going to see right through it. She'll know what it really is."

"I'm sure you'll figure out a way." Dad sent me an amused smile, like he knew exactly how difficult it was going to be. "Have fun with that."

"And don't be surprised when we show up and Bree starts interrogating her."

I scoffed at Uncle Konrad's words. "Why would I be?" I sat there for a second, then conceded with a sigh: "But if that's what they want, I'll figure something out. I'll ask her soon."

The three of us fell into a silence as we looked out at the gray ocean. It'd been a perfect morning for surfing, and it was getting bright enough outside that more people would be coming out soon. But we'd been coming here as long as I could remember; my dad and uncle long before that. We knew the perfect time to come for the waves and to have as much of the ocean as we wanted without many others around.

Uncle Konrad let out a sharp laugh, and my lips curved up in a smile at what was coming. It happened every time we surfed, and I knew today would be no different. Just like it was no different that Brian mentioned "Chachi" every time I was around him.

"Brandon. Remember that first day I went out surfing with all of you? Chase was being a dick about Harper, and you both started throwing punches that only lasted for a minute before all your housemates were pulling you two off each other."

Dad sighed, and a wide smile covered his face. "Those were some damn good fights. Didn't like them or him that much while they were happening, but I miss those times."

"You two looked like a couple of chicks fighting over the last pair of shoes at a store."

Dad barked out a laugh and looked over to me. "Have I ever told you about the first time I met Chase?"

"At McGowan's? McGowan set you both up in the ring to show everyone the new fighter he'd found in you."

Dad's eyes got a faraway look, and his smile softened. "Good fucking day."

Looking down at a tattoo on my right inner forearm, I stared at it for a second before saying, "Why don't you tell me again? It's been awhile since I've heard that one."

Uncle Konrad knocked into my side, and I turned my head for a moment to see him offer me a grateful smile just as Dad started in on the story. Looking back at the tattoo on my right arm, I didn't once take my eyes off it as I listened to a story I'd heard hundreds of times, and had no doubt I would hear hundreds more. A story about a guy I knew as well as I knew myself, and a guy I would never get the opportunity to meet.

July 17
Kennedy

I STEPPED THROUGH the door of Kira's and my condo and immediately knew something was wrong. Not with our place, everything still looked exactly how it had when I'd left earlier . . . but there was definitely something. I'd only been out for a walk for forty-five minutes, and I couldn't begin to figure out what could have changed in that time. I started walking in the direction of my room to get ready for work, but turned and headed toward Kira's instead.

Kira's mood hadn't changed at all—or if it had, it was only getting worse. I only saw her for a split second after we got home from work yesterday afternoon, and once again, she wouldn't talk to me. I didn't know if she was eating, I didn't know if Zane had called her last weekend, I didn't know anything because she refused to talk to me unless it was to ask me to leave her alone.

With a knock on her shut door, I let myself in and my face fell when I found Kira curled up in a ball on her bed—again.

"I don't want to go to work," she responded automatically.

"Uh . . . okay? Did you call Brandon, or do you need me to?"

When she didn't respond in any way, I walked over and sat on her bed so we were facing each other.

"What's going on with you, sis?"

Her eyes filled with unshed tears as she shook her head.

"Is it Zane?" When there was no confirmation or denial, I suggested, "If it's so hard for you, why doesn't he just come here to visit you at least?"

Seconds after my last question, a hard sob tore through Kira's throat and she buried her face in her hands as she cried.

I wasn't sure how to react or what to say. Kira had cried over him so many times that I'd stopped being surprised. But she hadn't once offered up any piece of information for me to know what exactly it was she was crying about this time. Kicking off my shoes, I curled onto the bed so I was again facing her and put one of my hands on her arm until the crying eventually stopped and she was looking at me again. Well, looking in my direction—I wasn't positive she was actually seeing me, though.

"You ready to tell me now?" I asked a couple minutes later. "We tell each other everything, Kira, and it has been at least a week of you walking around like there's no more life in you. You just got past something like this a month ago, you can't go through it again and expect me not to do something about it this time."

Again, no response from her.

"I'm not sure if I should call Mom, or Zane, or . . . I don't know."

"Don't call Zane," she whispered hoarsely.

Her sudden demand startled me enough that it took me a few moments to figure out what to say. "Okay, I won't. Do I need to call Mom?"

"He probably wouldn't answer anyway," she mumbled before clearing her throat. "No, don't call Mom . . . and don't call Dad either. The three of you would probably have a celebration over it, and I don't need to hear how happy you all are."

"Happy?" I laughed hesitantly. "Is this because of Liam? Because I've been spending time with him?"

Kira exhaled heavily and shook her head again, but this time I waited because there was nothing else I could think of that might be wrong. "Zane is cheating on me."

My head jerked back. "What? Kira, no, he's not. It's just hard because of the—"

"No, Kennedy, he's cheating on me. I know he is, he's not trying to be secretive about it." Her eyes welled up again, but she spoke through the tears. "Well, I don't even know if you can consider it cheating anymore. He broke up with me a week ago."

I was too shocked to even know how to respond to what she'd just told me, but now I understood why she thought I would have a celebration with our parents. Kira had been the only person in our family to actually like Zane.

"I knew this would happen," she muttered. "As soon as Dad told me that we needed to leave for California, I knew."

"You couldn't have known, I mean . . ." I drifted off, once again not knowing what to say. "How *could* you know he would do something like this?"

"Because I wouldn't be around to keep him interested anymore."

"That's bullshit, Kira. Keep him interested? You've been together for years! If anything, the distance should have made your relationship stronger . . . isn't that what they say? Distance makes the heart . . . I don't know. Whatever that stupid saying says?"

"Grow fonder," she finished for me on a huff. "Not with Zane. He needs . . . well, he needs to have someone within reach. Someone he can touch. Someone to satisfy him when he wants it. That's the only reason he went to the same college with us. I practically bribed him into going there."

"What? I thought he was just following you to be with you."

Kira shook her head. "That's why I was always near him in Florida, I was afraid he'd lose interest if I wasn't around."

"Why the fuck would you stay with him? And why didn't you ever tell me?"

"Because we were in love! Because I *still* love him!" she shot back defensively.

"That is not love, Kira, that's—I don't even know what that is. He was just using you to get laid whenever he felt like it!"

"That's not true!"

"It's not?" I asked incredulously. "You knew the second you found out you had to move away that he would cheat on you. You weren't in love with him, you were scared of being alone!"

Kira sat up and stared down at me. "Oh, and suddenly *you're* the love expert? You don't even believe in love, Kennedy! You think it's something people have made up to trick other people into marrying them. But then again, I guess you would know all about *that,* now, wouldn't you? You would run screaming in the opposite direction now if anyone ever mentioned the idea of loving you. And why is that? Because of some bullshit relationship that you won't even talk about anymore?"

I sat there in shock for a moment, then slid off the bed. Grabbing my shoes, I walked toward the door. "Fuck you, Kira." Just before I was out of her room, I stopped, but didn't turn to look at her. "Get ready for work and cheer up. I'm not going to cover for you again because you're too upset to leave your room. I'm sure I'm not the only one who's tired of watching you bitch and complain over Zane—especially if it's been over for him since we moved here. It's been long enough, you need to get over it— you're starting to look pathetic."

I ignored her next screams, just went to my bathroom and took a quick shower to rinse off. A feeling close to panic mixed with a deep sorrow filled me as I slowly got ready for work, and by the time I was ready and we were leaving, it was consuming me.

Kira and I didn't talk on the way to the gym, or after we were there. I knew I'd been harsh, and I should have been more caring about how upset she was, but I didn't know how to be. Not now that I knew the real reason she was so obsessed with her relationship with Zane, not when she'd known about his cheating for months and hadn't even been blindsided by it, and not when she'd kept something like that from me for years.

I wanted to apologize to her, but knew I wouldn't because I was being childish. I was mad that she'd purposely used something against me to hurt me simply because she was hurting.

And, unfortunately for me, she was right. I didn't believe in love anymore, and her words had me on the edge of panicking over my situation with Liam. I'd pushed him away for so many reasons in the beginning. Being afraid of getting involved with someone, afraid of the way I easily lost all control around him, and afraid of the way I couldn't stay away from him. But now, after I'd finally given in to him, Kira's words had slapped me with the reality of what I was doing—and now I didn't know how to let the relationship continue when all I could remember was why I'd built walls between us in the first place.

July 17
Liam

I JOGGED UP to the girls' door that evening and knocked, trying to mentally prepare myself for whatever awaited me, but I couldn't do it. I didn't know what was going on with either of them, and Kennedy hadn't answered any of my calls or responded to my texts all day. Dad said Kira had walked out mid-shift, but both girls had been acting strange from the moment they'd come in.

After knocking for a second time with no answer, I pulled out my phone and started looking for Kennedy's number when the door suddenly swung open.

"Hey, what—Kira," I muttered when I noticed the way her eyes were watching me. No matter how identical she and her sister were, it was always clear in their eyes who was who. "What's going on today? I can't get ahold of Kennedy and Dad said you walked out of work."

"Am I fired?" she asked in a dead tone.

"No . . . uh, he didn't say that. He was worried I'd done something to upset you. What's wrong?"

"Kennedy's in her room. I think," she called over her shoulder as she walked away from me.

I stared at her retreating figure until she was in her room and the door was shut, unable to figure out what had just happened. I cautiously walked inside and made my way to Kennedy's room. With a deep breath in, I opened her door and looked inside. Kennedy was lying on her bed staring up at the ceiling.

Her head rolled to the side to face me, and her lips curved up for a split second. "Hey."

"Hey," I responded hesitantly, and took a few steps in before leaning back against a wall. "Do you want to tell me what's going on since Kira didn't?"

After a few seconds passed, she blew out a heavy breath and looked back up at the ceiling. "Zane broke up with Kira. He was cheating on her for . . . I don't know how long. Probably since we left."

Of all the things I'd been thinking, that hadn't been one of them. The girls were moving back to Florida—possible. Kennedy was going to suddenly go back to pushing me away for another unknown reason—too likely for my peace of mind. Someone in their family had died—once again, possible. All of those scenarios plus a few others had been running through my mind for the last five hours, but definitely not Kira losing her boyfriend. For a moment, my body sagged in relief until I realized I still didn't know why Kennedy had been ignoring me all day.

Pushing away from the wall, I closed the distance to her bed, but didn't get on it. Once her eyes were back on me, I asked softly, "And you?"

Her eyebrows pulled together in confusion, and she shook her head. "And me, what?"

"I haven't heard from you all day. You haven't answered my calls or returned my texts. I'm sorry for Kira, but right now I'm a little more worried about whatever is going on in that mind of yours."

Kennedy's face smoothed out, and she didn't move or speak as she watched me for countless seconds. "I didn't know what to say to you. Kira . . . she said some things to me this morning that left me wanting to run as far away from you as I could."

"Kennedy, I'm not Zane. I'm not going to—"

"No," she said, cutting me off. "No, I know you're not him. I don't think you're going to be like him either. I guess Kira just reminded me of who I am. That's the only way I can figure out how to put it."

Folding my arms across my chest, I raised one eyebrow and studied her. "And who you are made you want to run from me . . . again? I think I proved you can't do anything to make me want to give up on you."

A bright smile briefly flashed across her face. "I know, Liam. That's part of the reason why I haven't talked to you today." She pulled herself up into a sitting position and immediately began speaking again, this time without looking at me. "After Kira reminded me of my past this morning, I was so mad, but I knew she was right. And I knew that my initial reaction of wanting to run from you would just make what she said true. So I've spent practically the entire day thinking about it. I knew what I thought I had to do was just a knee-jerk reaction, and wasn't what I actually wanted. But I knew if I talked to you, then I would go through with it—whatever *it* would end up being. But it wasn't as simple as just needing time until I knew I wouldn't push you away again. I told you that Kira reminded me of who I am; and I am—or I was—that way *because* of my past. And that past is such a huge part of me that it made me rethink everything I'm doing here . . . with you."

"That past . . . it's the one we talked about in the ice cream shop?" When Kennedy nodded, I asked, "And you're still not going to tell me about it?"

"It's complicated," she said softly, and I knew from her tone that she once again wouldn't be going into detail about it.

"Okay," I said, and studied her closely. "So what are you thinking now?"

Her dark blue eyes met me again, and she shrugged slowly. "I'm thinking that it was my past, and it's always going to stay there, so I need to move on from it."

I walked around the bed until I was directly in front of her, and leaned down so my face was within an inch of hers. "What does that mean for us?"

"It means I'm not going to run. You're safe." Her lips spread into a wide smile and she closed the distance between us until our lips were barely touching. "For now."

11

July 17
Kennedy

"WHAT ABOUT THIS one?" My fingers trailed over what looked like a combination of two letters on Liam's right forearm, close to the inside of his elbow.

He'd been lying on my bed for the past couple hours with his shirt off as he told me stories about all the times he'd gotten his ass handed to him by his dad in the ring, and I'd studied the art covering the left side of his upper body.

When he didn't respond, I traced the letters again and asked, "Is this a *T*?" I glanced over to his arctic-blue eyes, and he simply nodded. "Does that mean this is a *G* it's connected to?"

Liam nodded again, and I pursed my lips, contemplating asking him more about it since he wasn't offering anything. Unfortunately for him, I was one of those people who didn't know how to stop talking even when I knew I should.

"Obviously you don't want to tell me about it, but can I ask one more question before I drop it?"

"Sure." The word was soft and deep, and rumbled up from his chest in a way that had me biting down on my lip.

"Um, is it—is it a girl's initials?"

His eyebrows pinched together and he laughed once. "What?"

"Well, this is the first time you've kind of shut down while we were talking. Not that I can say much about that since shutting down is my favorite thing to do—but I've *never* seen you respond this way. And I can't think of any other reason why you would have two letters tattooed on you."

He sent me an amused smile. "Do you have a guy's name tattooed on you somewhere?"

"No."

"And there isn't a girl's name, or anything to do with a girl who has been in my life, on my body."

"Got it."

I stopped tracing the tattoo when he looked away from me, and tried to figure out why he was acting like this suddenly. There was an anxious energy rolling off him as he continued to stare up at the ceiling, and the minutes continued to pass without him saying anything. Just when it started to become too much, I began climbing off the bed and he grabbed my arm to stop me. When I looked back at him, he pulled me closer and sighed heavily.

"Don't leave. I've just never had anyone ask about that tattoo, and it caught me off guard. I've never told anyone about it. There's a certain group of people who know the whole"—he paused as he tried to find the right word, and finally just blurted out—"weird and confusing-as-shit story, and not one of those people is someone I've told. They all knew long before I did—or before I understood, I guess. The reason behind actually getting the tattoo . . . well, it was kind of for my mom because I'd been a dick to her and my family. It was an apology of sorts."

"You don't have to tell me," I whispered. "I get it, it's personal. What you've already said explains enough, so it's okay."

He stared at me for a while before admitting, "But I want

to tell you. I don't know why, I just do. You have this normal family and I have the exact opposi—"

"My family is far from normal," I scoffed.

Liam raised an eyebrow at me. "Really," he said, his tone full of disbelief.

"I'm sure there are people who have families far different from mine and Kira's. I've already told you that my dad and uncle Mason are detectives in the gang unit, and you met Mason, so I'm sure you can somewhat understand, and having them hovering over us and just being the way they are as we grew up was an experience in itself. But the older we got, the more stories we heard . . . and I don't know how to wrap my head around the kind of men that they had to be. So it's not like I had this insane life growing up, or crazy family who had weird rituals in the backyard on full moons or anything. We just weren't a cookie-cutter family. I grew up learning how to escape being kidnapped, how to defend myself, how to shoot, and basically having two bodyguards instead of a dad and uncle," I finished on a laugh.

Liam watched me for a few seconds with a soft smile on his face. "Okay, well, my family wasn't like *that*. Things were . . . normal—for the most part, I guess. Mornings were spent surfing with my dad, sometimes my friends and his. Grew up in his gym, as you already know. My family is really close. I've already told you I have a different relationship with my dad than most sons have. I've always seen him more as a best friend. I see him almost every day at the gym even though we spend the mornings at the beach, and I see Mom a couple times a week. Even if my sister didn't live with them, I know she'd be the same way."

I felt my brow pinch together. "That doesn't seem like an abnormal family."

He laughed hesitantly. "It's not my *family* that's abnormal. It's the circumstances behind my family that are. I have three sets of grandparents. And I'm extremely close with all of them. I have an uncle and aunt on my dad's side, and the same on my mom's side. But the part where it gets confusing . . . is it's not really my mom's side. My mom has her real dad and his wife, and they're great. We all love them. But then she has this other family she considers hers, who we all consider her side of the family, who is my *real* dad's family. And that's where my aunt and uncle come from on that side; and that uncle is Konrad . . . you know him from working at the gym."

"Wait. What?"

"Exactly." He sighed.

"So your parents were related before they got married?"

His wide blue eyes met mine before he burst into laughter. "No. Not even close. I meant that my mom's family is technically not *her* family but my biological father's family. His real sister is my aunt Bree, and her husband is Konrad."

My confusion quickly disappeared, but then I was left feeling surprised. "Brandon isn't your real dad? I never would have known."

"No. I mean, he is. He's my dad, but he's not my biological father. And this is where it goes from confusing to fucked up. Apparently my dad and mom were together, and my mom cheated on him with his best friend—my biological father. Nine months later, and here I am."

"Holy shit," I said before I could stop myself. "And did your dad know?"

"Yeah, he knew. My mom and biological father, Chase, were together for a short time while she was pregnant. According to everyone, she loved him and my dad both. She knew she'd made a mistake, but was trying to make it right by being with Chase. And then halfway through the pregnancy, my biological father died in a car accident."

My eyes widened and my jaw dropped, but no sound came out.

"Few months later she and my dad got back together, and he's raised me as his own, but they raised me to know who Chase was. And before Mom and Chase ever got together, Chase's family had pretty much already adopted her because she was best friends with my aunt Bree and wasn't talking to her dad or something, I guess. So we have this weird family that consists of my dad's family, my mom's dad, and then Chase's family—who my mom considers her family. It's confusing as shit, and we're all close."

"That is confusing," I mumbled. "And just . . . just oh my God."

"Yeah." He took in a heavy breath, then released it and stared up at the ceiling again. "But you need to know all that to understand the tattoo."

When he didn't say anything for a while again, I squeezed his hand. "You don't have to tell me, Liam."

"I told you I grew up knowing about Chase," he began, his eyes still glued to the ceiling. "There wasn't one morning of surfing with Dad and Uncle Konrad that there weren't stories of him. Then, of course, whenever we were with my grandparents— *Chase's* parents—stories were told. No one wants his memory to fade even after all this time, and I get it to an extent. Kristi and I don't understand completely because we didn't know him, but we know how important it is for them. But as I got older, I stopped looking like my mom, and started looking more and more like Chase. Because of that, there were times where my grandparents, Aunt Bree, or Mom would just start crying when they were looking at me. Even my dad sometimes, I'll catch him staring at me with a distant look, and I know he's back in college with his best friend.

"The stories—shit, I could tell you stories about Chase like I had been there. But I have no *real* emotional connection to them, and to have my family randomly crying or accidentally calling me Chase when they saw me started getting on me. On my nine-teenth birthday, my mom was trying to get me to do a bunch of things—I don't even remember. But everyone was there, and she was busy, so she rambled off a list of things really quick that she needed me to do, and I said something to her. Two words. Just two fucking words, and my entire family went dead silent and then all the women started sobbing."

"What did you say?" I asked when he didn't offer anything else.

Liam finally looked over at me and shrugged. "I said, 'Okay, Princess.' I was just being a dick because she was giving me a list of things to do on my birthday. Out of all the stories they'd told me about Chase, no one had ever mentioned that he called my mom 'Princess.' Ever. So my dad finally told me why everyone was crying, and that, mixed with how I looked just like him . . . it was too close to home, and I kinda lost it. I went off on all of them. Told them to get over what happened, that it'd happened long enough ago that they shouldn't be upset anymore. My dad was yelling at me to shut up, and I just kept going. I was pissed and said I wasn't Chase and it wasn't fair that they all kept put-ting his life on me, like they wanted me to be him *for* them or something. I said it wasn't my goddamn fault I grew up to look like him . . . and then I looked at my mom and said, 'If you would've kept your fucking legs closed, I wouldn't have to deal with everyone's bullshit now,' and then I left."

"Liam . . ." I said on a breath, shock apparent in the one word.

"I know. I went back to my dorm and didn't talk to any of them for a week, and not one of them tried to contact me. I didn't blame them. I said the worst thing I could to them. They don't want me to be him, I knew that even then. I knew all they wanted was for me to know who he was. Like I said, I was being a dick. It had just started feeling like the Chase thing was forced on me all the time. My middle name is Chase, and a friend of the family only ever calls me LC—for my first and middle name—or Little Chachi. He and his wife always called Chase 'Chachi,' so once I started looking like him, the nickname transferred over to me. But I didn't really start looking like him until I got into high school, and then that's all anyone could talk about. So for the few years before that birthday, I just felt like I couldn't get away from his ghost . . . if that even makes sense. And then I let it get to me when I shouldn't have.

"So when I'd cooled off and realized what I'd done and how I'd hurt my family, I went to get this tattoo. Brian—the guy who came up with the Chachi nickname—is a tattoo artist who worked with Chase and is still close with my parents; he does all of our work. I went to see him, and of course he'd already heard about what I'd done on my birthday. When I told him what I wanted, he just smiled and sat me down. Once it was done, he told me something I still remember like it was yesterday—probably because it was the first time he'd ever been serious around me. He said, 'What you did was fucked up, LC, but we've put a lot on you that no kid should have to deal with. When Chase died we all had to cling together to keep going— this family of strays loved that guy, and I think we were all terrified of forgetting him. So we made sure we wouldn't. Your mom and dad's intentions were from the heart. Chase meant a lot to both of them, and they wanted you to know the dad you would never get to meet. Did we put too much pressure on you? Maybe. Even though having you here and seeing Chase through you has been the biggest blessing of my fucked-up life, I don't want you to be him, and I know they feel the same. Is it crazy looking at you and seeing him? Yeah, dude, it's a fucking trip. But it's the best goddamn trip I've ever been on.' "

My lips tilted up in a small smile at the remembered words. "And then you went to apologize?" When Liam nodded absentmindedly, I asked again, "So what do the letters stand for?"

"My last name is Taylor. Chase's last name was Grayson—that side of my family's last name is Grayson. They want to remember him, and they wanted me to know him for a reason. So this is my way of accepting and embracing that part of my life."

I watched him for a couple minutes before whispering, "I think that's beautiful."

His light blue eyes flickered to me, and he huffed softly.

"You've never told anyone that story?"

"No, none of my friends even know about Chase," he admitted.

Moving over so I was sitting in his lap, I rested my head in the crook of his neck and my body melted against his when he tightened his arms around me, holding me close. "Thank you for telling me."

He pressed his lips to the top of my head, and kept them there as he murmured, "Thanks for listening, Moon."

July 23
Liam

AFTER I PULLED up in the driveway, I looked over at Kennedy and my body relaxed when I noticed her carefree expression. I'd been dreading this night, afraid of what it would mean for us, and what it might cause her to do—like run. But when I told Kennedy that my parents wanted her and Kira to come over for dinner, she'd surprised me by immediately agreeing like it was nothing . . . like she was agreeing on what movie to watch.

"Nice house!" Kira said from the backseat before stepping out of my car.

"You ready for this?" I asked cautiously.

Kennedy turned to face me with an easy smile and a confused expression. "Of course I am; why wouldn't I be?"

I huffed softly and raised my eyebrows—like the answer to her question alone could have her panicking. "Well—"

"The question is, Liam, are *you* ready for this? I don't have family here ready to embarrass me in front you. I'm hoping to get some juicy details about you tonight. Maybe your mom will even pull out baby pictures to show me. But don't worry, since they probably won't be playing twenty questions with Kira, I'm sure *she'll* be on your side." With that, she stepped out of the car laughing, and left me sitting there staring at where she'd just been, completely speechless.

I'd spent an entire day trying to figure out how to ask her and Kira to this dinner, and then had rehearsed the question a few dozen times before finally mentioning it casually, acting like it didn't matter if they came or not. But given how she was acting right now, she knew exactly *why* this dinner was happening, and she seemed more than fine with it.

The girls waited by the front door of the house until I joined them and let us in. We'd barely made it past the entryway before Aunt Bree was in front of us.

"Hello, friends! I'm Bree, but you probably already knew that since I'm always snooping around the gym. Now—" She cut off quickly and looked between Kennedy and Kira a few times then up to me. "Which one?"

"This one," I said, nodding toward the girl standing at my right.

"Right, right."

"Aunt Bree—"

"No!" she said sharply, and held up a silencing finger at me. "You and I are not friends, you do *not* get to speak to me anymore. I'm going to busy myself with these two, and you can figure out how to beg me to forgive you."

Uncle Konrad came up behind her and shrugged. "I told you she was mad. Can't say I didn't warn ya."

Aunt Bree looked up at her husband and gave him her best glare. "You don't talk to the enemy either unless you want to sleep on the dog's bed for the second night in a row!" She grabbed both Kennedy's and Kira's hands and began walking away while still looking at them. "Now I have time to—wait, which one of you is the girl again?"

"Me, I'm Kennedy," Kennedy said at the same time as Kira said, "*She's* the girlfriend."

I could just barely make out Kennedy's grumbled "I'm not his girlfriend" before Aunt Bree had them seated on the couch with her on the coffee table so she could face them both.

As I looked at my uncle Konrad, my eyes narrowed. "Couldn't you have at least told her to take it easy on them?"

"Why do you think she said I'd be sleeping on the dog bed for the second night?"

My lips pulled up at the corners, and I nodded once. "Figures. Thanks for trying."

He grunted and slapped a hand on my shoulder as we began walking into the living room. "Don't forget, your mom is still pissed. I'd be more worried about her than your aunt. You should probably get to her before the twins get away from Bree."

Uncle Konrad had been right. Mom was beyond pissed, but it was hard to feel bad when she barely came up to my chest and was trying to talk down to me. I hadn't been able to handle being scolded without laughing since I was twelve. She started getting even madder when my neutral expression began breaking and my mouth kept twitching, so I finally picked her up in a big hug for a few seconds, then set her down. And like every time I'd ever done it before, she melted and her anger was gone by the time she was on her feet again.

"Okay, okay. Let's go talk to them," she said as she walked away from me. I followed her out of the kitchen and into the living room until she was standing close to where Aunt Bree was sitting. "Oh my word, we just need to make you two wear name tags all the time. This is so confusing."

The girls laughed and Kennedy said, "I'll make it as easy as I can for you. Kira has a scar just above her top lip."

My head jerked back for a second, then I was leaning forward to find the faint scar. "Why haven't I ever been told that?"

Kennedy's eyebrows rose, and I knew she was enjoying the fact that she'd helped my family and not me. "You've never had trouble figuring us out except for that very first meeting. There was never any reason to tell you."

"Still would have been helpful," I mumbled at the same time as my mom finally saw the scar.

"Oh, you can barely even see it! But I guess it will have to do. How did you get it, sweet girl?"

Kira laughed and glanced at Kennedy. "I hid Kennedy's stuffed bear when we were four, and she threw a Barbie car at me. She's a little violent."

"Oh, *I'm* the violent one? *You* chased me with a knife when we were ten. *I* was just trying to scare you, it's not my fault I have bad aim and it ended up hitting you in the face."

Kira's laugh got louder and she shrugged unapologetically. "You deserved it, you—"

"Anyway," Kennedy said, cutting off Kira. "That's the easiest way to tell. We have different tattoos, but that usually doesn't help people. Sorry, we've probably scared you all off now."

Mom snorted. "Not even close. Liam tried to melt Kristi's dolls in the oven, cut her hair off while she was sleeping, and put her in a headlock when she was three. Nothing can scare me after raising a boy." She rolled her eyes and looked up at me, but gave me a little wink as she nodded toward the girls—and I knew right then that she already approved of Kennedy and Kira. "Well, I wanted to introduce myself. I'm—"

"Mom, they already know who you are."

She smacked me in the stomach, her smile never faltering. "Like I was saying. I'm Harper, Liam's mother, and I'm so happy you both agreed to come to dinner. Brandon and Kristi talk about you two so much, I couldn't wait to get to spend more time with you."

Kennedy gave me a soft smile before looking back up at my mom. "Well, we really appreciate this, thank you so much for having us. Liam's told me a lot about you, it'll be really nice to get to sit and talk with you instead of just saying hello and good-bye at the gym. Besides, I told Liam in the car that I'm really hoping to get some juicy stories about him while we're here."

Aunt Bree laughed and stood up from the table. "I like her. We can keep them both." Walking up to me, she tilted her head back like Mom did when she was about to get mad at me, and poked me in the chest with each word she spoke. "And we're still not friends! It better be an epic groveling I get from you!"

"I'm sure it will be," I called after her as she walked into the kitchen with Mom not far behind her. Looking back at the girls, who had just stood up from the couch, I released a heavy breath. "So that's Mom and Aunt Bree. I think they're the worst you'll get."

"I like them," Kira said as she turned to go to the kitchen.

Kennedy walked up to me until she was pressed against my chest. "I like them too. So," she said huskily, and gave me an amused look. "You tried to melt your sister's dolls in the oven, huh? I'm sure that's somewhere in a book on the makings of a serial killer."

I pinched her side and brushed a kiss across her cheek. "I was six, give me a break. Come on, let's get the rest of this night over with."

With a soft kiss to my lips, Kennedy slowly backed away from me. "Like I said, *I'm* not the one who's going to be embarrassed tonight. I'm excited about what I'll find out next."

"Meeting your parents will be the sweetest payback I've ever received."

"Who said I'd ever let you near my parents?" she asked teasingly. With a wink, she turned around and went to join my family in the kitchen, and for long moments all I could do was stand there and watch her as I realized Brian was right.

For the first time in my life, I knew I was falling in love. And it was with a girl who was terrified by the idea of relationships. But nothing about the challenge was scaring me at the moment.

12

October 23
Kennedy

"Are you ready for this?" I asked Kira, and was beyond happy to see her eyes immediately light up as she nodded her head.

"As long as you are."

For a moment, my chest constricted with a years-old panic that was hard to break, but the feeling passed within seconds. "I'm ready."

Grabbing the door to the tattoo parlor, I swung it open and followed Kira inside.

"Good afternoon, ladies, wha—" The man greeting us did a double take, and his mouth stretched into a wide grin as he raised his arms in the air. "Oh yeah! Twinsies! Double the fun for me. What can I do for you two today?"

I eyed the massive head of long, curly dark hair on the guy standing in front of us, and guessed, "Brian?"

His face immediately fell and he cocked his head to the side. "Trip. Such a trip. I don't remember twins."

I laughed and pointed to Kira, then at myself. "Kira and Kennedy. We're friends of Liam's."

"Ah! Little Chachi's girlfriend and her equally hot sister! Welcome, welcome!"

I decided to let the "girlfriend" slide this time. "We want small matching tattoos, nothing crazy today. Shouldn't take long; do you have time?"

"Do I have time for you? Of course I do, you're practically family already. Dudes, Riss is gonna hate me for meeting you before she gets to."

"Riss?" Kira whispered to me.

"His wife," I whispered back, and held up the bag I was holding toward Brian. "Liam said you like tacos."

"Oh, sweet sustenance. Where have you been all my life?" he asked as he gently took the bag from my hand—like it was precious and would break if he moved any faster. "Liam tell you that Riss starves me?"

My mouth curved up when I eyed his beer gut. "You look like you're doing okay to me."

Brian's face lost all emotion, but his eyes look horrified. "No. Dude number one, you don't understand. She's on a plant-food-only kick. She. Starves. Me."

"Eww."

He looked at Kira and nodded. "Tell me about it, dude number two. Okay. Now that I've gotten my payment, what matchy-matchy do you want today, and where do you want it?"

Kira immediately pulled out her phone to show Brian the tattoo and talk placement with him.

It had been five months since our quick and unexpected move to California, and while there were still things we hated about this place—like the fact that we were still in motherfucking California—I'd been right all those months ago. This move had been good for both Kira and me.

In the last three months, Kira had slowly but surely gotten better, and gotten over the whole Zane thing. It didn't take long

for her to admit just how messed up their relationship had been—
once she stopped torturing herself by stalking Zane's social media
accounts. It was after that that she'd been able to realize the
reason she'd tried so hard to continue to make it work between
Zane and her was that she'd wanted a perfect marriage like our
parents have, but wanted to be able to say that she'd married her
high school sweetheart on top of it. I could understand that to an
extent. It was hard not to want the kind of marriage our parents
had, but Kira's would have been anything but perfect with Zane,
so I was glad she was moving on from that dream and him. And
to be honest, I think the guys at the gym had a lot to do with it too.
There were a handful of men who talked specifically to her whenever they came in, and although she had yet to give it over, she'd
been asked for her number more times than I could count.

As for me? I was doing better all the time in dealing with my
past and the fears that came with it. I knew what had happened
to me had happened for a reason, just like I knew I needed to let
the past stay in the past without letting it keep me there; but letting go had been harder than I'd ever imagined. It wasn't until
Kira had brought it up last week that I'd realized how little of a
hold it still had on me. And it was because of the progress of us
both that we were meeting Brian today.

Kira and I didn't get matching tattoos often. Our tastes were
too different, just like our polar opposite personalities. But our
deep love for art on our bodies was something we'd always
shared with Dad, and every now and then something in our
lives called for "matchy-matchy," as Brian had called it. This
was definitely one of those times.

Because of the relationships that had been life consuming and
life altering for both of us, we were getting "free hearts" tattoos
to show how we felt like we'd finally been released from the past.
A tattoo of a small red heart with *free* in black inked across it, as
if the word had been stamped on top.

After Kira was done and Brian was set up again, I was lying next to him with the outline on my left collarbone, and the familiar buzzing started up. Nothing was more soothing to me than the buzzing of these machines, and I couldn't help but smile as I waited for the process to start.

"You in love with my boy yet?"

And there went my smile.

A short laugh bubbled past my lips, and my eyebrows pulled down as I looked over at Brian. "Uh, what?"

"Have you finally figured out you're in love with him?"

"No," I responded, slowly drawing out the word. "Why?"

"Because it's gonna happen," Brian said, like the fact that I didn't already know this was blowing his mind.

After a few minutes passed with him focused only on what he was doing, he moved his head so it was directly above my face. "He loves you, you know."

"Really?" When Brian nodded, I laughed again—but this time there was no humor behind it. "Liam Taylor loves me," I stated blankly. "I think you might be high, Brian."

"Not today," he boasted proudly, and sat back to mess with the ink before he started tattooing again.

I'd been joking, but his response had my forehead pinching. "Liam said you don't do drugs . . ."

"No, ma'am, not for thirty years. No drinkage or drug-gage. Not since the night I almost lost my lady love when I was twenty-three. She gave me an ultimatum, and that was it for me. Doesn't mean I don't feel like I'm high most days. This job and my life give me all the high I need, dude number one. What else did LC tell you about me?"

"Your hair," I replied immediately with a smile.

"Dude. The hair *is* me. I *am* my hair. I made this hair look cool way before Troy Polamalu started getting paid mad bucks for his."

"Who?"

"Eh." Brian leaned back and shrugged. "Football player who jacked my style. Retired when you were just a young'un. So, what else? Did LC tell you how dead sexy I am?"

"Oh yeah," I mumbled sarcastically. "That was our very first conversation."

"Damn straight it was. LC knows what's up."

I bit back a laugh and let another minute pass before I said, "He told me about his tattoo for Chase, and what you said after you finished it."

"Was I high?" he asked teasingly, but the humor quickly died and he stopped tattooing and sat back. After a few beats of silence, I turned my head to find him staring at me with a look of shock. "He told you about the initials?"

"And the entire story behind it," I confirmed with a nod.

"No shit?"

"No shit."

"Dude number one, LC doesn't tell anyone that story." Brian was silent again for a while, and with a laugh, he shook his head and got ready to keep going. "Christ. I knew my boy was in love with you. But, homie, he is *in* love with you."

"You're wro—"

"No, I'm not," he said, cutting me off. "You in love with him yet?"

"Again, no, Brian."

"That's okay. I'll ask again when I'm done to see if you've realized it yet."

There was no stopping my smile over the next couple minutes as Brian finished up. Despite how crazy Brian seemed, I could easily understand why Liam and his family liked him so much. His weird personality was addicting.

"Dude number one," Brian said when he finished. "You in love with my boy yet?"

I laughed in frustration and amusement, and shot him a look. "No, Brian!"

" 'Kay, 'kay. I'll check back with you tomorrow."

"Do it, I can't wait to give you the same answer."

"Uh-huh. We'll see."

I rolled my eyes, but didn't say anything else regarding the topic as he got me ready to go, and Kira and I paid.

"Come back to me, dudes!" he called out when we reached the door to leave, and pointed at me. "Tell my boy to come feed me!"

"Will do! Thanks again!"

"Strange one," Kira said as we walked back to the car, and I nodded in agreement.

"Strange but fun." I grabbed my phone to see the time. "Let's make a coffee run and then get home. Liam will be over in an hour."

Kira stopped walking and pointed back to the shop. "Oh, don't you mean the love of your life?" she teased.

"Shut up," I grumbled, and pushed her away.

WITH A QUICK knock, the front door opened and Liam came walking in half an hour after we'd gotten home. "You really need to lock your door," he murmured, then pressed a quick kiss to my neck.

"We do lock the door, I just unlocked it about five minutes ago because I knew you'd be here soon."

"Doesn't matter," he said, and Kira nodded and pointed at him as she finished off her coffee.

"I agree," she said, and dropped the empty cup on the table. "With our family, leaving the door unlocked for anything is probably a big no-no. Can you imagine how Dad would react if he showed up and found it open?"

"Exactly," Liam continued. "A detective's daughter should know better."

I glanced at Kira and pursed my lips. I knew she was talking about the Juarez threats, which had only continued and multiplied as a few of the members of the crew had been released from prison, but Liam didn't know a thing about it, nor did I want him to know.

I didn't feel the need to worry him about threats that I doubted would find their way to California, and knew telling him would only cause him to become overly protective. Kira and I already had that with Dad and Uncle Mason, and now we hadn't seen them or Mom for almost half a year because of their paranoia.

Kira's eyes widened when she remembered that Liam didn't know about Juarez, and she sent me an apologetic look.

"Yeah, sure. I won't leave it unlocked anymore." Looking up at Liam, I asked, "Happy?"

"Yep."

"Good. As much as I love having you two gang up on me over an unlocked door, how about movie time?"

He started walking toward one of the couches with me, but came to a stop, then took a few steps back. "I left my candy in the car."

"You brought candy?"

"Movie night means candy," he answered simply.

I bit back a smile and held my hands up in surrender until he turned and jogged out of the condo.

Less than a minute later he was back, and as soon as he was inside he was yelling, "You didn't lock the door."

"You weren't even gone for sixty seconds!" I yelled back, and narrowed my eyes when I caught sight of his amused expression. "You're so—" My words caught in my throat, and I froze as I eyed the offensive boxes in his hand. "What the fuck is that?"

Liam seemed startled by my horrified question, and glanced around him for a few seconds before looking at the candy in his hand and holding it up to show me. "This? It's Sour Patch Kids candy."

"Oh my God," Kira whispered, her voice expressing the same horror as mine.

"Yeah. Saw that. Why are they in our condo?"

"Well, shit, are you allergic to these too?" Liam asked quickly. "You need to tell me these things."

"We're not, but we might as well be!" I waved my hand at the boxes and made a gagging noise. "You need to get rid of those."

"Fuck no, they're my favorite."

"Since when?" I asked dramatically, like Liam had just told me he had an incurable disease.

"Since always! What is your deal?"

"You need to get rid of them," Kira repeated my earlier words.

"Tell me what's wrong with them first!"

" 'Sour Patch' is our dad's nickname for Mom," Kira explained. "They've never told us why, and we've never asked. But they eat Sour Patch Kids like they need them to breathe. Kennedy and I can't stand them because of our parents—they gross us out."

Liam's lips turned up. "Seriously?" He dropped one of the boxes on the kitchen counter and walked toward us as he opened the other. "I'm sure you'll get over it."

My eyes and mouth widened. "You're really going to eat them?"

"Yeah, Moon. And I'm gonna kiss you as soon as I'm done."

"I will castrate you," I swore, and his smile widened.

"That's not nice." As soon as Liam was sitting on the couch, I started walking over to sit near Kira on the love seat, but Liam grabbed me and pulled me back, so I was sitting on his lap. "Movie time, and you're sitting with me."

Kira laughed as she started up the movie.

"So you're allergic to anything that comes from water," Liam muttered, and tapped my nose before popping a couple pieces of candy in his mouth. "What about you, Kira?"

"No allergies."

"And you're both abnormally disgusted by the best candy ever made. What else?"

I started to say, "Nothing," but Kira cut me off. "Pancakes."

"Ah, yes!" I said, and pointed at her. "Pancakes."

Liam stopped chewing, and looked at me like he was worried about my well-being. "What in the hell is wrong with pancakes? Pancakes are a Sunday-brunch tradition in my family."

"Oh, fuck that. Don't ever ask us to brunch with your parents. And pancakes are another thing between my parents that we don't understand. But their little inside jokes about pancakes have made Kira and me steer clear."

"Don't worry," he said on a laugh. "Sunday is family day."

"Then I'm safe."

"Are there any foods in particular that you love?"

"Bananas," I said on a sigh. "I freaking love bananas."

"Amen to that," Kira said distractedly.

"I probably could have guessed that from the never-ending supply in your fruit basket. Now, you don't see me flipping out over that, do you? You're both a little dramatic when it comes to—"

"Can we stop?" Kira pleaded. "You're going to make me sick if you keep talking about those two things."

"So dramatic," Liam whispered, and repositioned me so we were both more comfortable. "That's new," he said awhile into the movie, as he traced just below the new tattoo.

"Yep. Kira and I got the same one. We went and met Brian today." I turned my head to smile at him, and Liam's eyebrows shot up.

"Did you? And what did he have to say?"

I readjusted myself so I was curled against his chest with my legs across the couch and Liam's arms around my waist. "He said you needed to go feed him."

Liam rolled his eyes. "Figures."

"But we took him tacos today, so he should be good for a while."

The shock from finding out we'd gone to meet Brian was suddenly gone, and Liam was looking at me like he was trying to figure me out. "You brought Brian food?" he asked softly, and I nodded.

"Of course. You said you always did, so I thought we should too."

"You know you didn't have to."

I shrugged. "I know. But I thought he'd appreciate it."

"I'm sure he did. Thank you," he whispered, and passed his lips across my jaw. Tapping on my skin just below my left collarbone, he asked, "What does this mean?"

For a fraction of a second, I considered telling him. About the tattoo, about my past, and what it had meant for me over the years . . . but I quickly pushed back the thought. Now was not the time while Kira was sitting right next to us with a movie playing in the background. When I finally told Liam everything, we needed to be alone. He deserved that much after everything I'd put him through before we'd started dating.

My chest warmed when I realized that this was the first time I'd ever thought—and wanted—to tell him about anything from back then.

Grabbing his face in my hands, I pressed a slow kiss to his lips. "For now, just know that it means we're still okay . . . and it means I'll be ready to tell you all about it soon."

Liam's eyebrows were pinched together for a few seconds, then they relaxed when he understood I didn't mean *just* the tattoo, and his entire face looked like I'd just given him a gift he'd been desperately wanting. "Really?" he asked in awe.

"Really. Just not tonight."

After we watched two movies and takeout had been delivered

and devoured, Kira called out a good night and headed off to her room. As he normally did, Liam stood up and started grabbing his phone and keys. The times we slept over at each other's places weren't usually planned, and they were rare. If it happened, it was because we'd fallen asleep while talking or watching TV, or if a few hours in the bedroom had left us with only enough strength to crash in each other's arms.

Getting the tattoo with Kira had been a big enough step for me, and then promising Liam I would tell him about my past soon had just added to it. While I expected to feel the usual panic over what that could all mean, there was nothing. Well, nothing bad at least. Right now, all I wanted was for Liam not to go home. I knew this would be taking us in a new direction. I knew he would see a deeper meaning in this than most people might, but I was pretty sure I was ready for it.

"Hey," I said, and grabbed his arm to stop him. "Do you think . . ." I drifted off, and stared into his patient eyes. "Do you want to stay?"

That same smile that had crossed his face earlier when he'd asked about the tattoo was there again. And without a response, he bent down and lifted me into his arms, and walked me into my bedroom.

I'll take that as a yes.

October 24
Liam

"WHY DON'T YOU both come with me tomorrow?"

"Come with you where?"

"To my parents' house," I answered hesitantly.

Kennedy's body stilled in my arms for a second before she looked up at me; her eyes were squinting like she was trying to figure something out. We'd woken up in her bed a little over an hour ago, and I'd been explaining all about how my family spent Sundays. This was different from the first time I invited the girls over to my parents' house. And even though I'd told her what Sunday was all about in my family just the night before, I wanted her to know *exactly* what she was getting herself into before she agreed to go and ended up being blindsided. I didn't want Kennedy thinking it would be just another day when no one in my family would see it that way, not if I brought the girls with me.

"You want us to go to your parents'? But . . . tomorrow is Sunday, and Sunday—you're really asking us to go with you?"

I laughed softly and tightened my arms. "Yes."

"But Sunday is *family* day," she said with wide eyes, like she was trying to get *me* to understand what I was asking.

"It is, and I want my girl there."

"This is kind of a big deal, Liam." She leaned forward and smiled against my lips as she slowly moved one leg over my body so she was straddling me, and I pulled her closer as I nipped at her bottom lip.

"Does this mean you're going to come with me?"

"If I say yes, does that mean we have to eat pancakes?"

I smiled and nodded. "Tons of them."

Kennedy sighed dramatically, but her lips were tilting up by the time she was done. After a few silent seconds, she asked, "So now I'm your girl?"

I looked up into her gleaming eyes, and narrowed mine, trying to judge her expression. "That's not anything new."

Her lips spread into a smile as she pressed her forehead against mine. "For you, maybe. But I haven't heard you call me that before."

"Maybe because you're always so quick to reject any title that would signify that we're together."

Kennedy's smile fell, but her blue eyes stayed locked on mine when she said, "Brian called me your girlfriend yesterday."

"Did he?" I asked in a monotone voice. I was worried about what else Brian might have said.

"I think I'm starting to be okay with it."

Not trying to hide my surprise, I grabbed her waist and pushed her back until she was lying on the bed and I was hovering over her. "Really?"

One eyebrow rose in confirmation, and a soft smile slowly crossed her face again. Her long legs easily wrapped around my hips, pulling me closer as her fingers threaded through my hair.

"It's about time, Kennedy Ryan. How many times did I have to tell you that you were mine before you finally started being okay with it?"

"But it never stopped you from telling me."

I shook my head and brushed my lips across her forehead. "No, it didn't. I've known you were mine, just as much as I've been yours."

"I have never claimed you as my own," she responded, but there was no bite to her words. She was looking at me in wonder, and I knew this was a turning point for us.

"Not yet, but you will."

"Oh, will I? You sound a little sure of yourself."

"I haven't been wrong when it came to you yet." I pressed my mouth to hers, and then only moved far enough away that my lips brushed hers when I asked, "So what's your answer? Are you going to come with me tomorrow?"

Before she could say anything, there was a knock on the front door. I almost told her to let Kira answer it when I realized no one else knew where the girls lived except their family, and I currently had a naked Kennedy pressed between my body and her bed.

I pushed away from her, my body tight as I stared at her beneath me. "Are you or Kira expecting someone?"

She shrugged and started to move out from underneath me. "No, but it's probably just a solicitor or something. They're always in this complex."

I pushed her back gently to where she'd been. "I'll get it. Just wait here."

"I can get it," she said on a laugh.

"You're not dressed yet," I argued, and quickly climbed off the bed. Grabbing my jeans off the floor, I stepped into them and snatched my shirt up as I began walking out of the room. "Put some clothes on."

"Don't tell me what to do!" she called back as I reached the hall.

I smirked and walked over to the entryway, the entire time wondering if any member of their family other than Eli knew about my relationship with Kennedy. But my worries of Mason and Kash coming after me died as soon as I opened the door to a guy I'd never seen before.

The guy's forehead creased in confusion, and he took a step back to look at the number near the door.

"Can I help you?"

His hard eyes shot back to me. "I'm looking for Kennedy."

I straightened and held his stare. "And you would be?"

"Look, just tell me if she's here. Or do I have the wrong building?"

Before I could answer, I heard Kira's door opening and Kennedy's voice coming from down the hall. "Who is it, Liam?"

The guy's mouth twisted into a mocking smile, and he looked behind me, at whom I guessed was Kira.

"I need your name," I told him, stepping closer to him and closing the door enough that I was all he could see. "You're out of your mind if you think I'm letting you in here without knowing who the fuck you are."

"Liam, seriously, who is it?" Kennedy touched my arm as she came up behind me, and I hated that every time he heard her voice, the man standing in front of me looked like he'd just won a prize. Kennedy ducked under my arm, and immediately scrambled back when she saw the guy, but was blocked by my body. "Holy shit!"

Releasing my hold on the door, I pushed Kennedy back and slammed the door shut before locking it. "Who is he?"

Kennedy just stood there staring at the door with wide eyes, not saying anything. I looked over to Kira, and she shrugged.

"I didn't see him," she replied, and walked up toward her sister. "Is it—" She cut off abruptly and looked up at me for a few seconds, then turned her body so she was facing away. That didn't stop me from hearing her when she asked, "Is it one of Juarezes?"

"Who the fuck is Juarez? Someone tell me what's going on," I demanded. I had to know if I needed to go outside and beat up the guy who was asking for Kennedy, or call the cops.

"No, it isn't," Kennedy replied to her sister, but her eyes stayed locked on me—nothing but confusion and pain in them. "Kira, it . . . it's Rhys."

Kira looked at Kennedy with a confused expression, then her head jerked back and she turned quickly to look at the door and I saw the sudden surprise and confusion in her eyes. "Uh . . ."

"For fuck's sake, will one of you tell me what's happening. Is this guy dangerous? Do you need me to call the police?"

"I don't think he's dangerous," Kira said, her voice sounding a little unsure. "But maybe *you* shouldn't open the door for him again."

As soon as Kira took a step toward the door, I stopped her and turned to get it myself. I still had no idea who Rhys was, or why he was here, but I sure as hell wasn't letting the girls talk to him until I knew.

Unlocking and opening the door, I eyed the guy still standing there.

Before I could say a word, he asked, "Do you mind if I see my wife now?"

13

October 24
Liam

WHATEVER QUESTION I had for Rhys quickly escaped me, and I stood there staring at him as his question played over and over in my head. The guy was asking to see his wife . . . to see Kennedy.

I took a step away from the door and turned to look at the girls standing there with a mix of emotions on their faces. Kennedy looked like she was worried and hurt, and Kira's face was full of confusion and anger.

"Kennedy?" I asked softly, and her head snapped around to look at me before going back to Rhys, who was standing in the doorway.

"Well, *I* can say that I've never been more surprised by anything in my life," Kira sneered. "Who'd've thought that you would show up after four years? And what is this, the second time I've seen you . . . ever?"

"Kira, stop," Kennedy whispered, and even though there was no force behind her words, Kira obeyed. "You're here. How? How did you know I was here?"

Rhys started to say something, but I spoke over him. "So he wasn't lying? You're his—you're married to him?"

The sharp tone of my words had Kennedy looking at me again, her face apologizing when her words couldn't do the same. "Liam," she pleaded, and reached for me when I stalked past her toward her room, but I didn't stop or respond.

As soon as I hit her room, I was searching for my phone and keys. Just as I was turning to leave, she was beside me, tears streaming down her face.

"Please, you don't understand."

"*I* don't understand? You're fucking married, Kennedy! What isn't there to understand?" I laughed harshly and ran a hand roughly through my hair. "So he's why you continued to push me back? *He's* your past? He's why you're fucking terrified of letting yourself get too close to me?"

"Liam, please!"

"No. No, I fucking get it. Message received. What I don't get is why you waited this long to tell me that you have a goddamn husband!"

"He's my ex-husband," she said weakly. It sounded more like a question than a statement.

"Ex?" A hard laugh sounded in my throat, and I nodded past her. "Does he know that? Better yet, do you?"

October 24
Kennedy

LIAM STORMED PAST me, but I didn't try to stop him. I didn't know what to say. I didn't know what to say at all now that Rhys was here. Like Kira had said, it'd been four years since any of us had seen him.

Minutes after I heard the front door shut, I turned at the sound of someone walking toward me, and found Rhys there.

A million memories hit me. Our whirlwind romance. Eloping after knowing each other for only two weeks. Being devastatingly in love with him, and then being simply devastated when he left me. I'd never loved anyone before or after him. Dated guys, sure, but no one had been like Rhys until Liam came back into my life. What we'd had was something you only ever see in fairy tales. Rhys had been my entire world, and I'd thought I was his. Obviously I had been wrong.

My family had been furious when we'd gotten married. Partly because I had barely turned eighteen when I met him, but mostly because we barely knew each other and none of them had even met Rhys before we eloped. I married him just days after graduation, and even though I'd been positive I wouldn't end up going to college with my sister since Rhys's job was in Tampa, college had ended up being an escape when he'd asked for a divorce just two weeks before classes started.

He'd fed me a line about how he couldn't give me the life I deserved—complete with tears and the most heartbreaking expression I've seen on anyone's face—and I never saw him again. He didn't return to his apartment, which I'd been sharing with him over the summer, and his phone was taken out of service that day. I received the divorce papers in the mail just days later. That was the day I stopped believing in love.

My mom and sister were equally mad at him and sad for me, but my dad had been the confusing one. Where I thought he'd be happy that Rhys had left me, he'd done nothing but hold me as I cried for days. Only leaving my side if Uncle Mason was there to take his place. Neither of them ever said a word, but their worry and sadness had been unexpected.

And now, after four years, Rhys was standing in my room, in my condo, in motherfucking California.

"Why are you here? How! *How* are you here?" I asked him when I felt like I could finally speak again.

"Are you asking how I knew where to find you?"

"Yes, Rhys, I want to know how you knew where we were." And I wanted to do anything but start crying again.

"Your dad told me."

I waited for him to correct himself, or to tell me the real answer, but instead of speaking, he stared at me with the same heartbroken expression on his face as he'd worn on the day he told me we were over.

"Who was—"

"My dad told you where we were?" I asked, cutting him off. "Why?"

Rhys looked off to the side, his dark eyes wide, like he was having trouble understanding something. "He, uh . . . he knows how much you still mean to me. I hadn't said anything other than your name before he was writing down the address here."

The air left my lungs in a hard rush. It felt like he'd just punched me. "How much I still mean to you," I said, the statement almost sounding like a question. "What do you—Rhys, you *left* me! You divorced me and then you just disappeared! I never heard from you again! I didn't know where you went when you left, and you gave me no way of getting ahold of you so I could try to change your mind."

Rhys's expression changed to something between surprise and awe. "He never told you?"

"No—what? Who never told me what?"

"Your dad. He gave me his word, but you're his daughter. I didn't think for a second that he would actually keep it from you."

When he didn't offer more, I threw my arms out to the side. "Are you going to tell me what you thought I already knew, or just leave me wondering?"

Rhys looked around again, and his eyes stayed on the bed for a few seconds. When he spoke, his voice was dark. "I want to sit down while I tell you this, but if he has been in here with you, I will not touch that bed." His eyes shot over to me and he took a step back. "Please give me the chance to explain everything."

He didn't wait for me to say anything else; he just turned and walked out. When I followed him, I found him standing in the living room, waiting for me to decide where to go from there. I didn't want to sit on the couch with him, because I was afraid he'd get too close to me, and I couldn't handle that right now. Turning, I went into the kitchen and sat down at the small table. As soon as we were sitting, he began talking.

"Kennedy, what did you think I did for a living?"

My forehead creased. "What did I *think*? You're a cop. Or, you were."

Rhys nodded and leaned forward to put his arms on the table. "A cop for the city of Tampa. You never found it odd that I didn't know your dad or Mason, and they didn't know me? We worked for the same police department."

"No, because they're detectives, you were on patrol."

"The two still cross, Kennedy."

I sat back in my chair, trying to put distance between us without being obvious about it. I didn't understand what he was saying. I'd seen his uniform, I'd seen his patrol car . . . I knew he worked for the Tampa police. "What are you getting at? Did you steal the uniform and car?"

A startled laugh left him, and his lips curved up into the smile I'd fallen for so long ago. "No, nothing like that. What I'm saying is, we did know each other. When I met you, I had no idea that the two of you were related. I *knew* Detective Ryan. I'd had to talk with him and Detective Gates a few times when they were looking for certain gang members, but never once did I think you had any connection with them. Two days after we got married, I got called in to talk with the chief; do you remember that?"

"I don't know—I mean, I guess I do. I knew you were supposed to be off work and you went in for a few hours, but that's it. All I really remember from that day was going to tell my family later that night that we'd gotten married."

"Yeah," Rhys said on a sigh. "In that meeting with Chief, I was asked to change jobs in the department for one assignment. He told me some things about the job, and I immediately accepted it. I knew it was important, I knew it involved getting some bad people. I had no idea until after I'd agreed that I would no longer be able to have a relationship with you. For some reason, I never once realized the seriousness of this job until two detectives came in to talk to me about it. Your dad and uncle."

I sat there staring at him with wide eyes. "My dad and uncle? What . . . what was the job?"

"To go undercover," Rhys responded immediately. "Your dad and uncle were going to be the ones training me over the next few months because of the work they'd done while they were undercover. At the end of that meeting and their going over what we would be doing for training and when . . . they told me to start cutting ties with everyone. They said I couldn't tell anyone, but I had to start distancing myself from even my family."

"You're lying."

"I'm not, Kennedy."

"I had my dad look for you in the department after you left me, and he said you just disappeared! He said you stopped coming in for work and no one could get in touch with you!"

Rhys's eyebrows rose, as if he were trying to get me to understand what I was saying. "Exactly. They knew where I went, but I couldn't have any contact with them, just as they couldn't have contact with me or act like they knew me if our paths crossed. But that night, when I got home, you were so freaked out about telling your family about our marriage that I don't think you even noticed how dead I felt. Knowing that I'd have to leave you, and fighting with myself over whether or not I should tell you why. I didn't want to go to your parents' house after that, but realized that we needed to. I knew your family needed to see me—the guy who would soon be leaving their daughter—so they would have a face to go with the name of the person they blamed. And I needed to see them to know that you would have people there for you once I was gone. Imagine how much worse it got when you and I walked in, and there was your dad expecting you and wanting to know where you'd run off to for the past few days . . . the same man who just hours before had told me to cut ties with everyone in my life."

I couldn't say anything once he was finished. I couldn't remember how to speak, and wouldn't have known what to say if I could.

When minutes passed without a word from me, Rhys cleared his throat. "The assignment ended almost two weeks ago, and I had to go through some debriefing and tests to make sure I was . . . well, to make sure I was still me. The minute I could, I found your dad and asked about you. And now I'm here."

"So . . . what? Now that you're here, things just go back to how it was? We get married again on a whim and see what happens? I had three months with you, Rhys. Three! And in those months, you took everything I knew and turned it upside down in the most incredible way before tearing my entire world apart! I waited for you for two years before completely giving up. I kept thinking that you would show up and it would be okay again. Or that it really had all just been some horrible nightmare and I would wake up in your arms again. But there was nothing. And you can't come in here after four years expecting us to go back to how we were and try to make me believe that you still feel something for me."

"Kennedy, I'm sorry. I'm so fucking sorry for leaving you, but I love you. I have always loved you. I have never met anyone—"

"No, you don't and you didn't. If you ever had, you would have turned down the job." I stood from the chair and turned, but Rhys's whispered words stopped me from leaving.

"Your dad was so sure that you would be waiting for me . . . that our marriage was something you still wanted."

I looked back at the mixture of confusion and hurt on his face, and shook my head slowly, ignoring the tears streaming down my cheeks. "He was wrong. You shouldn't have come back here, Rhys."

"Kennedy!" he called when I began walking toward my room, and I whirled back to face him.

"You *ruined* me!" I screamed. "Don't you get that? Leave!"

I didn't wait to see if he did. I just walked into my room and locked the door behind me before sliding down it until I was on the floor. I sat there crying for hours with my heart torn now that my past had just collided with my present.

14

October 27
Liam

THERE WAS A soft knock on my office door three days later, but I didn't respond to it. If it was Eli, he'd have come in without waiting for me to invite him. If it was anyone else, they could call me. A minute later, I heard another few knocks and then the door slowly opened.

"I have it shut for a reas—" I cut off quickly when I looked up and saw the girl standing in front of me.

Seeing her there felt like a weight settled on my chest, and conflicting thoughts rushed through my mind. I wanted to hold her, I wanted to yell at her, I wanted to demand she tell me *now* why she never told me she was married, and I wanted to press her against the wall and show her what exactly we'd had and what she had thrown away.

Instead, I cleared my throat and looked back at the screen of my computer. "I'm busy."

Another minute passed without her leaving or saying anything, but the second I heard her voice, I couldn't stop myself from looking up at her. "Do you remember that night in your apartment—the night I stopped fighting what you already knew I felt for you?" I didn't respond, but she continued anyway. "You told me that you wanted to face whatever I was fighting from my past head-on."

"But I didn't know that I would be fighting your *husband*."

"Ex," she corrected. "Rhys is my ex-husband. And before you go repeating what you asked me the morning you found out about him, yes, I know he's my ex. I am fully aware of it. But you don't understand; I was eighteen when I married him and he divorced me three months later and disappeared until just the other day. I looked for him for two years after he disappeared before giving up, and only now do I know that he had to leave me because he had to go undercover—just like my dad and uncle."

"Well, good, I'm happy for you. Now he's back, and you can pick up your marriage where you left off," I said, but it was obvious that the last thing I was feeling was happiness over the situation.

Kennedy shook her head as tears gathered in her eyes. "What I'm trying to tell you is that his reappearance had me too shocked to figure out what to say or do the other morning, and that's why I wasn't able to stop you from leaving. I never expected to see or hear from him again—especially not while Kira and I were here in California—but I didn't want you to leave then, and I don't want you to leave me now."

I sat there for a while just staring at her as tears slipped down her face. "I don't know what you want me to say."

"I want you to say you're still here with me! I want you to keep fighting for us instead of just leaving me!"

"I can't, Kennedy! He was your husband, and now he's come back for you. I can't compete with that," I said, my voice and body showing how defeated I felt.

A hushed cry burst from her chest, and she tightened her lips into a hard line as she tried to regain control over her emotions, but her voice still shook when she said, "That pain you used to talk about? That fear? That was me not wanting to have another Rhys in my life. That was me being terrified that my world would be shattered again by you, because I knew you had the capability of doing that. I knew it in the way you silently commanded control, I knew it in the way I easily and willingly gave in to you again and again, and I knew it in the way you made me feel just by being near me. No one had ever done that except for Rhys until you came into my life."

All the air in my lungs left in a heavy rush. It felt like her words had just landed a blow to my stomach. Never once since Rhys had shown up at her door had I imagined that the entire time I'd known Kennedy, I'd been reminding her of him. "So is that why you fought me, or is that why you were with me—because I reminded you of him?"

Kennedy's face tightened in pain at my words, but she nodded, acknowledging their truth. "I fought you because of all the ways you were like him. I'm with you because of all the ways you *aren't*."

My legs ached from the force I was using to keep myself in my chair instead of going to her, but just as she'd protected herself over the past five months, I needed to protect myself until I knew what exactly was going to happen with us. "Sit down," I ordered softly, and waited until she did. "What happened after I left?"

"We talked. He told me about why he left and how he found me, and—"

"How did he?" I asked, interrupting her.

"My dad. As soon as his undercover assignment was over, he found my dad and asked about me. Dad gave him the address to the condo."

I kept my face neutral, but behind my desk, I was clenching my hands into fists. "So I guess we know who your parents want you to be with."

"Not necessarily," she whispered. "Neither of them liked him when we got married because they didn't know him, and they never got the chance to. I've talked to my mom about you a lot, my dad just knows *of* you because he doesn't really care to know about Kira's and my relationships. I think my dad just remembers how I was when Rhys left, and in his mind, he was doing me a favor by sending him to California. Besides, I think he sympathizes with Rhys because of his own time spent undercover—and he knows what it can do to a person and those closest to them. But that doesn't mean he would rather I be with him than you."

"So did you just forgive him when he told you everything?"

"No," she responded immediately. "It made me more mad to finally know all that. I told him to leave."

My eyebrows rose, and I straightened in my chair. "You did?"

Kennedy started to speak, but stopped and her face pinched together. Like she was worried that what she said next would crush my hopeful expression. "I did, but he never left. He's been sleeping on the couch the past three nights. When I came back into the living room after leaving him out there and found that he hadn't left, he told me he was going to stay until I was ready to talk to him again, and I haven't been. And to be honest, I don't think he's ready to talk to me again either. He was really upset about you. He didn't say that exactly—but it was obvious in the way he looked at me when he asked about you, and he gave me that same look when I told Kira where I was going today."

As much as it pissed me off that he was still there, I couldn't help but be glad that Kennedy hadn't talked to him again even though he was waiting for her to. But not one part of me enjoyed hearing that he didn't like my relationship with Kennedy, because I was right there with him. I hated *his* relationship with her. "If you didn't want me to leave then, why did it take you three days to come to me?"

"Because I didn't know what to do," she said honestly. "And I didn't know what I was supposed to say to you after you stormed out. Having my past and present collide was something I never thought would happen."

I studied her for a few seconds, then asked, "Were you ever going to tell me? I mean—Christ, I feel like I don't know a damn thing about you after finding this out."

"You do," she assured me. "You know more about me than Rhys ever took the time to try to know. And, yes, I was going to tell you about him. I told you during the movie on Friday night that I would tell you soon. I just didn't know when that would be."

I laughed in frustration. "So you're saying it's possible that one day you would've found a guy that you wanted to marry, and then sometime after the wedding, it may or may not have come up in passing that you'd been married once before? That's something guys want to know right away! That's something *I* would've wanted to know!"

"Would it have changed things for you? Would we still have dated if you'd known?"

"Yes, of course we would have. But finding out like this after I've already fallen in love with you? It's bullshit, Kennedy."

Shock covered her face, and for a moment, she didn't say anything. "You've fallen in love with me? That—you can't. You're incapable of falling in love with anyone."

I laughed once and threw my arms out to the side. "Since when?"

"Your sister said you were incapable of being with only one person and loving anyone who wasn't family."

"I don't give a fuck what Kristi said. If you hadn't noticed, whatever bullshit she said is already moot since I've been with you! I am perfectly capable of loving someone; I've just never *wanted* to love anyone until I met you. You're the one who doesn't believe in love, which is why I haven't said anything about loving you until now. But now I'm betting that's not even the case. It's not that you don't believe in it, it's that you're afraid of loving someone after Rhys because he broke your heart."

She didn't respond, but I took the look in her eyes as a confirmation.

"People get hurt, Kennedy. That's life. If you were to go back with your husband, would I be hurt? Yes. I can't even begin to tell you what it would do to me. But I wouldn't spend the rest of my goddamn life shielding myself from loving someone again, or letting them love me." I searched her dark blue eyes for another minute, then continued, "Now, I need to know if you're going to hurt me, or if you're going to finally let yourself love again, and be loved by me. I'm letting you know now that I won't take anything less from you this time, Kennedy. Not after everything we've gone through just to get to this point."

"I don't know what to tell you. I don't know what to think or feel about Rhys being here, but I am terrified of losing you, Liam."

"No matter how much I hate saying this, it *has* to be him or me."

"I can't lose you!" she cried, but the way she said it left me waiting for what would come next.

"But?" I prompted, and she shook her head.

"But I married him. *I* promised him forever, and even though I want to, I can't blame him for his reasons for breaking *his* promise and leaving me four years ago. I don't know what I'm supposed to do about my vows to him now that he's back. This would be hard enough if I didn't have you, but I do. Trying to decide between what's right, and figuring out what I want, is tearing me apart, Liam."

"Well, this isn't a game where you can pick and choose who you want on each day, Kennedy. Like I said, it can only be him or me at the end of this if you even decide to choose one of us.

It's tearing you apart. I get it. I can assure you that Rhys and I feel the exact same way waiting for you to decide. I'm not leaving you, but I can't be physically with you while you make your decision. So I'm going to step back so you can have time to figure things out without me pressuring you to make the decision or choose me. Because no matter how much I want to, fighting for you is only going to confuse you more. Not only am I not about to do that to you, but I'm sure as hell not about to go through what either of my dads went through with my mom."

"Liam," she begged, but I shook my head.

"I can't, Kennedy. I'm sorry. I'll be right here waiting for when you decide. But until then, I will *only* be right here."

Countless moments passed with her sitting there crying before she left my office. As soon as the door was shut behind her, I dropped my head into my hands and spent the next hour holding back my own tears as I continued to remind myself that running after her would only make the situation worse.

October 27
Kennedy

I SOMEHOW MADE it home despite barely being able to see the road through my tears. After taking a few minutes to collect myself, I got out of the car and walked into the condo. I'd barely made it a step inside when I paused with my hand still on the door.

There was laughter coming from inside my condo.

Kira had gotten so much better, but I hadn't ever come home to this sound . . . and it felt out of place considering the mood when I'd left, and my mood now.

Taking my hand off the door, I took the last few steps inside so I could see into the living room, and paused again.

Both Kira and Rhys stopped laughing and stared at me with wide eyes when they caught sight of me from where they were sitting on the couches, and an awkward silence engulfed the room for long seconds until I gestured to the front door.

"Uh, we—Kira, we need to go to work."

Kira quickly got up from her spot on the love seat and walked over to me. When she reached me, she grabbed my hand and whispered, "Are you okay?"

I looked at her in confusion, then glanced at Rhys. "With you laughing?"

Rhys's worried eyes stayed pinned on me as Kira stepped closer. And even though I knew she was trying to get my attention, I couldn't stop looking at the man sitting on our couch—just like I did every time I was in the same room with him.

"You're crying," Kira whispered, and squeezed my hand.

I finally tore my eyes from Rhys to look at my sister, and put my hand up to my face to find it wet. "Oh, I thought I . . ." I trailed off and shrugged. Apparently I hadn't pulled myself together as much as I'd thought I had.

"We'll talk about it in the car. I'll go get ready."

Once Kira walked away and had shut her bedroom door behind her, I looked back at Rhys to find him now standing—the same look of worry in his eyes. I dropped my gaze to the floor and walked toward my room, but stopped when I heard his voice.

"Are you okay?" he asked softly. His voice was just as deep as Liam's, and the rough tone was something I had loved once and craved for long after he was gone. But now the sound was only a reminder that Rhys was back in my life—as if his standing in front of me wasn't enough—and that I now had to choose between him and Liam.

"I'm fine."

"You talked to him," he stated. There was no question; I doubted my face left any room for one.

"Yes, I talked to him. But whatever you're gathering from the way I look right now, I can tell you that you have it wrong."

Rhys nodded but didn't say anything else, and after a few seconds, I began walking toward my room again.

I'd only been in there long enough to change when I heard two knocks on my wall. I turned to find Rhys leaning against a wall with his arms folded across his chest.

"Why *are* you crying then?"

"I'm crying because I have no fucking clue what I'm going to do, and this entire situation is tearing me up!"

He watched me for a minute before asking, "Do you want me to leave, Kennedy?"

My first thought was to yell at him that I'd already told him to leave, and he'd stayed. But I found myself saying, "I want you to leave because you broke my heart. I *don't* want you to leave because like I said, I have no idea what I'm going to do . . . and if you leave now, I'll always wonder later what I would have decided if you'd stayed."

With a nod, he pushed away from the wall and took a step back toward the door. "I, uh . . . I used your shower while you were gone."

"That's fine, Rhys."

"If you need anything while you're at work—"

"I know. But we're fine," I said, cutting him off. He'd made the same offer yesterday, but I didn't need anything from him at the moment—nor did I want him to do anything *for* me.

A few more seconds passed before he took another step back and grabbed on to the doorframe. Just before he turned to go, he said, "I'm sorry, Kennedy. I'm so sorry."

"I know," I repeated, but this time the words were barely audible.

Kira turned the corner in the hall to walk toward my bedroom, and mumbled an apology to Rhys when she bumped into him before looking up at me. "You ready?"

"Yeah. Yeah, let's go."

The only good-bye between Rhys and me was a long look as I walked through the living room. He looked hurt again, like he had when I'd left the house earlier . . . but I couldn't let myself get too focused on his expression. While I didn't like that he was hurting, I couldn't feel bad for him. I didn't know how he'd expected me to be waiting for him after all those years, and after the kind of good-bye he'd given me. I didn't know what he'd expected to find when he showed up at my door. But he couldn't blame me for going on with my life.

"Okay, tell me what happened with Liam," Kira said as soon as we were in the car and she was reversing out of the spot.

"He was mad . . . obviously. He was mad that I'd kept my marriage from him, and wanted to know if I ever would have told him. He told me he loved me—"

"He did?" Kira asked, surprise coating her short question.

"Yeah."

"What did you say? Did you leave—wait, is that why you were crying?"

"No," I said on a humorless laugh. "We kind of fought about the whole love thing because of something I'd heard about him, and what he knew about me. But I'm pretty sure I was already crying before that. I'm not sure, though, I don't know when I started."

Kira was quiet for a few seconds, then asked, "Would you have?"

"Would I have what?"

"Told him," she explained. "Would you have told him about Rhys?"

I told her all about the mini-conversation Liam and I'd had

during the movie on Friday night. I told Kira his question about
our new tattoos, what my response had been, and what we'd
talked about Saturday morning before Rhys had shown up.
Unlike her usual self, Kira never once interrupted me while I
told her everything. She just looked over at me with shocked expressions every once in a while, and when I was done, she let out
a huff.

"Wow."

"That's pretty much how I feel," I mumbled, and stared out
the window.

"Dad called me again . . ." She trailed off, her tone hinting at
what she wasn't saying.

"I know, he called me too. I didn't answer."

"Kennedy, you can't keep ignoring him. He's our dad."

I glanced over at her with wide eyes. "Yeah, and I just found
out a few days ago that he'd kept a secret from me for four years!
I think I'm allowed to not want to talk to him after that. From
what Mom told us about when they met, you think Dad would
understand by now that keeping the whole undercover thing a
secret while you're in a relationship is a bad thing."

Kira sighed, and I knew she didn't agree with me. But she
couldn't understand. Dad hadn't kept anything from her the
way he had with me. And from what I was hearing from Mom, I
wasn't the only one who was ignoring him. She was just as mad
as I was that he'd let me go through all that pain without ever
saying a word to anyone—including her.

"So what happens now? With Liam," Kira clarified a few moments later.

I exhaled heavily and lifted one shoulder in a lopsided shrug.
"Now I have to figure out what I want to do. Liam said he was
going to back off while I decided. He basically said it was to
make it easier for me to decide; but nothing about that sounds
like it'll be easier for me. Even though he said he wasn't leaving

me, that's exactly what it sounded like. It sounded like he was giving up."

"I think he's right to back off," Kira mused. "I'm sure it's hurting you right now, but just imagine what it would be like trying to decide between them if Liam stayed around you. With Rhys staying in the condo, there would be so much tension between the two of them. And right now, you're really too upset with Rhys for him to sway your decision in his favor. If Liam was always around you, you'd only be able to think of him because you've been falling for him for months now; and right now, you *only* want him. What was it you said to me this morning before you left? That you didn't know how to decide between what you thought was right and . . ."

"Who I wanted," I finished for her.

"Right. You think staying with Rhys is right only because of your past with him. You know you want Liam, but you don't know if you'll end up wanting Rhys again once your anger is gone. So right now Rhys is more like an obligation, and Liam sticking around would only make that more apparent and not give you a real chance to make up your mind." Kira waved her hand between us and said, "All that to say I agree with what Liam's doing—even if it does hurt."

"I guess," I whispered. "I can see what you mean, but right now it hurts too much to understand."

Kira squeezed my arm, but didn't say anything else about Liam. Once we pulled up to the gym, she put the car in park and looked at me. "I know I've never been a fan of Rhys's, but I never really had a chance to get to know him. In those months of you meeting him, marrying him, and being with him—you basically shut out everyone else in your life, including me. I get why now, I do. You were very in love with him, and even though you didn't know that he would be leaving you, I bet you could sense his worry over what little time you two had left together, and that made you throw everything into that summer. But now that he's been here for a few days and I've talked to him a lot, I just want to say that I like him. He's really nice, Kennedy, I can see why that relationship destroyed you. And I'm sorry that I didn't understand before."

"No hard feelings, sis. It's in the past, right?"

"Right," she agreed.

"Come on, let's get this day over with. I'm not exactly thrilled to face another day of Kristi glaring at me."

We got out of the car and made our way into the gym, and before we even got to the drink station, Kristi walked past us with a death glare directed right at me.

I groaned and looked over to Kira when she patted my back, and mumbled, "So, this should be fun."

15

November 29
Liam

SHUTTING THE FRONT door of my parents' house, I called out
to them as I walked through the entryway and into the living
room. I found my parents, both of my aunts and uncles, and
Kristi in there . . . and fourteen eyes locked on me—none of
them giving me a welcoming look.

"Your cousins all already went back to school a couple hours
ago," Aunt Bree bit out. "If you were wondering or cared."

"Um, okay? I do care . . . thanks for telling me," I said uncer-
tainly.

"And all six of your grandparents are wondering why you
barely said a word the other night, and then left as soon as
dinner was over."

"Okay? I'm sor—"

"*And* you already missed pancakes, if you were wondering.
I'm sure you can run back to wherever you've been hiding and
make some for yourself," Kristi added, cutting me off.

I raised my arms out to the side before letting them fall back
down. "What the fuck? What did I do to get this kind of reac-

tion as soon as I walk in? And what do you mean by 'hiding'? I just saw all of you on Thursday."

"You said you would be around this weekend to spend time with everyone," Mom explained. At least she looked more worried *for* me than pissed off *at* me.

"I said I would try. I have a lot going on, and I'm sorry that it cut into time with everyone, but they'll all be back for Christmas, I can see them then. There was a huge account I was finishing up that should have been done before Thanksgiving. I've been working my ass off to finish things before the end of the month."

"Or maybe you've been gone because you were still moping around over a lying whore!"

"Kristi," Dad warned.

"Fuck off, Kristi," I growled. "What is your deal?"

"My deal is that it's been a month, and you're still waiting for her to choose you when we all know that isn't about to fucking happen! Her husband is back, that alone should have told you all you needed to know in regard to her. She's not coming back for you, Liam!"

"That's enough," Dad said with his eyes directly on my sister.

I backed up a couple steps and held out my arms again. "Is this really what today is going to be about? I'm not putting up with this shit from you." Looking at the rest of my family, I said, "I'm sorry. I'll apologize to everyone later, but I'm gone. See you all next Sunday."

"Bye, Liam! *Bye*. Go hide out again because a girl you were with for four months doesn't want to be with you anymore."

"Kristi," Dad barked. "I said enough."

"Oh, but what a shock it was!" she continued. "She wouldn't even let anyone call her your girlfriend—did you really think she would just change one day?"

"Again, fuck off, Kristi!" I yelled, and turned back around to face them. "You don't know *anything* about what happened between Kennedy and me. Got that? None of you do—well, except maybe Dad. Finding Kennedy and fighting for her is something I would do again, and again." I looked at all of their expectant and frustrated faces, and shrugged. "I didn't meet Kennedy at the gym. I met her a year and a half ago in Vegas."

"What?" Mom whispered, and looked at Dad. "You knew this?"

Dad's eyes didn't leave me, but I couldn't tell if he was mad that I'd just thrown him under the bus, or if he was simply waiting to see what I would tell everyone.

"I met Kennedy one night and we hooked up," I started again, but Kristi cut in.

"Wow. She just keeps getting better and better."

"Think whatever you want about that, but know that *I'm* the one who initiated it then . . . so don't go putting your bullshit theories on her." Looking back at everyone again, I said, "It was only one night, but I thought of her for months. I would've done anything to find her again. And I mean fucking anything. But I had no name, nothing. Six months ago, my boss told me about his nieces who had just moved here from Florida, and weren't happy about it. He wanted help introducing them to people, and anything else I could offer them. I knew Dad was looking for new people at the gym, and he agreed to interview them. Nothing more. I didn't know until *after* the interview that it was the same girl from Vegas and her twin sister." Narrowing my eyes on my sister, I said, "*That* is why Kennedy freaked when she saw me at the gym during her first week. Not because she dropped a drink—she dropped it *because* I was there."

Kristi scoffed. "It doesn't change what she did to you, or what she's doing now."

Aunt Bree looked like she wanted to agree, but I was sure the reason Uncle Konrad was whispering to her was to try to stop her from saying anything else. My mom looked shocked and mad that she was just finding all this out. Aunt Aubrey and Uncle Jeremy, my dad's brother and sister-in-law, were staring at me just like Dad was . . . without judgment. Just waiting for what would come next.

"No, it doesn't change what she did. But now you know why I wanted to be with her so bad. She fell back into my life, and I wasn't letting her go again no matter how hard she tried to fight her feelings for me. No matter how much I fucking hate what's happening now, everything finally makes sense. Why she was cautious, why she tried to push me back, why she still wouldn't let anyone actually define our relationship . . ." I trailed off and focused on my sister again. "Yeah, I was mad when I found out. I was mad she'd waited so long to tell me. But *you*? You have no room to sit there and judge her or be a bitch about what's going on because all you know is that she was married. Think about everything she did when it came to my relationship with her in the five months from when she moved here until her ex showed up, Kristi, think about it. And now think about her ex. They were married when she was eighteen, and he left her and disappeared out of the blue one day only a few months in, and just showed up again four years later. I fucking hate what is happening, and I hate not knowing who she's going to choose. But really, you can't blame her for being confused when she found out that the reason he left her was because he had to go undercover for the police department."

Kristi's pissed-off expression disappeared when I finished, and was replaced with wide eyes that were filled with shock. But she never said anything. No one did.

"Yeah. So there's the whole story. Have fun with that." Without another word, I turned and walked out of my parents' house. No one tried to stop me, not like they could have after everything that had just gone down in those few minutes. And now that I'd just told the entire story, I was right back where I'd been for the last month.

Hurting. Frustrated. And waiting. Always waiting.

November 30
Kennedy

"Did you notice the way Kristi kept looking at you today?" Kira asked as we walked up to our condo.

"Yes! You noticed it too?"

Kira gave me a look and laughed. "Kind of hard not to. She looked like she couldn't figure out what to say to you, so she just kept telling me everything."

"Oh well. At least she doesn't look like she wants to kill me anymore. I wonder what changed." I was about to put the key in the door, but stopped and looked at Kira with wide eyes. "Do you think . . . do you think Liam is seeing someone?"

"No. No way. If he were, Kristi would be throwing it in your face after how she's been acting the last month." Kira didn't look worried about the possibility that Liam had found someone, but when she saw my face, her expression softened. "Have you talked to him?"

I shrugged. "I've tried. Whenever I call him or text him, the first thing he asks is if I've decided yet. When I tell him I'm still trying to, he says, 'I'll be here,' and then hangs up . . . or stops responding."

Kira suddenly looked uncomfortable, but before I could question her expression, she asked, "And are you getting any closer to deciding?"

I thought about that for a minute, and finally said, "If I had to make a decision right now, I know who I would choose. But whenever I think about making the decision, I feel like I'm still not giving Rhys the chance he deserves—so I don't."

"It's been more than a month," she reminded me.

"I know," I groaned. "I know it has. I really need to spend some time actually talking with Rhys . . . I've been ignoring him even when I'm near him."

Kira didn't respond; she just nodded her head as she turned to face straight ahead.

Unlocking the door, I pushed it open and followed Kira inside. A few steps in, she turned to look at me with wide eyes.

"Smells good in here," I mumbled.

"It does," she agreed, and turned toward the living room.

It wasn't uncommon for the condo to smell alarmingly good. Rhys had nothing to do all day, and was still on paid leave for another month from the department to regroup from his time undercover, so we often came home to a clean house. Once he explained how he'd been living for four years, and how, now that he was away from that life, he felt like nothing was ever clean enough, I'd stopped asking him not to clean, and let him do what he wanted.

"Wow," Kira said in amazement when she rounded the corner to look into the kitchen. "What is all this?"

"Oh, wow!" I echoed when I looked into the kitchen. There were plates and bowls filled with amazing-looking food, and Rhys was standing in front of the sink rinsing off what looked like the last of the dishes he'd been using. "Where did this come from?"

"I made it," he answered with a nonchalant shrug. "I went to the store today and bought enough food to stock up the pantry and fridge."

I glanced over at Kira, who was looking in the pantry, then looked back at Rhys in awe. "Really? You didn't have to do that. It must have cost so much."

"I don't think I've ever seen this so full," Kira whispered from where she was now standing in front of the refrigerator.

"You didn't let me help pay any of the bills from last month. I had to do something."

"Because you sleep on the couch and clean all the time!"

Rhys smiled. "Kennedy, that does not come close to equaling out."

"Wait," I said, and held up a hand. "*How* did you get to the store to buy all of this?"

Kira turned to Rhys for his response, but quickly moved her eyes away and looked down at the food.

"Uh, I went and bought a truck today."

"You bought a truck?" Kira asked, her voice and face showing her excitement.

"How?" I asked again.

Rhys's smile turned sarcastic. "Well, I picked it out, signed the papers, and drove it back here. But if you're asking how I could afford it, you have to remember I came back to four years of back pay with absolutely nothing that I needed to pay for except my ticket here."

"Huh, well, that's fun—wait! How did you get to the dealership?"

Both Kira and Rhys laughed, and after a quick look back at Kira, Rhys's eyes were on me. "They have these cars called taxis now. You call the number, they pick you up, you pay them to drive you somewhere. They're pretty cool."

"Shut up," I said on a laugh, and rolled my eyes. "You could've just said you called a cab, jerk."

"But then you might have asked, 'How?' "

This time I was laughing with them, but my laugh died and I blurted, "Wait! How did you call a cab?"

"Rhys asked if he could use my phone today, I left it with him when we went to work."

For a second, I wondered why he'd asked Kira instead of me, but figured he probably didn't feel comfortable asking me seeing as I was always either at work or at the beach, and if I was home, I was locked in my bedroom. And he and Kira had become friends over the last month, so I just nodded. "Okay, I swear I'm done with the *hows*."

"Good," Rhys said with a wink. "You girls hungry? I just finished getting everything ready about a minute before you walked in."

"Yes!" Kira and I said in unison, and helped him carry all the dishes over to the table.

"THAT WAS SO good." I placed a hand on my too-full stomach, and groaned. "I can't remember the last time I ate that much."

"Or had a home-cooked meal," Kira added, and I agreed.

"Very true." I looked over at Rhys and nudged him. "Did you cook while you were undercover? Or were you just still good at it when you came back?"

He laughed and shook his head once. "Definitely didn't cook while there. I'm glad I still know how to boil water after being gone for that long."

"Poor guy," Kira said with an apologetic look. "You only ate takeout for four years, and then you come here and we're too lazy to cook anything, so we force you to have more of it. Good job, us."

"No, nothing like that. There was an older woman at the house I was in. She did all the laundry and cooked every meal except breakfast."

"Huh," I huffed. "Well, that's nice, I guess."

"No!" Rhys disagreed with a laugh. "Definitely not nice either. The way she did laundry, everything still came out dirty. She never cleaned the house with anything more than a paper towel, and would yell at us if we tried to. And her cooking? It was okay. I mean, it wasn't horrible, but she only made three different meals. There was always a soup, but only lentil, vegetable, or cabbage. Then there would be fried chicken, enchiladas, or pasta with this red sauce that you had to choke down. And then there would be mashed potatoes, rice, or garlic bread. Everything was seasoned beyond the point of being edible, and if you'd already eaten before you got to the house, she'd still make you eat everything she gave you. So after four years of that, takeout was the most amazing thing."

Kira and I were laughing, and I asked, "Well, why didn't they just get someone else to cook and clean?"

"She was the leader's mom. He cherished that woman. If you said anything negative about her, the cooking, or the house . . . it was over for you."

"Oh my God, are you serious?" Kira asked with wide eyes.

"Very." Rhys sighed. "You didn't mess with that guy's mom."

"Apparently not," I murmured. "Can you tell us anything about your time undercover? We've heard stories from Dad and Uncle Mason. But we obviously heard the stories years after anything happened."

"Uh," Rhys began, and his dark eyes got a faraway look. "We dealt, mostly. That was the big thing. Well, *we* didn't. We were the suppliers."

"Did you have to use?" I asked.

"Did your dad?" he shot back.

Kira and I nodded, and Rhys raised his eyebrows in confirmation.

"Not often, thank God. Getting in . . ." He trailed off. "Getting in, there was a lot I had to do that I hated—including a lot of using. But once I was in, it was easy to just act like I'd been using, and my stash would always be gone since I was handing it over to the department. There would only be a handful of times a year when they'd wait and watch you use. But there was always other stuff there was no way out of, as I'm sure you can imagine from hearing your dad's stories."

"Yeah," Kira breathed. "He said he and Mason were obsessive about getting tested because of what they had to do."

Rhys agreed, "Yep. I was lucky; but none of the test results ever stopped me from being terrified. Just never knew what could happen before the next test."

I studied Rhys's distant eyes for a few moments and cleared my throat. "Sorry, it wasn't really fair of me to ask you to tell us all this. That's probably hard for you to talk about, especially so soon. You don't have to tell us anything else. I guess we're just so used to hearing about the horrors of working undercover that it never seems like it's a big deal or shocking to us. But we didn't have to go through it. So like I said, I'm sorry."

"It's fine," he insisted, but I could tell that I'd brought up things he didn't enjoy thinking about.

"New subject?" I offered.

Rhys shrugged like it didn't matter. "Sure."

"What are you going to make us for dinner tomorrow?"

He laughed, and just like that, the haunted look in his dark eyes disappeared behind his smile. Rhys started listing off everything he'd bought at the store that day and things he'd been craving and wanted to make, and every now and then he'd make suggestions just to see what we thought about different meals and types of food.

The conversation over the next half hour was much lighter, and I found myself smiling along with Rhys and Kira and enjoying having him there. But I couldn't help but notice that even though it was nice having him around, I still no felt no connection to him romantically or physically. He was attractive, that was impossible to miss. Nearly Liam's height, but with dark messy hair and equally dark eyes; and while he was nicely built, he was much leaner than Liam.

And then I realized that not only did I not have any feelings toward Rhys, but all I could think about when I looked at him was how he wasn't Liam.

"Who the fuck . . . stay here!" Rhys demanded suddenly, and jumped out of his chair to take off running toward the back sliding glass door.

I'd jumped at his loud words, but even if I hadn't registered what he'd said, I don't think I would have been able to get up just because of the shock of his sudden outburst. I turned around in time to see him slide the door open and take off running out into the grassy area behind our condo and disappear off to the side.

"What on earth?" I mumbled when his shouts reached us through the open door.

Kira and I stood at the same time and walked over to the open door, and although we could still hear him, we didn't see him.

"Did you see someone?"

"No," Kira answered softly, like she was still trying to grasp what had happened as well.

When another moment passed, I asked, "Do you think he has problems from being undercover that maybe the tests the department did didn't catch?"

Kira snorted, causing my lips to curve up at the corners. "I think we would have noticed something like this before tonight if he did have a—who is that?" she quickly asked when Rhys finally rounded the corner of the building with a gangly guy stumbling behind him.

"I told you to stay at the table," he said harshly when he got close, and my eyebrows rose at the anger in his tone.

Kira looked down at the ground, and I scoffed, "You can't just pull that shit and expect us not to wonder what's happening."

Rhys's eyes narrowed, but it was clear now that he was closer that his anger wasn't directed at either of us—he definitely looked annoyed that we'd chosen not to listen to him, though.

"Who is this?" I asked when he got close enough with the guy in tow that Kira and I had to step away from the door.

"We're about to find out," he answered. "I'm guessing you won't give me time alone with him?"

"If you want," Kira offered while she shut and locked the door, and I shot her a look.

I folded my arms over my chest and returned Rhys's stare. "I know we were only married for three months, but you should know that there's no way you could expect me not to stick around for whatever's about to happen."

Rhys smiled in amusement, and his dark eyes brightened with memories of us from four years ago. "Never hurts to try, Kennedy." He continued dragging the boy behind him until he got to the couch and yanked him closer. "Sit. Don't even try to move."

Kira stepped back slowly until she got to the table where we'd been sitting, and silently sat down, her wide eyes on the three of us in the living room.

"Who are you?" I asked the guy when he looked up at us.

"I'm asking the questions," Rhys grumbled, and gave me a dark look that I reciprocated. The action had his expression lightening again before he could control it to look back at the guy on my couch.

"Who are you?" Rhys repeated my question.

"Wait, I don't even know what he was doing to make you chase after him and drag him back in here," I said when the boy refused to respond.

Rhys didn't look at me this time; he kept his stare on the boy. "He was looking through the sliding glass door. I thought I saw him when I was cooking, but he was gone when I checked out back. When I got back from the grocery store this afternoon, he was leaving a paper on the front door."

"Was it a love letter?" I asked sarcastically, and the boy's blank expression morphed into a mocking smile.

Rhys just sighed. "No, will you let me—"

"Well, then where's the paper? I want to see it."

"I threw it away, it didn't have anything on it but a symbol."

I was already confused that this guy—who didn't look like he was a legal adult yet—would be scoping out our condo, but as soon as I heard the word *symbol,* I gasped and glanced at Rhys, then looked at Kira's worried face. "Get the paper," I ordered, then eyed the boy as I asked Rhys, "It's in the kitchen trash, right?"

"Yeah," he said hesitantly, drawing out the word to sound like a question. "Why?"

I didn't respond, I just kept my gaze on the mocking face of the boy in front of me. "Name. Now."

"Juarez," he replied immediately, and my lip curled.

"I fucking doubt that. Name."

"Kennedy," Kira called from the kitchen, and held up the crinkled paper.

I pointed to the paper and asked the boy, "What does the symbol mean?"

"Juarez," he answered again.

"What the hell is happening?" Rhys asked on a harsh whisper, and grabbed my arm to pull me back a few steps. His eyes widened when we heard Kira calling 911 from the kitchen. "Kennedy, what the fuck?"

"No, no. Don't do that!" the boy said quickly, and suddenly his mocking expression was replaced with worry as he started to stand. "It's just a joke! I swear, I mean . . . they just sent me here to see if you're here."

"Shut the fuck up, and sit down," Rhys demanded, then looked at Kira and me again. "What's happening?"

I gave him the quickest explanation I could of what had been going on back home, and every few seconds Rhys would have to look over at the boy to stop him from trying to stand up again.

"No one thought this was important to tell me?" Rhys bit out when I was finished. "Including your dad?"

"I swear they just pay me!" the boy said frantically, and stood again. "Don't call the cops, I'll—"

Rhys shoved him down and caged him against the couch,

then leaned close so his face was inches from the boy's. "Tampa PD; if you don't sit here and shut up, I will personally fly you back to Florida and arrest you there."

"Man, I don't know anything," the boy cried as his eyes welled up. "They just pay me, man, I swear!"

"Pay you to do what?" I asked.

The boy shrugged and sniffed. "To mail letters, and to leave them at the police department and your parents' house."

My face smoothed out and I choked on a laugh when a snot bubble came out of the boy's nose as he sobbed. He looked terrified, and now I was worried he was going to pee on the couch. "Juarez pays you?"

The boy shrugged again. "Someone does. Juarez just tells me what to say and draw."

"What's your name?" I asked again; this time my tone was softer, but still held a hint of amusement at how the situation had drastically turned around. Not that I would have ever been scared of the boy himself, it was the situation that had me freaked out. He looked like he weighed no more than a hundred and twenty pounds, and having him come in trying to act like a badass only to start crying had me seconds from bursting into laughter.

"Matthew. My name's Matthew."

"Okay, Matthew, how do you know Juarez?" I looked over to Rhys when I realized he had stopped questioning the boy, but his eyes were wide as he watched the boy break down in hysterics.

"I was visiting my pop in prison. My pop owed Juarez a favor from the inside and told me to go to him, so I went to visit him to see what he wanted."

"How did you know the girls were here?" Rhys asked.

"I d-didn't, I swear. It was just a possibility. Juarez said there was family here, so I came. I've been following your uncle for almost a week, and saw you all go to his place for Thanksgiving, so I followed you back here. But I didn't know if these were even the girls I was looking for. I had to get a computer so I could search for their social media accounts to get pictures of—" Matthew cut off on loud sobs, and I had to bite my cheeks in order to keep myself from laughing.

"Police are coming," Kira mumbled from the kitchen, and Matthew cried harder.

I sighed and shrugged when Rhys gave me a confused look.

"What were your orders this time?" he asked gently, and I smiled, knowing that Rhys understood how to handle this situation. It was so hard to be mad at this boy since he'd just gotten mixed up with the wrong people because of his dad.

"Just to scare them with the symbol. But you'd gotten it earlier, so I've been waiting for the girls to come back. I was going to leave another note and knock once they were here."

"This poor kid," I whispered when Rhys took another step back so he was next to me.

"I don't know what to say now," Rhys said low enough that it wouldn't carry.

"I know," I agreed, and studied the kid again. "Matthew, do you know if Juarez has anyone else harassing my family?"

Matthew shook his head and choked out a sob. "I don't know, maybe. I'm sorry, I just wanted to help my pop and make money."

"And you don't know who's paying you?"

He looked up to me. "No. They mailed me a bank card and they just keep putting money in it for me. Oh no! No, please don't let them arrest me!" he cried out when sirens sounded close by.

I gave him a sympathetic smile, but didn't know what else to say. It was ridiculous that a kid who had been harassing my family could have me feeling so bad for him, but I couldn't help it. And from Kira and Rhys's expressions, they felt the same.

To be honest, I'd never thought anyone would find us here. But I was sure that if they did, it would have been a lot more action-packed than the last ten minutes had been. What a letdown.

Rhys helped the kid stand, and started leading him over to the front door. He was holding Matthew's hands behind his back like a cop without cuffs would do, and the action made Matthew cry even harder.

"Wait! Matthew, does Juarez know we're here in California?"

"No. He calls me every Wednesday. When he called me last week, I'd still only been following your uncle." He tried rubbing his wet cheeks against his shoulder, and looked between Kira and me. "I'm sorry," he cried.

"We know," I answered for us. Kira was still standing there with a guarded but sad look on her face. "We'll tell the police exactly what you told us, I promise."

He nodded, then let Rhys lead him outside.

"Do you think he was the only one doing everything?" Kira asked.

"I don't know. Let's hope so."

Kira's face clearly said she didn't agree. "We need to be a lot more alert from now on."

"I know, we will." I sighed heavily and clapped once. "Well! You ready to spend Monday night in a police station giving statements?"

Kira groaned and rolled her eyes, and I laughed at the look. "I'll go change my shirt so I don't smell like smoothies. Meet you outside?"

"Last one out has to call Dad to tell him!" I called over my shoulder as I ran toward my room.

I heard Kira's mumbled curse, and laughed louder as I stripped off my shirt and ran to my closet to grab the first one I touched. The worst part of this entire night would be telling Dad and Uncle Mason that one of Juarez's boys had found us . . . and I sure as hell didn't want to be the one stuck having to make that phone call.

16

December 4
Liam

I LOOKED UP at the sound of my office door opening, and my body immediately tensed when I saw the expression on Eli's face. He looked like he was nervous about talking to me, and while I still wasn't worried about my job, I *was* worried that he'd have news from one of his nieces.

"Hey," I said cautiously. "What's up?"

He sighed as he sat in the chair opposite me. "I just wanted to see how you're doing."

"I'm fine, why?"

Eli's face went blank. "Well, that's some bullshit."

"I don't know what you want, Eli. I've landed more accounts *and* finished more jobs in the last month alone than I normally do in a quarter. I'm fine."

"Yeah, your work is fine. It's great. But you never leave. You never leave the office and you never talk to anyone. So from what I'm gathering, Kennedy still hasn't called you, and as your friend, not your boss, I want to know how you're doing."

I sat back in my chair and folded my arms across my chest.

"I don't know," I finally admitted. "I don't know how I am. She calls, but she hasn't made a decision, so I don't talk to her. I can't until she knows. Because talking to her will only give me hope, and right now my chances aren't looking that great."

"Well I don't know about that. From what I saw when the girls showed up with Rhys for Thanksgiving, Kennedy's pretty miserable herself."

My eyebrows rose. "He came with the girls?"

"I wouldn't go reading anything into that. It was very much a we-don't-know-what-to-do-with-him situation since he's still staying at their place."

"Still doesn't change the fact that he's there, which means she's probably no closer to making a decision."

"Maybe not," Eli mumbled. "If you want my suggestion, I would go talk to her."

"I can't do that, Eli. I told her I was stepping back, and I need to stick with that."

He tilted his head to the side and looked at me like he thought I was making a mistake, but didn't say anything else as he stood and began walking out until he got to the door. "My other suggestion is for you to take the rest of the day off, you need this weekend away from the office, and the weekend is starting right now for you." Eli stepped out of my office, but popped his head back in. "And by 'suggestion,' I mean that's an order from your extremely stern boss."

I smiled and huffed, but listened to what he said. Gathering up my stuff, I drove home, changed, and grabbed my board to head out to the beach. I usually only surfed in the early mornings, but since I wasn't able to distract myself with work at the moment, I needed to do something to clear my head.

I'd only been out there for about thirty minutes when I caught sight of a man not far up the beach, standing up, watching me. Instead of paddling back out, I hung my head and walked over to him.

"Is this the day for people to give me lectures? Should I go see Brian after this?" I asked sarcastically, and dropped down next to where my dad was standing.

Once he was sitting down next to me, he asked, "What other lecture?"

"It wasn't really. Eli just wanted to know how I was doing with the Kennedy situation, and told me he thinks I should go talk to her. And then he ordered me to leave early for the weekend . . . so I came here. Speaking of, how did you know I was here?"

Dad shrugged. "Saw your car. I had to run an errand since your mom's and my anniversary is coming up, and saw your car on my way out and back. Decided I'd stop to see why you were here—but I figured it had something to do with Kennedy."

I sat there for a couple minutes trying to figure out if I wanted to ask him what I'd been thinking for the past couple weeks. Dad just sat there waiting for me to begin. "When it was you . . . what did you do? And would you do it again?"

"With your mom and Chase?"

"Yeah."

Dad exhaled slowly and leaned back so he was holding himself up on his elbows. "Well. When I found out she was pregnant I asked her to leave, and that was it for us for a long time. I knew you weren't mine, and it didn't take more than a minute to figure out who your dad was. I'd known how Chase felt, and I saw how your mom looked at him. While Chase waited for your mom to decide between the two of us—before she knew she was pregnant, and after—he did what you're doing. He stepped back. And if he were here, I have no doubt he would tell you how big a mistake that was."

"Mistake?" I blurted out. "Why?"

"Because your mom ended up taking a long time to decide. Even after Chase found out that we had broken up, she still told him she couldn't be with him, and didn't tell him that she was pregnant for months."

"Months," I echoed, my voice dead even though I was fucking terrified that Kennedy would draw this out for the same amount of time.

"Months," Dad repeated. "By the time your mom was ready to tell him, and ready to give him a chance, they didn't have very long before he died. He missed a lot of time with her because he stepped back. If he would have pushed it more, or been around instead of hiding from her, I have no doubt your mom would have broken down sooner."

"And what were you doing during that time?"

"Staying away."

I laughed, but it didn't sound right. "So are you saying it was a mistake for you to do that too?"

"Nope," he said simply, and I looked back at him.

"How is that supposed to help me right now? You said Chase would've regretted stepping back, but you stepped back and didn't regret it." I paused for a second, and then said, "But at that time, it wasn't really a decision between the two of you anymore since you and Mom were broken up. So your situation wasn't exactly the same as mine."

He thought for a minute before saying, "It was, and it wasn't. Your mom knew she'd hurt me, and one of her main reasons for waiting so long was because she didn't want me to get hurt even more by being with Chase and shoving their relationship in my face all the time. Then, when Chase died, even though your mom had broken up with him right before, she was still too torn to be with me. She thought it would be spitting on his memory."

"But you were together a couple months later," I hinted, and he nodded.

"The way your mom has put it was that she loved Chase, and

was *in* love with me. From the beginning, and through the whole thing. Even though she told me she wanted me to find someone else, she and I both knew that we would eventually be together again one day. But then Chase died, and it confused things as well as sped them up."

I shook my head and stared back out at the ocean. "Doesn't matter how many times I hear the story . . . I'll never understand how you went through any of that."

"I went through it because I loved your mom and you."

"Dad?" When he made a grunting noise, I asked, "When it was back to being a choice of being with you again or not . . . did you still stay back?"

"No. Hell no. She told me she couldn't be with me, and because of Chase's death I was questioning what I thought I'd already known about us being together again. But I told her I would be there for her and you. Not just because of how much I loved the two of you, but because Chase was my best friend and I know he would've done the same if the roles had been reversed. So I was there, at your grandparents' house, every day. Never pushing her, just always being there. Well—I may have pushed her a couple times."

I smiled and looked back to see him grinning. "She was with you, then no one, then Chase, then no one, and then you again. So Chase was there waiting for a relationship, then you both stepped back, and then you were there."

"Pretty much."

I sighed heavily. "What does that mean I should do?"

Dad looked up at me and laughed. "It is the most complicated and simple decision. In this situation with Kennedy and her ex, you need to figure out what stage you are all currently in, and then you need to figure out if you're me, or if you're Chase."

"Nothing in that sounds simple."

"I'm sure you'll figure it out."

December 4
Kennedy

"HEY, RHYS!" I called out as I walked down the hall and turned into the living room. I was caught off guard and took a step back when I found both Rhys and Kira looking at me—Kira with wide eyes that held a tinge of an apology, Rhys like he was afraid of what I was about to say. "Uh, everything okay?"

Rhys glanced over to where Kira was sitting on the love seat then back to me. "Yeah. What's up?"

"Er, well . . ." I drifted off and shot Kira a confused look that immediately had her snapping out of whatever weird state she'd just been in. "There's a farmers market in town tonight, they have one every Friday night. There's live music, fresh veggies and fruits we can grab for the kitchen, and I saw them putting up a stand for corn dogs and funnel cakes. It's my favorite part of a fair and the produce section from a grocery store all in one, and I thought you might like to go."

"Do you think it's a good idea to go walking around town when there's a possibility of more people looking for you?"

My face fell. "After how much Matthew cried on that couch, I'm really not worried about how another one of Juarez's guys will be."

"Kenne—"

"Please!" I whined, cutting him off. "Funnel cake!"

Rhys laughed at my excitement over the fried goodness, and conceded with a sigh, "Yeah, okay. Sounds great. When did you want to go?"

I shrugged. "Whenever. It started an hour ago, and I'm ready when you are."

"I'm ready." He stood from the couch, and I once again caught Kira staring off with a weird expression.

"Kira, you coming?"

"What?" she asked, her head snapping up to look at me.

"Farmers market. Are you coming with?"

Her eyes widened and her mouth formed a small O, like she was just now clueing in to what I'd been talking about. "Oh no. You two should probably go alone."

"Really, it's not a big deal, I want you to come."

"You're not going to come?" Rhys asked, and I pointed at him.

"See? He wants you to go too. Come with us!"

I stood there silently praying she would say yes. As much as I'd been enjoying having Rhys around, I was terrified whenever we had to do something alone. I was worried he would start taking it as a sign that I wanted to be with him again, and he and Kira got along so well that it usually took the awkward tension away from us. Besides, Kira had started withdrawing back into a shell, and I wanted to do anything that prevented her getting sucked into it. It had taken long enough to get her away from the one Zane had put her in, and now I didn't know how long it would take for this one since I didn't even understand what had caused it. All I knew was that whenever I entered a room, she wouldn't talk to me and always had weird looks on her face; and when I was talking with Rhys, she'd go to her room. If she was giving me the opportunity to be alone with him . . . it wasn't appreciated.

"No, really. You two go. You'll have fun." She was already off the couch and walking toward her room before she was even done talking.

Seriously? "So anyway, you ready?" I asked Rhys, and began walking toward the front door.

Rhys followed me out of the condo and walked with me over to the farmers market. It was only a mile away from our complex, and I doubted we would have gotten much closer if we'd driven and tried to find a place to park.

We didn't talk about anything important on the way over, or as we browsed the booths filled with produce. By *important,* I mean anything that I should have talked to him about. Like what had happened to me after he left, what I really felt the day he showed up at the condo, and just getting to know him again on a deeper level. All we talked about was Kira's and my job, the differences between California and Florida, and Matthew and Juarez. Rhys never really offered up anything about himself, he just continued directing questions at me.

And like with Kira, I felt like something was off with Rhys.

He was still smiling, polite, and funny, but there was a distance between us that hadn't been there just a few weeks ago, and it was nothing like the distance I'd placed between us when he'd first showed up. There was just something in his dark eyes that left me wondering why he looked so worried and, at times, unhappy.

I was afraid it had something to do with the fact that he'd been in California for over a month now and I had yet to make a decision. But the truth was, the closer and closer I got to making a decision, the more scared I got. Scared I still hadn't done enough to give both Liam and Rhys a fair chance, scared I would make the wrong decision and not be able to reverse it, and even more scared of hurting one of them. Both men meant too much to me to want to hurt them—and that thought had me wondering when I'd become such a wimp when it came to voicing my feelings.

But then I looked over at the guy walking next to me, and knew I had my answer. I'd become a wimp about voicing my feelings after Rhys left me—and only to men who held my heart.

"Kennedy, I have a question for you," Rhys said suddenly, his deep voice rumbling in the dark as we walked back to the condo with tons of fresh food and full stomachs.

Oh God. Oh no, he's going to ask me to decide!

"It's going to be personal, and probably awkward for you

to answer because it's kind of awkward for me to ask . . . but I really want to know. I've wanted to for some time now."

"Okay," I said hesitantly.

"This Liam guy. It was obvious he didn't know about me." It hadn't been a question, but Rhys still looked at me with a raised eyebrow.

"No, he didn't," I confirmed. "I had actually just told him the night before you showed up that I was going to tell him about my past soon."

Rhys laughed. "Looks like I had great timing, then."

I rolled my eyes and scoffed.

"But if you didn't tell him about me, did you . . . did you tell him . . ." He drifted off and mumbled a curse as he stopped walking and turned to face me. "Do you still have to be in control?"

"Yes," I admitted softly.

"And with him?"

I shook my head for a moment. I didn't want to get into this with Rhys because he knew that my needing control was purely physical and sexual. But then I remembered how he'd started this conversation, and how hard it had been for him to ask his question, and my shoulders fell as I said, "I lose it with him. There's not even a fight anymore—or, there wasn't. At the beginning I would try to stay in control, but I wouldn't hold on to it for more than a minute. He demands it—silently . . . I don't want you to think he orders me around or anything. But it's just how he is. He takes control."

"And you let him," Rhys stated.

Even though it wasn't a question, I nodded. "Yeah, I did."

Rhys started to look uncomfortable again, and he stumbled over his words when he asked, "Anyone else?"

"No. I was always in control except for when I was with you and Liam." Rhys wasn't looking at me anymore; he was staring at the ground. "Rhys . . . why are you bringing this up?"

With a heavy exhale, he looked up at me and said, "Because I wanted to know how much he means to you."

A hard laugh burst from my chest. "And knowing that I lose control with him answers that for you?"

Rhys watched me for a second with a sad smile. "Yeah, it does. Knowing how you were when we met, I knew exactly what I meant to you when you stopped trying to maintain control physically. Because right after that was when you stopped trying to control the relationship, and you just let *us* happen. Everything about you and us changed then."

"Wait, what? Control the relationship? I never tried to control relationships, I control anything physical."

One dark brow rose, and his lips twitched in amusement. "Trust me, Kennedy, you control relationships. You tried to control ours. If you think about it, I know you already know this." When I shook my head, he said, "Tell me why you think you control physical times."

"Why I *think*? You already know why I do."

"Humor me, Kennedy."

"Because I never wanted to feel like a man had control over me. I wanted to be the one to say how things went."

"That last part is why you try to control relationships. You told me the night I met your family that you'd grown up wanting a marriage like your parents have, and a lot made sense after you told me that. The way you were before you gave up control was like you wanted to make sure our relationship *was* like theirs. But the second you stopped trying to make our relationship a certain way was when I knew you had fallen for me as much as I had for you. At the time, I didn't know your parents or what you were doing, I just knew that you were right there with me for the ride instead of trying to make us something we weren't. The night you told me about wanting what they have, I knew I'd been right."

"I don't—" I began, but he cut me off.

"You do. Or, you *did*. We'd already talked about the physical part when we were still together, so I knew that I'd been the first person who you'd let control that. But I've wondered for years about the rest. Because like I said, when you lost control with me I knew what our relationship meant to you. You just confirmed that you've never been that way with anyone else . . . except for him. So now I know what he means to you."

I stood there completely silent, not knowing what to say. Because as much as I wanted to continue denying what he was saying, a part of me knew he was right. I had grown up wanting what my parents have, and now that Rhys had explained it to me, I could see that I *had* done things in my past to try to ensure I would have that kind of marriage and love—even in the smallest of relationships. But I hadn't done any of that since the man standing in front of me had completely rocked my world.

I rocked back on my heels and shook my head once. "That doesn't make sense now. I tried to *avoid* a relationship with Liam . . . and that was because of you. I didn't want to go through what you'd put me through again, and I just knew that he had that power to crush me like you did. But I never once tried to make my relationship with him something it wasn't. When I gave up with him, I was giving up trying to keep myself from him."

Another sad smile pulled at Rhys's lips. "Then I guess that tells both of us exactly what he means to you." He watched my confused expression for a second before gesturing in the direction we'd been walking. "Come on. Let's get all this stuff back and make Kira dinner, and we'll stop with the heavy conversation for tonight. Deal?"

"Deal."

THE NEXT AFTERNOON I was walking into Brian's tattoo shop with a bag of greasy food in hand. The air in the condo had been thick with tension as Rhys, Kira, and I had absentmindedly watched TV just so we wouldn't have to talk to each other, and soon it had been too much for me to handle. With a quick good-bye, I'd gotten in the car and driven around for almost thirty minutes before I found myself in a drive-thru buying food for Brian.

"Dude number one!" Brian called out excitedly. "To what do I owe this pleasure?"

"Why is it you don't have an issue with figuring out which one of us is which?"

Brian looked offended. "As if I would? I had my share of twinsies before I met my lady love. I'm what everyone should call an expert."

"Should?" I asked on a laugh. "Here, brought you something so you wouldn't starve."

"Glorious!" he sang out as he reached for the bag—once again like it was precious and fragile. "You here for some ink?" he asked over his shoulder as he walked to his station.

"Not today," I said on a sigh, and took a seat. "I came for your crazy-worded wisdom. Liam said he always went to talk to you whenever anything was going on his life, so I figured I would try."

"Smart boy." He pointed at me and grinned cheekily. "And very smart girl! Lay it on me."

"Has Liam been by in the last month to maybe talk to you about . . ." I trailed off, and my face twisted up as I tried to figure out how to explain the situation in as few words as possible.

"About your ex-boo? Oh yeah, I've heard all about it. My boy is torn up, my dude. Completely. Torn," he emphasized by tearing a fry in half.

"That makes three of us," I muttered. "I don't know what to do, Brian."

"What's your heart tell you?"

I thought for a second, trying to sort through all the emotions I'd been fighting with for the last month. "It tells me that I can't lose Liam—just like it told me the day Liam walked away from me."

"Uh-huh. Uh-huh," he mumbled around a bite of food. "But what about your ex-boo? What's it saying about him?"

"That I'm so scared of hurting him. I don't love him anymore, Brian," I confessed out loud for the first time ever—and Christ, did that small confession feel good. "I don't love him, not in the way I did, and not in a way that could make me possibly want him in the future. I enjoy his company, he's fun to have around, but that's it. That piece of my heart that I gave him all those years ago still belongs to him—but only in a first-love-memory type of way. But he thought we would be together again for four years. Four. Years. I was devastated when I lost Rhys after only having him for a few months, and I'm so worried about what I'll do to him if I tell him I don't want him."

Brian had stopped chewing, and continued to sit there with his burger halfway to his mouth for a few moments before shaking his head. "You can't be with someone just because you're afraid of making their heart hurt. Because their hurt will be temporary, but think about how much your heart will hurt if you spend the rest of your life avoiding hurting his."

"I know," I whispered, and my shoulders fell with the weight of the decision that was looming over me.

"Dude number one, tell me something, 'kay 'kay?"

"All right."

"When you met the ex-boo, what was it like?"

I shrugged. "Easy. We both fell hard and fast, and I was so sure at that time—and even for years after—that I would never again experience what I had experienced with him."

"And my boy? When he found you here in his dad's gym, what was it like for you?"

"Terrifying," I answered with a laugh.

Brian nodded and took another bite of his burger with a smirk on his face the entire time. "That's all you need to know right there."

"What? What is?"

"LC terrified you."

I huffed softly. "Okay . . ."

"My lady love terrified me. Finding your true love is the most terrifying experience of your life, dude number one. Well, unless you have kids. I've heard that shit is pretty fucking scary."

"Brian, no. I—"

"Tell me why you were terrified," he demanded, cutting me off.

"Because of the way he made me feel. That, and his personality reminded me of Rhys."

"Is that really why he terrified you? Because he made you feel like your ex-boo did?" There were a few beats of silence between us as I waited for him to realize that I'd already answered his question. "Who can't you live without?"

"Liam," I said without hesitation.

Brian clucked his tongue. "If you're asking me, dude number one, then I'd say my boy terrified you because he made you feel more than you ever felt for your ex-boo. And finding that, after being hurt by the ex, only made the fear of finding your true love that much greater."

"But I don't lo—" I cut off quickly, and my mouth dropped as my eyes widened. "I love Liam," I whispered. "Brian, I'm in love with him."

"I already know that, dude."

I laughed and looked around me, like I couldn't seem to grasp the epiphany I'd just had. Even last night I would have continued denying my true feelings for Liam. But something about this conversation with Brian—something about finally voicing the fact that I no longer loved Rhys—had made the last of my walls finally fall.

"Oh my God, Brian!" I said in awe. "Do you know how absolutely amazing you are with your nonstoned mind?"

"Like I told my boy when I informed his denying ass that he loved you not long after you came back into his life: I should be Cupid's sidekick. I've got this love shit down."

"Twins expert. Cupid's sidekick. Badass tattoo artist. And a fucking genius."

"Ha! You get me, my dude!" He took another large bite of his burger and waved it at me as he spoke around the mouthful. "Well, now that you're done acting like you don't know what the fuck's up with your heart, you better go tell my boy what you just realized."

I stood, but Brian's voice stopped me from leaving.

"Not that I know much about anything. But it's Saturday."

"Yeah," I said a little breathless. I was anxious to get to Liam, and the anxiety had my heart racing. "And?"

"*And,* dude number one, all I know is that every Saturday my boy comes to see me and feed me after he gets done sparring with his daddy-o. So if I'm not as high as I think I am . . . he's at the gym, or he's on his way there."

I barreled forward and wrapped my arms around Brian's neck. "Thank you. And don't tell your wife that you got two cheat meals in one day!"

"Who's tellin?" he called out as I raced toward the door to leave. "Go get him, dude!"

17

December 5
Liam

"I FIGURED IT out," I said in way of announcing myself.

Dad turned around from where he'd been talking to Kristi at the drink bar with his brow pinched together. "Figured out what?"

"Kennedy, and what I need to do."

A smile crossed his face, and he folded his arms across his chest. "Really? Well, let's hear it."

"I'm you *and* Chase. And my entire relationship with Kennedy has been what Mom went through with both of you."

Both of his eyebrows rose, and he nodded. "Explain."

"At first, I pushed for a relationship that she tried to stay out of *because* she'd been married before. Granted, I didn't know, but I kept pushing until she was mine. When I found out about Rhys, I thought there was no way that she would end up choosing me, which is why I wanted to step back. I did it for her, but I knew I had to start protecting myself from what I thought was coming, so in a way it was also for me. So that's Chase, right?"

"Right," he said with an amused grin. "I feel like I know where this is about to go."

"I gave her time, but I can't keep staying away. I can't sit still without feeling like I'm losing my mind. I need to be working, surfing, running . . . anything so I don't think about her. And if I sit there for any amount of time, I get up and grab my keys. But I only ever make it to my car before I talk myself out of it, and I don't want to keep talking myself out of it. I want to be there. I want to show her what we had, and to fight for my chance even though I may not get it again."

"And that's me," he assumed.

"Yeah," I said on a breath. "That's you. Looks like I got the best of both of you."

Dad's smile changed into something softer, and for a second, his eyes welled up before he was able to blink the tears away. "That has to be the best thing I've ever heard come from you, Liam." Clearing his throat, he took a deep breath and studied me for a second. "I guess that means we're not sparring tonight?"

"Hell no. I need to go to her." I heard a voice call my name, but before I turned to look, I grabbed my dad in a quick hug. "Thanks for everything, old man."

Dad pushed me back and took a few steps away. "I don't think you're about to get your chance to—"

"Liam!"

I didn't hear the rest of what my dad was saying as a wall slammed into me from behind and almost knocked me over. I stumbled forward a few steps, and quickly understood why my dad had backed up. A pair of slender, tattooed arms crossed in front of my chest, and long legs wrapped around my waist.

Grabbing on to the arms I knew so well, I helped her slide down, and turned to face my girl standing there with the widest smile and brightest eyes.

"Kennedy—"

"I'm in love with you!" she blurted out, and her smile seemed to widen.

I shook my head and leaned closer. "What?" I asked, knowing I hadn't heard her correctly.

"I love you!" Her chest fell and rose with her heavy breaths, and she seemed to bounce even though her feet were firmly on the ground. "I love you, and I'm sorry I never told you that before. I'm sorry it took me so long to realize it, and I'm so damn sorry I didn't tell you about—"

I cut her off by crushing my mouth to hers and pulling her into my arms. "Fucking hell, Kennedy, tell me I didn't just dream this," I begged against her lips before kissing her again.

She laughed and pressed her hands against my chest so she could lean back. "Not a dream. I love you, Liam Taylor."

"Thank God," I growled as I captured her mouth. "Rhys?"

"I still need to talk to him. I've known what my decision would be for a couple weeks now—well, I've known since you walked out of my condo that last time—but I just started trying to get to know Rhys again so I could give him a chance in the last couple weeks. I was so worried that I would do something wrong that I hadn't been able to voice my choice, but now I know who I want *and* what is right for me."

My lips curved up in a slow smile, and I shook my head in amazement. "I told you, Moon. One day you would claim me as yours."

Her eyes narrowed playfully. "I still haven't done that."

"You're about to," I assured her, and faintly brushed my lips over hers. "You are mine, Kennedy Ryan."

"And you are mine," she responded as her arms wrapped around my neck to pull me closer.

"As much as I'm happy that you two finally figured your stuff out, I'm pretty sure you're either grossing out the members of my gym, or making them wish they were in Liam's place."

I turned to glare at my dad before glancing around at the handful of guys staring at us.

"Take it outside so you don't have this audience. And Kennedy," he called out just as we began walking toward the doors and waited until we were facing him. "Thank you."

"For?"

"For choosing correctly."

Kennedy's bright smile crossed her face again, and she buried herself in my side. "It was my pleasure, Brandon. Really."

I pulled Kennedy out of the building and, as soon as we were outside, grabbed her up in my arms and kissed her enough to make up for every kiss I'd missed in the last month. We were both breathless when I set her back on her feet, and she swayed back toward me a bit.

"How did you even know I was here?"

She laughed and her eyes widened for a split second. "I was with Brian, he told me you'd be here sparring with your dad."

"Fucking Brian," I mumbled, but couldn't stop smiling with the way she was smiling at me. I'd never seen her this happy before, and it was contagious. "Didn't end up sparring. I came in to tell my dad that I was going to go to you because I was done waiting for you to make up your mind."

Her dark eyebrows rose high. "Were you?"

"I needed to remind you of what you were missing."

Her features softened, and she tightened her arms around me. "Trust me, Liam. I knew exactly what I'd been missing. It just took me a little bit to stop wasting time."

"That's an understatement."

Kennedy punched my stomach teasingly.

"I'm kidding, Moon. As long as I was the one you chose in the end, you could've taken years."

"Years," she stated skeptically.

"I never said I'd fight fair during that time." I shrugged unapologetically.

"Well, a month was long enough for me." She took a deep

breath in and released it slowly. "There's a lot I need to tell you, but nothing that I want to tell you outside of your dad's gym. And I still need to tell Rhys what I've decided . . . alone."

"You're sure you don't want me there with you?"

"Yes, I'm sure. I need to do it alone. After the conversation I had with him last night, I have a feeling he's going to understand. Besides, if my decision had been different, would you want me showing up with him to tell you?"

"Fuck." I rubbed my forehead, but conceded, knowing that this was something I had to let her do. "No, I wouldn't want that. If you need to talk to him alone, you should."

"So I think maybe you should go fight with your dad, then go take Brian his second greasy meal of the day, and maybe if you're up for it, I'll come over after. I think Brian would be mad at me if I made you miss your Saturday night with him."

"Miss my Saturday with him? I see Brian whenever, it's not always on Saturdays."

Kennedy's face fell. "That greedy bastard," she muttered, and sighed. "Whatever, I'm sure he's expecting you after this. Just don't take burgers to him, he already had some."

"Okay, no burgers, and I'll go work out with Dad as long as you can tell me you'll come back to me tonight."

"I said if you—"

"I'll be up for it, Moon. I'm going to need you tonight—especially if I know you're about to go talk to your ex about all of this."

She nodded and pressed a lingering kiss to my lips before backing away. "I'll see you in a few hours, Liam Taylor, I promise."

And just like that, the last month fell away like it had been nothing. Everything I'd been worrying about and afraid of suddenly felt like it had been worth the trouble. Turning around after she'd driven off, I went back into the gym and caught my dad's eye.

"Let's do this, old man."

December 5
Kennedy

I GOT HOME as fast as I could, and practically ran to the condo. My sudden entrance seemed to have caught Kira and Rhys off guard, but I had too much adrenaline to think about it much.

"Hey, I'm sorry for interrupting your conversation! Apparently I like to do that," I said with an awkward laugh, and looked directly at Rhys. "Do you think we could go to dinner . . . alone? I was hoping to talk to you about something."

Rhys's eyes darted over to Kira, but didn't stay there for more than a second. "Yeah, sure. Let me change really quick." He pulled out his bag from behind the couch, and carried it down the hall and into my room.

"I'm sorry," I said to Kira, who was staring off into space. "I swear it's nothing against you, I just need to do this. I need to talk to him."

"Yeah, no. I get it," she mumbled, and stood up from the love seat.

"Hey," I said, and grabbed her arm when she started walking past me. "Are you okay? You've been so weird the last week or so."

"I'm fine."

My eyebrows pulled together. "Kira, what's wrong?"

"Nothing, I'm just tired and I've had a headache all day. You two going to dinner will give me a chance to relax."

"I can bring you something back," I offered, but she shook her head as she pulled her arm free.

"No, I'm good. Food doesn't sound good right now. I'll see you when you get back."

I stood there staring at her closed door until I heard Rhys walk back into the room.

"Ready? And can we take my truck? I haven't had a reason to drive in a while."

"Yeah, sure," I murmured, then shook my head. "Yeah, I am. Do you know if Kira's okay?"

Rhys shrugged. "Yeah, she's seemed fine all day, why?"

"Huh. Okay. Well, yeah, I'm ready."

The entire ride was tense, and I wondered if Rhys somehow knew what decision I'd made. Conversation was short and strained, and I was thankful when we pulled up to the restaurant so we would have the distractions of food and other people. We didn't speak or look at each other as we glanced over the menu and placed our orders, and as we waited for the food, the conversation became as awkward as it had been in the car. It wasn't until the food had been placed in front of us that I finally felt like I could tell him—like the food was a shield in a way.

"Rhys—" I began at the same time he said, "I need to talk to you, Kennedy."

My heart raced, and I quickly pleaded, "Can I please go first?"

Rhys's face looked like a mix of panic and uncertainty.

"I'm sorry, but I'm worried that whatever you have to say will make me unable to say what I need to."

"Okay," he finally said. "Talk to me."

I opened my mouth, but shut it really quick and pointed at the food. "Could you eat while I talk? It'll make this easier."

The corner of his mouth tilted up, and with an amused look, he grabbed his fork and started eating.

With a deep breath in, I said, "I chose Liam, Rhys."

Rhys's eyes widened, and like Brian had done earlier, he stopped eating and just stared at me.

"Keep eating, please." As soon as he was doing so, I con- tinued. "I'm sorry—you'll never know how sorry I am—that I couldn't make a decision sooner. I've just been going crazy wor- rying about hurting you, and I—"

"Kennedy, Kennedy . . . it's fine," he said, cutting me off. "You do not have to explain why it took you this long. Not at all."

"But I—"

"I showed up after four years and confused you. I get it. No one could blame you for taking a month, and I promise you that I don't. Can I say what I wanted to tell you now?"

I blinked quickly and nodded. "Yeah, sure." The first part had gone so well that I almost didn't know how to react. Rhys looked pointedly at my food, and I quickly grabbed my fork and dug in like he'd done earlier.

"Okay . . . Kennedy, I fell in love with you the minute I saw you. As ridiculous as that sounds, you already know it's true. Those three months with you were full of more life and passion than I'd ever imagined I'd have. When I had to leave you, I felt like I'd left myself with you . . . which, to be honest, made going undercover easier. I wasn't myself anymore, I felt like I had noth- ing to live for, and that ended up helping. But the entire time I was gone, I was positive your dad would have told you the truth, and that you would be waiting for me whenever I got back. That hope, and remembering what we had, was what got me through those four years. But when I came looking for you and I realized how wrong I was . . . I was . . . I don't even know how to explain what was going through my mind when I saw you again. But in that first moment of seeing you, I felt whole again, only to feel like half of me was ripped away when I realized the guy who opened the door wasn't there for Kira. I couldn't understand how I could be so in love with someone who no longer loved me.

"It didn't take long, maybe a week since I had nothing else

to do but think about it, but I quickly realized that it was the *idea* of us and loving you that I'd clung to for those years. All I thought about was how it had been between us when we were married, what I'd continued thinking about while I was gone, and how it felt now that I was near you again. I figured out that I loved you, but I had fallen out of love with you sometime while I was gone. Not consciously, but probably because in my mind I was still cutting ties—and that included not loving you—and I knew that I had to prepare for you not to be waiting. Like I said, it wasn't conscious, because I'd been hoping for the opposite that whole time, but it didn't change the reality of my feelings for you now.

"I should have left then. I should have apologized for turning your world upside down again, and left you to go back to your life. But I couldn't. You'd moved on, but you were still giving us a chance like I'd asked for, and I knew I had to give us that chance too. I knew no matter what you decided, I would be happy. But something has changed in the last couple weeks, and to be completely honest with you, I've been terrified that you *would* choose me. I just didn't know how to ask you not to after asking you to give me a second chance."

Throughout his entire speech, I sat there with wide eyes, and I was pretty sure I'd stopped eating at some point during that time. As he got closer to finishing, I couldn't believe what I was hearing. "You're not mad? Wait! What's happened in the last couple weeks?"

A secretive smile I'd known well a long time ago crossed his face, and he dropped his head. When he lifted it again, he asked, "Is it okay if I'm not ready to tell you yet? There's someone else I need to talk to first."

The question surprised me, and I opened my mouth to respond but shut it when I realized I had no idea what I'd been about to say. "Uh, yeah. Yeah, it's okay. I wasn't expecting this, but I know I've said that exact same thing before . . . so I have to be okay with waiting."

"I *will* tell you, Kennedy. Just not yet."

I smiled and nodded. "I know you will." I looked at our half-eaten meals and laughed. "Well! We just got a conversation I've been dreading out of the way. And I'm guessing you feel as relieved as I do?" He sent me a confirming smile, and I asked, "How about we finish this dinner and then get out of here?"

"Sounds perfect."

Once we were finished and the bill was paid, we stood to leave. Rhys walked directly behind me out of the restaurant, and helped me into his truck. We talked about the dinner, and the relief we felt now that everything was out there in the open. Everything about our conversation felt perfect. It felt easy. It felt like a friendship. A friendship I should have had with him for over a month.

When we pulled up to the condo, I touched his arm to stop him from getting out of his truck. "I'm going to grab the keys to the car, and then I'm going to leave so I can talk to Liam. I want you to know that just because we know for sure nothing will happen between us, you do not have to leave. Kira and I both really like having you here, and if you want to stay, please do."

That secretive smile was back. "I appreciate it."

Leaning over the console, I wrapped an arm around his neck and pulled him closer so I could press a kiss to his cheek. "Thank you, Rhys. For everything. You showing up in California was the best gift you could have ever given me."

18

December 5
Liam

I'D BARELY BEEN home long enough to take a shower before Kennedy was at my door, but that knocking couldn't have come soon enough. The hours while she was with Rhys had dragged.

As soon as the door was open, she was launching herself at me and clinging to me like she was afraid I'd disappear.

"Hey, did it go okay?"

"Better than okay. I'm still in shock at how okay it went. Rhys said he'd realized soon after he moved here that he was no longer in love with me. But he felt like he owed it to me to give us the chance that he'd asked me for."

My eyes widened. "Are you serious?"

"Ye—" Her words cut off abruptly when I pushed her against the wall and pressed my mouth to hers.

Kennedy's hands immediately went to the bottom of my shirt and began lifting it, but just as fast as they got there, she released the fabric and pushed against my stomach. "Liam, wait. I need to talk to you, and if you keep kissing me then I'll skip the talking."

I grinned wickedly, and she giggled against my next kiss.

"No, I'm serious. This has to be said before we do anything else. So we're going to go sit on your couch—on opposite ends—and I'm going to tell you everything I've been keeping from you. Well, except the whole Rhys thing, I'm pretty sure you understand that by now."

As much as I wanted Kennedy underneath me in my bed, I knew I'd been waiting months for this talk and didn't want to put it off any longer if she was ready. Once we were seated on opposite ends of the couch with her feet in my lap, she blew out a long breath like she was collecting herself, and then waited another few seconds.

"Okay," she said. "There are three things that you need to know. First is the tattoo that Kira and I got the day before Rhys showed up." Grabbing the collar of her shirt, she pulled it to the side to show me, as if I would have forgotten. "Kira, as you know, had been with Zane for *years,* and you saw what happened to her when he left her. You now know about Rhys, and sometime during the months with you, I realized that Rhys and my past with him no longer had the same control over me that they originally had. Before, that past controlled my life, but as I got deeper into my relationship with you, I got further and further from that past, and its hold. So Kira and I both felt like we were finally free from our past relationships—relationships that had completely changed us. That is what the free hearts stand for." Kennedy laughed and shook her head. "And then my past came back into my life the next day, and you saw how that went."

I smiled, but remained quiet as I grabbed her feet in my hands and started rubbing them. I didn't want to interrupt her, but I wanted her to know how much I was appreciating that she was finally telling me this.

"The second is, I like being in control of my life . . . eh, well, mostly my sex life. It makes me panic when I'm not in control of kisses, touches . . . everything. Like I told you that day in your office, only you and Rhys have ever been able to make me willingly give up my control. But only Rhys has ever known *why* I needed that control."

I waited somewhat patiently while Kennedy looked like she was trying to gather her thoughts. But this was something I'd wanted to know since Vegas, and knowing that I was seconds away from finding out had me almost begging her to tell me.

"This is probably going to be so jumbled and confusing, but I'll try to make it so you understand. Before I met Rhys, I needed control for a completely different reason from when I met you. My mom is a very strong-willed person, and that's something I've always admired about her. I'm just like my dad, but having a strong will was definitely the one thing I've taken from my mom, and I took pride in being that way. After my first real kiss I realized just how vulnerable I felt during it, and it made me really uneasy because that wasn't the kind of person I was. So I made sure from then on that there wasn't a way for me to feel like that again. I always took control after that. With Rhys, there was something about him that made it so easy to just let him take control. I never once had that vulnerable feeling, but I still fought him because I had been unknowingly trying to make all my relationships be just like my parents'. Do you remember I told you that I used to want what they have, and then I realized that that kind of love didn't exist?"

I thought for a second, then nodded. "Ice cream shop."

"Right. Rhys was what made me realize that . . . or *think* that. But I never understood that I'd been trying to force my relationships to be perfect until I talked to Rhys about it last night. To be honest, I always thought it was only Kira who did that. So with Rhys, losing control meant no longer controlling how our relationship went, then after him, I guess it was the same as before. I didn't want to go back to feeling vulnerable with any guy; but then I met you, and you demanded control from the start. The second you touched me I was already completely lost in you in a way I had never been, and it absolutely terrified me. I thought it was because you were like Rhys, but Brian is actually the person who made me see the differences. Everything was easy with Rhys, but everything was terrifying with you because what I felt with you was more than I ever felt with him, and I had thought at one point that he was the last person I would ever love. So it wasn't the similarities between you and Rhys that scared me, and it wasn't that I didn't stand a chance of keeping control with you. It was that I had finally found the guy I was meant to be with, and after what had happened with Rhys, I was too scared to let myself feel anything for you. Letting myself love again was the hardest and scariest thing I've ever done."

"Does it still scare you?"

"No," she breathed. "Liam, I crave the way you make me feel and the way you love me."

"And do you trust me not to hurt you now?" I asked as I pushed her feet to the side and leaned forward so my mouth was less than an inch from hers.

"I wouldn't be here telling you all of this if I didn't trust you with my heart."

I captured her lips with mine, and like before, her fingers gripped my shirt, then flattened against my chest as she pushed me away.

"Wait, wait. Last thing that you didn't know," she whispered against my lips. "I have to tell you about Juarez and why Kira and I are really in California."

"Yeah." I sat back and looked at her. "Who the fuck is Juarez? No one ever answered that question for me."

She waited until I was back against my side of the couch and rubbing her feet again before she started talking. "Juarez is the leader of a gang that my dad and uncle Mason infiltrated. To make a long story—that I don't actually even know—short, the gang wanted payback after my dad got most of their members thrown in jail. The remaining members kidnapped my mom right before my parents were supposed to get married. Obviously she got away from them, and the rest of the gang members were thrown in prison as well. A few months before Kira and I moved here, my dad started receiving threats from someone in the gang, or close to them, that were directed at Kira and me. Moving to California without our parents was just a precaution, but Dad thought it was necessary since a handful of the members were being released within just months of each other. Then last week we had a visitor from Juarez."

"You what?" I yelled.

"Let me keep explaining!" After Kennedy gave me a quick rundown on some kid named Matthew, and the hours she, Kira, and Rhys had all spent at the police station giving statements, she sighed heavily and held her hands up to emphasize her uncertainty. "We don't know if there are any more people working for Juarez yet, but I have a feeling that Matthew was it. All that said, I don't know when Kira and I will be allowed to move back to Florida, and that used to upset me, but not so much anymore. Even though there are so many things I hate about California, moving here was the best thing that could have happened because it brought me back to you."

"Aw," I drawled sarcastically. "You must like me or something."

"You like that last little cheesy part?" she asked with a wink.

"Love it. Best part of everything you just told me." Kennedy kicked at my stomach, but I caught her foot and started rubbing it again. "Now tell me why the hell didn't I know about all this Juarez bullshit before?"

The teasing look that had briefly crossed her face quickly left at my question. "I didn't want you to worry when Kira and I weren't really worried. Mom and Dad said the threats increased for a while when some of the members started being released, but they've had the police watching them. Besides, like I told you before, my dad made sure we knew how to escape bad situations if they happened, and Matthew definitely wasn't a bad situation. It scared me when he first showed up and started talking, but as soon as he started sobbing it was pretty funny."

"How can you talk about this like it's not that big a deal?"

"Because it's not to us," she said on a laugh. "I wasn't scared when my parents told us about the threats, and I'm not scared now."

"I don't think I'll ever understand how your mind works," I mumbled.

"Who said I wanted you to?"

Grabbing her ankles, I pulled her closer until I could wrap my arm around her waist to haul her onto my lap. "I like when you act like you don't care," I said against her throat before placing a kiss there.

"Oh, you like it now?" she teased as she turned so she was straddling me. "I don't remember you liking it about six months ago."

I made a confirming sound in my throat. "You were always so bad at lying to me anyway, it was funny to watch you try to make me believe you didn't want me. But now I've gotten you to admit your feelings, so your attempts at not caring are adorable."

"Adorable?" she said, deadpan.

"Fucking adorable, Moon."

I slowly inched her shirt off her body, and let it fall to the floor before reaching for the back of her bra, but my hands stilled when I looked down. Her black lace bra looked like it was barely able to hold her in, and was filmy enough that I was able to catch a glimpse of something I knew hadn't been there before.

"Kennedy . . ." I began; my voice had dropped low and was barely audible.

"If you say they're adorable, I will castrate you."

"Still not nice," I mumbled, and finished taking her bra off. *Two* somethings. "Holy shit. Not adorable." I gently traced around the small barbells set just beneath her nipples, and fucking loved the needy noise she made when I did. "When?"

"The day you walked out of my condo."

My eyes went up to find her looking down at me. "Really?"

Her eyes were filled with need as she breathily explained, "Rhys wasn't leaving, you'd left, and I didn't know what to do. I went to talk to Brian since you'd told me about all the times you went to him. I really had no one else I could talk to even though I'd only met him the day before. He wasn't in yet, but the woman at the parlor started talking to me about my tattoos and somehow I ended up back in her room getting new piercings after I'd told her about my other ones. We were done and I left before Brian ever showed up." She sucked in a quick breath when I traced around the piercings again, and moaned. "I've been waiting for you to do that."

"Has it been long enough for me to—"

"Close enough," she said, cutting me off, and a choked whimper left her throat when I leaned forward to suck one nipple into my mouth. "Oh God."

"You okay?" I asked, and gently bit down, eliciting another whimper from her.

"Yes, just don't stop."

I unbuttoned her pants and started pulling them down, but with the way we were sitting, they weren't going far. As soon as I released her breast, she was scooting off of me to lie down on the couch, and yanking at her pants while trying to pull me down with her.

I focused my attention on Kennedy's other breast and slid my hand inside her underwear before she'd even gotten her jeans off. Her back arched off the couch and a breathy whimper filled the room when I teased her clit, and it took a few seconds for her to go back to trying to rid herself of her pants. By the time she was tightening her thighs around my hand, her jeans were still on her ankles. With another gentle bite against her nipple as I teased her clit, her body started vibrating and her mouth opened in a soundless moan.

"Oh my God," she whispered when the vibrating in her body had slowed.

"I'm pretty sure that's a new record, and that's saying something for you."

"Shut up," she said on a laugh, and threaded her fingers through my hair.

Looking up into her bright eyes, I glanced down for a second and said, "These are gonna be fun."

Kennedy smiled playfully and lifted her eyebrows once. "I can see that."

Pressing her mouth to mine, she kissed me long and slow as I grabbed at her jeans and pulled them off of her one leg at a time.

"Is that all you have for me tonight?" she asked against my lips.

I smiled as I stood from the couch with her wrapped in my arms. "Not even close, Moon."

19

December 6
Kennedy

"MOON, IT'S TIME to go eat pancakes."

I was having a nightmare—a horrible one. There were pancakes everywhere and someone was telling me to eat them. *No. No, no, no. Pancakes mean secret looks between my parents that make me want to throw up. Pancakes are the food devil.*

"Wake up."

Yes, I want to fucking wake up from this pancake nightmare!

"Moon," Liam yelled, and my eyes flew open.

"Jesus Christ! You scared the shit out of me."

He smirked proudly. "You were impossible to wake up, not my fault I had to yell."

I groaned and slapped at his chest before burying myself under his comforter. "It *is* your fault because you're the one who had me up until almost four this morning."

"Are you complaining about that?"

My cheeks heated, and I shook my head quickly even though he probably couldn't see what I was doing.

Liam lifted the comforter away from me and passed his lips across my nose. "It's Sunday."

"Mm-hmm."

"You know what that means . . ."

No, I didn't. I didn't really care about what anything meant because I'd just realized that Liam still didn't have any clothes on.

"Pancakes with my family."

"Oh my God," I whispered, horrified. "That was supposed to be a nightmare!"

Liam's eyebrows drew together in confusion.

"I was having a nightmare that someone was making me eat pancakes and I was surrounded by them! It was awful!"

He burst into loud laughter and pulled me into his arms. "These won't be bad, you want to know why?"

"No," I mumbled against his chest.

"They won't be bad because you'll be eating them with me. You won't even be able to see your parents, so whatever it is with them that ruined pancakes for you and your sister will be nowhere near you."

"Still doesn't sound good."

"My mom makes banana pancakes."

I lifted my head and widened my eyes. "I love bananas."

Liam smiled. "I already know that, which is why I was using it to lure you in. So what do you say?"

"To banana pancakes, or to brunch with your family . . . including your sister, who I'm pretty sure hates me."

"All of the above. And Kristi doesn't hate you. She only knew that you had been married and that I was miserable, and she didn't wait to hear the rest of the story before she reacted. I don't know what she did to you, but I know how she was to me. But she knows now . . . the whole thing—even Vegas. My entire family does. So I can assure you no one there will hate you."

"Oh my God, they know about Vegas? What the hell, Liam? I can't go there now!"

He rolled his eyes. "Yes, you can. So are you coming with me?"

"No," I said stubbornly.

"Banana pancakes?" He waited a few seconds before repeating with exaggeration, "*Banana* pancakes."

I sighed dramatically and mumbled, "Well, I guess I know why Kristi stopped giving me the death stare every time she walked by me."

"Still waiting."

"Yes, Liam. Yes, I will go with you to brunch with your family and eat banana pancakes. As long as we get something straight, first."

He'd started pulling me out of bed when I agreed, but abruptly stopped. "Like what?"

"What am I?"

Liam watched me for a few seconds before saying, "A woman?" I shook my head and started to clarify, but he spoke again. "*Not* a woman? Uh . . . a unicorn?"

Hard laughs burst from my chest, and it took me awhile to calm down enough to speak. "No! What am I to you? What is your family going to think I am? I think we need to get that figured out before you toss me into a house with them."

"My girl, mine, girlfriend . . . whatever you prefer, as long as it's clear that you *are* mine."

"All of the above?" I offered.

With a nod, he agreed, "All of the above, then. Let's get ready and go."

THIRTY MINUTES LATER, we were walking up to his parents' door. I was wearing my clothes from the night before. I had no makeup on because it looked better than the half-smeared-off look I'd been sporting when Liam woke me up. And I was wearing Liam's deodorant. I. Felt. Fabulous.

"You do realize this is my first Sunday with your family, and I look like I spent the night in your bed."

"You did."

I smacked Liam's stomach as we continued walking. "Yeah, but *they* don't need to know that." I groaned and rubbed at my eyes. "Oh well, they probably already figured it out when you told them I was coming."

Liam glanced at me with a confused look. "I didn't tell them you were coming."

"Fuck this, I'm not going." I turned to go back to his car, but he caught me around the waist and started carrying me toward the door. Ass first. My hips were against his forearm, my arms and head were hanging down next to his butt, and the tips of my toes were just barely scraping along the cement so it was giving me a tease of being able to regain control if I could just put my feet down. I looked like a damn rag doll.

"Put me down!" I hissed when he rang the doorbell.

"Hell no. If I do, you'll leave."

"Since when do you ring—" Brandon's deep voice cut off as he started laughing. "Never mind. Understood."

"I'm starving," Liam mumbled as he walked us inside.

"Well, you came to the right place," Brandon said, his tone still light with the hint of laughter. "Is she misbehaving again?" he asked his son.

"I hate you both," I grumbled, but the defeat was clear in my tone. I knew this was about to be the worst day. Never mind that I looked like I'd been fucking their son all night, I was also being dragged into the house like some kind of object.

"I'm so glad—" A woman, who I was almost positive was Liam's mom by the sound of her voice, began saying, but cut off as she started laughing just like Brandon had done.

Within seconds there were numerous other people laughing too.

Fan-fucking-tastic.

"Well then, back to what I was saying. I *am* glad you showed up today, and I love that you came with him, Kennedy!"

"It wasn't voluntarily!" I called out.

"I can see that." Liam's mom sighed, and I listened to her light footfalls as she approached us. From the way Liam bent, I assumed she was giving him a hug, but then I heard a smack and Liam cringed. "Put the poor girl down! Gently! *Gently* put her down."

As soon as I was on my feet, I straightened and blew out a frustrated breath, then turned to see everyone watching me with amused expressions. "Hi," I said awkwardly. But no one said anything back; they just kept smiling as they looked between Liam and me. "Um . . . huh. So . . . the pancakes smell good."

"So you're in love with this loser, huh?" Liam's aunt Bree asked.

A startled laugh bubbled past my lips, and my eyes darted over to Kristi and then Brandon, who were both smiling patiently, and I could only assume from their looks that they'd told the rest of the family about my decision. "Uh yeah. Yeah, I am."

"And the ex?"

"Bree," everyone said at once, and gave her a look.

Konrad, her husband, pulled her back and put a hand over her mouth as he shrugged. "Don't listen to her."

There were mumbled words coming from Bree, but all I could catch were the words *dog bed* when Konrad dropped his hand.

"Don't you shush me," she bit out at him, then looked back at me. "Well, *I* still want to know."

I looked at Liam's parents and sister, and both sets of his aunts and uncles, and tried to find the right words. I knew Liam was close with his family, so I wouldn't have doubted that they all knew what had been going on between us over the past month. But he'd also told me about last weekend and the huge blowup over Thanksgiving and me on our way over here, so I felt like I owed them some explanation. I just couldn't figure out how much of an explanation I wanted to give them—not to mention that this was an incredibly awkward situation.

"You don't have to answer that," Liam leaned down to whisper.

Grabbing his hand, I held on to it as tight as I could. "There's nothing between Rhys and me anymore, and there's no chance of any relationship ever again. I told him last night that I'd chosen Liam, and he was surprisingly okay with it."

Bree still looked like she was hoping for more, but the rest of Liam's family was either glaring at her or giving me sympathetic looks.

"Well, now that you're done being rude," Liam's mom said to Bree, then looked back toward us, "I think it's time for pancakes. Everyone hungry?"

Liam must have felt the way I tightened, because he whispered, "Banana pancakes."

"I can do this," I said to myself, and Liam failed at holding back a laugh.

"Yes, you can. It won't be that bad, I promise."

He was right. They weren't that bad. Actually, the pancakes were to die for, and if Liam hadn't cleaned the rest of them out, I would have gone back for thirds. Liam and I were curled up on an oversized chair together, and everyone else in the family was spread throughout the living room and kitchen as they talked and finished eating.

"How many did you eat?" Liam asked when he set his plate on top of mine on the end table.

"Six," I boasted proudly. "My stomach is so happy and fat right now."

"Look at you eating pancakes. I'm proud of you. I should give you a medal or something."

"Don't ruin this moment. This aftereffect of the pancakes is better than the ones from the orgasms you give me."

Liam hooked an arm around my neck and pulled me close so he could whisper, "I somehow doubt that. But if you still think so in five minutes, I'll have to remind you how much better the latter is."

"Five minutes?" I asked, raising my eyebrows. "Are we leaving already?"

"Why would we have to leave? There are a lot of bathrooms and bedrooms in this house."

"Liam Taylor," I harshly whispered. "We are not doing *anything* in your parents' house."

"We are if I feel like you need to remember how easily I can start making you scream."

My eyes widened, and I glanced around to make sure no one in his family was close enough to overhear us. "I cannot believe you just said that here."

"When was it?" he asked in my ear, and nipped on it. "After your second orgasm last night? Yeah . . . after the second. And we both know just how fast it is to get you there."

"I hate you."

"No, you don't. You love me, and I fucking love those piercings and what they do to you."

My breathing had deepened, and I was now beyond mortified that I was getting turned on in front of his family. "Liam, you have to shut up."

"Are the five minutes up?" he asked teasingly. "Your choice. We can find a room, or you can tell me that you were wrong."

"You guys are so cute, it's kind of disgusting," Kristi said as she walked past us.

Her sudden presence had me jolting back into the arm of the

chair, and I wanted nothing more than to smack that triumphant smile off of Liam's face.

"Not disgusting," Liam's mom said from just a few feet behind Kristi. "I love seeing my son this happy." She grabbed my hand briefly as she walked past us, and murmured Brandon's words from last night. "Thank you."

"If your family keeps thanking me for being with you, I'm going to start feeling like I took you on as a charity case," I whispered when his mom was out of the room, and bit back a scream when Liam pinched my side.

"Five minutes are up, Moon. Your choice."

I turned my head to look at him, and leaned close enough so our noses were touching. "The banana pancakes were not nearly as good as what you do to me," I assured him.

Liam's face fell. "I was hoping to have a reason to find a room."

"Ha. Sorry, but that won't ever happen here. You can wait until later."

AFTER SPENDING THE rest of the morning and early afternoon with his family, Liam and I headed back to my condo so I could check on Kira and Rhys. And even though I told Liam that I would be fine going in alone, he wasn't having it. He'd already been worried last night about Rhys's reaction to the news of my decision, but because Rhys had been okay with it, Liam didn't trust him now . . . He said it was a guy thing.

"He's not dangerous," I said before we reached the door. "You need to calm down."

I unlocked the door and walked in with Liam so close behind me that he kept making me stumble forward.

"Really?" I sighed, then looked around at the empty apartment. "Did he leave? I could've sworn that was his truck outside."

I walked quickly through the living room and, when I caught sight of Rhys's bag stuffed behind the couch, continued down the hall and into my room. He wasn't in there or the bathroom.

"Maybe they walked somewhere," Liam guessed as we returned to the living room, but I shook my head.

"No, I could hear music coming from Kira's room. Maybe she knows where he went. Hey, Kira," I called out as I opened the door, and immediately began shutting it when I saw a man's naked ass as he drove into my sister, closely followed by their screams when they noticed me. "Oh my God, I'm so—wait! What the fuck are you two doing?" I screamed, and swung the door back open when I realized it wasn't just some random guy Kira had probably found at the gym. It was Rhys.

Rhys and Kira both started yelling their explanations as they tried to cover themselves, but I wasn't hearing any of the words they were saying.

"Holy shit," Liam hissed from behind me, and wrapped his arms tightly around my waist. I just wasn't sure if the action was meant to protect Kira and Rhys from me, or if it was meant to be reassuring to me after what I'd just seen.

"What. The fuck?" I screeched. "What are you doing—just what the fuck?"

"Come on, Kennedy," Liam whispered, and pulled me away.

I couldn't tear my eyes away from them until Liam had me out of the room and had reached around me to shut the door. He dragged me over to the couch and knelt between my knees with his hands covering my cheeks so he could force me to look at him.

"Are you okay?"

"What the fuck," I whispered again. I didn't know how many times I'd said it at that point . . . I only knew that I couldn't stop saying it.

"Shit, Kennedy, say something else to me, please," he begged. "I need to know what's going through your mind."

I pointed behind him toward Kira's door. "What's going through my mind is that I just walked in on my ex-husband fucking my twin sister! What the fuck?"

Liam's eyes and face were a mix of panic, anger, and sorrow. None of which I could take the time to think about at that moment. "I need—" he started, but was cut off by my screaming when Rhys scrambled out of the room buttoning up his jeans.

"What the fuck were you doing with her? How long has this been going on?"

"Kennedy, please, let me explain!" he rushed out.

"Let you explain? Let you *explain*? She's my fucking sister, you asshole!"

"You don't understand, I swear—"

"Oh my God, Kennedy!" Kira cried as she ran out of the room with Rhys's shirt on. It was inside out and backward, and I had no clue why I was so focused on those details, but I couldn't stop staring at the shirt. "You don't understand."

"Apparently not!" I yelled. "Someone needs to make me understand what I just fucking saw!"

Tears filled Kira's eyes before falling to her cheeks, and all she could do was shake her head.

"We didn't think you were coming back today," Rhys said, and I laughed mockingly.

"*Oh*. So because you didn't think I would be here, you thought it would be okay to have sex with her?" I looked at my sister and pointed to Rhys. "He is my *ex*, Kira! What are you thinking?"

"I'm so sorry," she sobbed.

"Not because we thought you wouldn't be here," Rhys answered my original question although it had been rhetorical. "I just—I don't know. Kennedy, I'm sorry, but you have to let me explain."

"I'm waiting, Rhys!" It was only then—when I felt the slightest squeeze on my arms—that I remembered Liam was sitting directly in front of me. He wasn't looking at Rhys and Kira, he was only focused on me with that same mixture of emotions still playing out over his face. But I couldn't keep my eyes on him for long; it was physically straining to not stare at the two people standing on the other side of the room.

"Last night I told you that something had happened over the last couple weeks."

My jaw dropped at Rhys's words. "My *sister* was what happened? You've been fucking for *weeks*?"

"No!" Kira cried, and clutched at her chest like that action would help her steady her breathing.

"No, Kennedy, God no. I told you that I would tell you what that something was, but I needed to talk to someone else first. Kira was who I needed to talk to. I never touched or kissed your sister until after you left last night."

"Kennedy, I swear," Kira said between sobs. "I didn't even know that he shared my feelings until last night."

"He's with you because you look just like me, Kira! Don't you see that?"

"No!" Rhys yelled. "Yes, you two are identical, but nothing about Kira reminds me of you. When I see her, I know exactly who I'm looking at—probably just like Liam knows exactly who he's looking at when he sees you. There's a difference, Kennedy." Rhys looked to Liam for help, and even though Liam was still facing me, he nodded.

"There is," Liam reluctantly said. His arctic-blue eyes captured mine and held them. "It's your eyes; even when you were mad at me in the beginning, it was there. There's so much passion in the way you look at me. When Kira looks at me, it's just like any other person I know. If I look at her too quickly, I'll think she's you, but only for a second until I realize that there is absolutely no draw to her."

"Exactly," Rhys breathed, his voice relieved.

For a few moments, the only sound in the room was Kira's crying as I watched Liam. And for the first time since he'd brought me to the couch, I understood his look. He was worried about why I was reacting so strongly when I'd chosen him over Rhys. But he didn't understand the depth of betrayal I felt over what I had seen.

"It's still you," I whispered so softly only Liam could hear. When I looked back up to my sister and Rhys, I shook my head. "How do I know that you won't just up and leave her too?"

"You know why I had to leave you, Kennedy. And you know I won't ever go back to that kind of work."

"I don't understand," Kira said, and brought her arms out to the side before letting them fall. "You have Liam. Why is it okay for you to have him, but it's not okay for Rhys to have someone?"

"Yes, I have Liam. I *love* Liam. I'm not upset because Rhys is with someone, Kira. I honestly would have been ecstatic for Rhys if it had been anyone but you."

"Why does your reaction have to change *because* it's her?" Rhys asked, and took a step closer to Kira, like he was ready to defend her.

"Honestly? Because I'm scared for my sister! I'm scared about the real reason you're with her. And I'm pissed off at both of you because you've been keeping your feelings from me while I've been going insane over the last month and feeling so fucking guilty because I thought I was going to hurt you."

"What was I supposed to say?" Kira yelled. "He came back *for*—"

I continued with my explanation as if she hadn't spoken. "And while there is absolutely no connection between us any-more, Rhys, I can't help but think that if we'd stayed married, you two would have had an affair eventually."

Neither of them responded, and from the looks on their faces, their silence was because they couldn't deny it.

"*That* is why I am mad. *That* is why I feel betrayed. And *that* is why I'm struggling to be okay with something you both obviously want." Looking at Liam, I grabbed his hands and pleaded, "Take me back to your place."

His only response was to nod and stand up—pulling me with him. Kira and Rhys didn't say anything to us as I packed the necessities and an extra outfit and left. And for the rest of the day, Liam didn't try to make me forget about what we'd walked in on. He simply held me in his arms on his bed, and let me talk through all of my thoughts before helping me by offering his own thoughts and opinions on the situation.

"Thank you," I said on a sigh as we curled up under his comforter that night.

"You're thanking me? Why?"

"For being there with me, and for helping me talk through it today. You have no idea how amazing you are for that."

"Anytime." With a soft smile, Liam pressed a kiss to my forehead and pulled me into his arms. "Good night, Moon."

A quiet giggle left my lips, and Liam looked down to eye me curiously.

"There's a sound I didn't think I'd hear the rest of the day. What's funny?"

"It's not really *funny*. Do you realize that every time we've fallen asleep together—even that night in Vegas—you've said 'Good night, Moon'?"

"I guess . . ." He drew the words out, making them sound more like a question. "I don't know why it made you laugh."

"Because it's a little children's book. I smile every time you say it, and after today . . . I don't know, it was just the perfect end. It was what I needed to hear."

"Best damn children's book I've ever read." Liam pulled me back against his chest and sighed. "Good night, Moon."

My lips curved up in a smile, and I squeezed him. "Good night, Liam Taylor."

20

December 19
Liam

MY EYES FLEW open and widened when I saw Kennedy lowering herself onto me two weeks later. I groaned at the feel of her around me, and my hands went to her hips so I could control her movements.

"Good morning," I mumbled groggily. "And what did I do to deserve being woken up like this?"

Her lips spread into a smile and she rocked her hips once, then paused. "I woke up and you were already ready . . . thought I'd take advantage. But if you want me to stop," she said innocently, and started lifting herself up before I slammed her back down.

"Don't," I warned her.

"That's what I thought," she mumbled, and started moving again, her husky voice even raspier from sleep.

"Fuck, Kennedy." I groaned and tightened my grip. The way she was changing from fast and hard to slow, as she lifted all the way off me only to lower herself back down teasingly, was driving me insane.

I palmed her heavy breasts and circled her pierced nipples

before pinching on them, causing her to clench around me as a loud whimper filled her bedroom. When I did it again a minute later, one of her hands left its place on my chest and moved to tease her hood piercing.

She moaned and quickened her finger movements, and as fucking hot as it was to watch her, I wanted to be the one who was making her moan.

Lifting Kennedy off me, I pushed her to the side and backward so she was lying on her back, and quickly followed so I was hovering over her. I pressed my mouth to hers and teased the seam of her lips with my tongue until she opened her mouth and began giving me the sweetest torture with only a kiss.

I lowered my hips, and she automatically wrapped her legs around me. She moaned into our kiss when I slid against her piercing, and when it got to the point where I couldn't continue forcing myself to stay only there, I moved slowly down her body. I pressed openmouthed kisses down her throat and chest, and spent time torturing each nipple before moving down her stomach to her hips, and then finally lower. I settled myself between her legs, and keeping my eyes on her expectant expression, I leaned only far enough forward that my mouth barely brushed against where she wanted me with each heavy breath she took.

She whimpered in aggravation and threaded her fingers into my hair when I didn't move, and begged, "Liam, please."

I waited another few seconds before leaning forward to taste her, and I had no doubt that if Kira and Rhys weren't already awake . . . they were after the sound Kennedy had just made.

Kennedy's fingers tightened in my hair, and her body shook from the combination of her first and second orgasms. She tried to shut her legs but was unable to since I still hadn't moved—and I didn't plan to. It hadn't taken more than three minutes for her to hit the first two, and I knew from experience she could give me another one. I'd never been with a girl who could have more than one, and definitely not within just a few minutes.

I would say it as long as she kept the piercing in . . . I fucking *loved* that thing.

"Stop," she breathed. "Stop, I can't—" She cut off and groaned. "I can't do any more."

"That's what you say every time. Besides, this is payback for last night." I growled against her, and went back to torturing her in a way I knew she would be begging for again that night.

"Oh my God!" she cried out as her body shattered for the third time.

I waited until her shaking had calmed before climbing back up her body and pressing against her entrance.

"I hate you," she mumbled weakly as I slowly filled her.

"Do you?" I challenged.

Even though she shook her head, she said, "Yes. So much—oh, that feels so good," she breathed.

I stopped moving, and her dark blue eyes flew open. "Are you going to apologize for last night?"

"Fuck no! Not after what you just did!"

I moved out and back in, and stilled again. "Are you really mad? I can always see if you can give me another one."

"No, no!" But even as she spoke, she clenched painfully tight around me and her eyes widened. She was such a bad liar. "I'm sorry for teasing you last night and not letting you finish for over an hour," she said on a rush.

I grinned boldly. "Apology accepted."

"That's what you get for letting me take control last night," she goaded when I began moving again.

"Are we really gonna keep doing this right now?"

She laughed huskily and tightened her legs around my back. "No, keep moving," she pleaded.

After that little argument, it took another minute to find the rhythm we'd had and to lose myself in Kennedy again, but once I did, her little moans and pleas had me struggling to hold on. I quickened my pace, and a couple minutes later buried my face in her neck as I found my release. I lowered my body onto Kennedy's, and a shiver went through me when she lightly trailed her fingernails across my back and over my shoulders while she waited for our breathing to calm.

Not thirty seconds later there were loud knocks coming from the front door of the condo.

"Are you fucking kidding me?" I groaned and shakily lifted myself off Kennedy. "If there's another ex-husband, I want to know before I answer the door."

"None that I can remember," she teased, and pushed me away. "I can get it."

"No, I got it. Not after who it ended up being the last time there was a random knock on the door, and not with the possibility of it being another person Juarez sent."

"Liam," she groaned. "Matthew was so not dangerous."

"Get dressed," I ordered as I finished buttoning my pants. Grabbing my shirt from the floor, I walked out of Kennedy's room and down the hall. I stepped into the living room at the same time Rhys stepped out of Kira's room. Like me, he was finishing getting dressed.

In the two weeks since Kennedy and I had walked in on Rhys and Kira, things had gotten easier. Kennedy still mumbled about how weird it was to see them together, but she was no longer mad at them, or afraid for Kira. It was obvious how much Rhys and Kira meant to each other, and I think that made the transition easier for Kennedy. But it was still awkward. For the most part, if we did anything, we did it at my apartment. I didn't like the idea of Kennedy's ex-husband being able to hear us, and I didn't think she liked hearing him and Kira. But last night we'd had a late dinner here after going to a concert, and after a lot of drinking, none of us really cared. In silent agreement, Rhys had taken Kira—who was already taking her shirt off—into her room, and I'd taken Kennedy into hers.

This morning, however, was beyond uncomfortable.

I followed Rhys to the door and stood next to him while he opened it.

If I thought I was uncomfortable before, that couldn't begin to explain how I felt when I saw an older version of Kennedy and Kira standing right in front of us, with a man at her side who looked like he had already thought of different ways to kill me. If only he knew what I'd *just* been doing to his daughter.

"Who the fuck are you?" the twins' dad asked as he eyed me.

"Kash!" their mom scolded. "That's Liam." Her wide eyes found me, and she shook her head. "I'm so sorry, he—"

"Who the fuck is Liam?" Kash looked at Rhys and gestured to me. "Who the fuck is he?"

"That's Kennedy's boyfriend, Kash, now shut up. I'm sorry, I'm Rachel—"

"No, Rhys is her boyfriend."

"Oh, Kash," Rachel mumbled.

"Uh, not," Rhys answered. "I'm actually with Kira."

"No, you're not," Kash said confidently.

"Actually he is." I extended a hand toward Kash and said, "Liam Taylor, nice to meet you. Eli Jenkins is my boss; he and Mason were the ones who talked to me when the girls first moved here. They work at my dad's gym."

"Isn't that convenient for you," he scoffed. "Why the hell are the two of you here at nine in the morning?"

"Anyway!" Rachel chimed in. "We came to surprise the girls for Christmas next week. Are they . . ." She trailed off and her eyes shot over to Kash. "Um . . . here. Are they here?"

"Yeah, of course." Rhys and I stepped back, and I whispered to Rachel as she passed, "They're decent too."

"Thank God," she whispered, and sent me a thankful smile.

"Mom!" Kira said excitedly at the same time as Kennedy rounded the corner and screeched, "Dad!"

Kash looked at Kennedy and pointed to me. "Who the fuck is he, and why is Rhys with Kira?"

"Oh Jesus," Rachel mumbled. "Coffee anyone? I'll show myself to the kitchen."

I had the urge to join her. I could only imagine how this day was going to go. I just hoped their whole trip wasn't a constant repeat of the first few minutes.

December 19
Kennedy

"Dad, stop it," I hissed.

He hadn't stopped glaring at Liam for the last hour and a half since he and Mom had shown up at our door. Kira and I should have known that they would come to California; we got together every year for a vacation around Christmas. But my parents hadn't mentioned anything, and I would have thought with Juarez's guys being able to find Kira and me, that would have prevented my parents from being anywhere near us now. Then again, I hadn't forgiven my dad up until a couple weeks ago for his role in the whole Rhys situation, and we had only talked once more since then on the night Matthew had shown up. So there was a chance that he knew there was no longer a threat against us. Regardless, a little warning about their arrival would have been nice. It was awkward sitting across from my parents with the guy who had just finished satisfying me minutes before their arrival.

"I don't like him," he stated.

"Dad!" Kira and I snapped at the same time Mom said, "For Christ's sake, Kash!"

"Mason didn't like me either, if that helps at all," Liam said with a shrug.

"Is it supposed to?" Dad asked. "If Mase didn't like you, then I have to wonder what you did to make that happen. It's weird that the only person who likes you is Eli."

"And us," I blurted out. "Kira and I like him, Dad. Even Rhys likes him."

He rolled his eyes. "Don't get me started again on the Rhys thing. I didn't send him here so he could go from one daughter to another."

We all groaned, and Mom just sat there shaking her head like she didn't know what to do with Dad anymore. "How about we go get some lunch?" she suggested.

"It's not even eleven," Dad shot back.

"I swear to God, Kash, you are still such a child. Get up and take us all out for some damn lunch."

I bit back a laugh when Dad immediately stood up from the love seat.

"I don't know how I put up with you sometimes," Mom mumbled, and then turned to look at Liam. "Do you see this? Take it all in because *that* daughter of mine is just like her daddy," she said with a nod in my direction.

"Wow, thanks, Mom."

She winked. "Love you, sweet girl. Okay! Everyone get ready, and let's go eat. I am in need of some Mexican food from California."

Dad sat right back down when he realized we all still needed to change, and Mom turned to glare at him. "What? They're not ready to go!"

"Get. Up. I need to talk to you outside."

Dad grinned at her, and I knew exactly what he was doing and what he was about to say. "Aw, come on, someone needs to be hard on him to get him initiated into the family. Don't be mad, Sour Patch."

And there it is, I thought to myself before making a gagging sound.

Liam burst out laughing at hearing Dad's nickname for Mom, and both my parents turned to look at him.

"Can I help you?" Dad growled.

"No, sorry. I just—I finally understood something that Kira and Kennedy told me awhile back, and I see why it's funny now."

"I don't like you," Dad reiterated.

Liam nodded and bit back a smile. "Understood."

BY THE TIME we got back from the restaurant, Dad was so in love with Liam he wouldn't let him stop talking. In Dad's defense, he *had* tried to continue hating him. He'd made sure to talk only to Rhys, and then it was only about stuff that was going on in the department and about undercover operations. I don't know how, but Liam had somehow injected himself into their conversation with a comment I hadn't been able to hear. All I knew was that my dad had looked shocked for about ten seconds before smiling and including Liam in on every conversation he'd had throughout the rest of lunch.

I'd asked Liam what he'd said to him when we were on our way back to the condo, and he had just looked at me with a serious expression and said, "I'd rather not be killed, so I can't tell you."

"Who would be killing you?" I'd asked in amusement. "Dad or me?"

"Guess we'll never know," he'd mumbled. That had been the end of that.

"Girls, we have something we're excited to tell you about," Dad announced suddenly after we'd been back at the condo for about half an hour.

Mom smiled widely and sat up on the love seat as she waited for Dad to tell us the news.

"I know originally we didn't know how long you'd have to be here, and I know this wasn't exactly something you wanted to do." He cleared his throat and looked pointedly at Kira. "But after almost seven months, I can now say that it's safe for you to come back to Florida."

"Really?" Kira screamed excitedly. "Oh my God, finally!"

But only she and Rhys looked happy about the news. My stomach dropped, and even though I wasn't looking at him, I could feel Liam's eyes on me.

"It's safe now?" I choked out. "But how do you know? Matthew found us." I wasn't worried about more guys finding us, but I wasn't ready to leave.

"Out of the five men who had the possibility of getting out, two of them were denied parole, one is dead, and the other two are already back in jail—as of a couple days ago. There was only one other man helping Juarez's crew, the guy funding that Matthew kid, and he was caught when we looked up the bank card Matthew had been given. He was one of the gang members' sons, and he didn't make it three days in jail before a couple members from a rival gang had him taken out. The three members who had been released retaliated, and it obviously didn't go well. One was killed, the other two killed a man and were caught."

"That's a nice bedtime story," Kira said sarcastically, but her face still showed how excited she was to be going home.

I finally turned to face Liam, and my chest constricted at the terrified look in his eyes. It looked like he wasn't even breathing as he waited for my reaction. Cupping my hand against his cheek, I said, "It's time for me to go back to Florida . . ."

He exhaled heavily as if someone had hit him, and his gaze dropped to my lap.

" . . . so that I can pack all my things and move to California for good."

Arctic-blue eyes shot back up to mine and widened. "Are you serious? You hate it here."

"It's not so bad." I shrugged. "But I do need to get everything from back home. I mean, after all, I have to get my cow."

Liam's lips twitched up before spreading into a wide smile. "Hell yeah, Bessie." He grabbed my face in his hands and pulled me closer to kiss me thoroughly—never once caring that my parents were sitting a few feet away.

"Hell. No. You're not staying!" Dad yelled.

"Kash, stop. I moved to Florida for you," Mom reminded him, and he scoffed.

"It's official. I don't like him again."

I leaned back an inch to look into Liam's eyes and laughed softly. "You really thought I would leave? I'm yours," I whispered.

"You are," he agreed, his voice equally soft. "And I'm so fucking glad you're staying, Moon."

Epilogue

December 23 . . . One year later
Liam

I OPENED UP the door to our new house and called out for Kennedy as I stepped inside. There were still random boxes scattered throughout the place that I knew I needed to unpack since Kennedy couldn't, but right now I needed to do something that was more important.

"Moon?" I yelled.

"In here!" she called back.

"Where is here?" I mumbled to myself as I walked through the house trying to find my wife.

Although our parents had tried to stop us, we had our wedding in Vegas at the beginning of July. We didn't have the cliché Vegas wedding, that had never been the plan. We just wanted to get married in the city where we'd met. Thanks to Kennedy devoting all her time to planning since we'd set a date that was only two months after we'd decided to get married, the night ended up being amazing.

Once our parents understood that we would be having an

actual wedding, and that everyone was invited, they stopped trying to push for a wedding that was in California or Florida, and just tried to get us to wait. We didn't see the point in waiting. We were already living together, we knew that we would eventually get married anyway, and as we revealed to our families at the reception, we'd found out that Kennedy was pregnant in May.

We'd bought a house and moved in just a couple weeks ago; and thank God we were finally in here, because Kennedy was already a few days past her due date.

I turned the corner into the nursery and found her folding clothes and putting them away.

"Hi! How was work?"

"Long. How are you feeling? How's Chase?" I asked as I came up behind her and wrapped my arms around her.

Kennedy placed her hands on her swollen stomach and sighed. "He's good. I'm just ready for him to be here."

"Do you think it'll be tonight?"

"We'll see. But the doctor said if it's not within the next few days, she's going to induce me on the twenty-sixth."

"Good," I whispered against her neck, and placed a kiss there. "I have a Christmas present for you." I brought the small, wrapped gift around her and held it up for her to take.

"It's not Christmas yet!"

"It's for you and Chase. Just open it." I let my hands rest where hers had been, and waited as she tried to find a spot to start opening the wrapping paper. "It's small, and kind of more for us than for him . . ." I trailed off when she opened the present and inhaled sharply.

"Oh my God," she breathed, and I knew those pregnancy hormones were about to kick in at any second. "It's perfect," she choked out, and held up a copy of *Goodnight Moon* before turning in my arms to look at me. "Thank you. I love it and I love you."

"I love you too." I smiled and wiped away the tear that had fallen down her cheek. "Merry Christmas, Moon."

THE END

Acknowledgments

AS ALWAYS, A very big thank you to my husband, Cory. I know I must have driven you crazy with this one! Thank you for helping out with even more than you usually do as I've sat around doing nothing but writing while waiting for our baby girl to arrive. I will never be able to repay you for how much you have done. Love you!

To my editor, Tessa Woodward, and my agent, Kevan Lyon . . . you're both incredible! Thank you for cheering me on through this story, and thank you for not getting annoyed with me when I trashed the first draft, just to do the same with the second draft a month before it was due. I think we can all agree that we love the third draft so much more.

To my readers . . . there will never be enough thank-yous to y'all. For helping promote, for reading, and for loving my characters, just *thank you*. I know this story will mean more than others, and I hope you enjoyed seeing how Liam turned out, as well as getting glimpses of all the other characters!

Immerse Yourself in the World of Molly McAdams

TAKING CHANCES

Her first year away is turning out to be nearly perfect, but one weekend of giving in to heated passion will change everything.

Eighteen-year-old Harper has grown up under the thumb of her career marine father. Ready to live life her own way and to experience things she's only ever heard of from the jarheads in her father's unit, she's on her way to college at San Diego State University.

Thanks to her new roommate, Harper is introduced to a world of parties, gorgeous guys, family, and emotions. She finds herself being torn in two as she quickly falls in love with both her new boyfriend, Brandon, and her roommate's brother, Chase. Despite their dangerous looks and histories, both men adore Harper and would do anything for her, including taking a step back if it would mean she'd be happy.

FROM ASHES

Aside from her dad, who passed away when she was six, Cassidy Jameson has only ever trusted one man: her best friend, Tyler. So of course she follows him to Texas when he leaves for college. She just didn't expect to be so drawn to their new roommate, Gage, a gorgeous guy with a husky Southern drawl. The only problem? He's Tyler's cousin.

Gage Carson was excited to share an apartment off campus with his cousin. He didn't mind that Tyler was bringing the mysterious friend he'd heard about since they were kids . . . until the most beautiful girl he's ever seen jumps out of his cousin's Jeep. There's something about Cassi that makes Gage want to give her everything. Too bad Tyler has warned him that she's strictly off-limits.

Despite everything keeping them apart, Cassi and Gage dance dangerously close to the touch they've both been craving. But when disaster sends her running into Tyler's arms, Cassi will have to decide whether to face the demons of her past . . . or to burn her chance at a future with Gage.

STEALING HARPER

A Taking Chances Novella

Chase Grayson has never been interested in having a relationship that lasts longer than it takes for him and his date to get dressed again. But then he stumbles into a gray-eyed girl whose innocence pours off her, and everything changes. From the minute Harper opens her mouth to let him know just how much he disgusts her, he's hooked.

But a princess deserves a Prince Charming who can make her dreams come true. Not a guy who can turn her life into a nightmare.

All good intentions go out the window when Harper starts to fall for the guy Chase has come to view as a brother. He wanted to protect her by keeping her away, but he can't stand to see her with anyone else, and he'll do anything to make her his. But when it comes down to Harper choosing between the two, will Chase have the strength to step back from the girl who has become his whole world if it means she's happy?

Lines will be crossed. Friendships will be put to the test. And hearts will be shattered.

FORGIVING LIES

A matter of secrets . . .

Undercover cop Logan "Kash" Ryan can't afford a distraction like his new neighbor Rachel Masters, even if she's the most beautiful woman he's ever seen. To catch a serial killer, he needs to stay focused, yet all he can think about is the feisty, long-legged coed whose guarded nature intrigues him.

A matter of lies . . .

Deceived and hurt before, Rachel would rather be a single, crazy cat lady than trust another guy, especially a gorgeous, tattooed bad boy with a Harley, like Kash. But when his liquid-steel eyes meet hers, it takes all of Rachel's willpower to stop herself from exploring his hot body with her own.

A matter of love . . .

As much as they try to keep it platonic, the friction between them sparks an irresistible heat that soon consumes them. Can Kash keep Rachel's heart and her life safe even as he risks his own? Will she be able to forgive his lies . . . or will she run when she discovers the dangerous truth?

NEEDING HER

A From Ashes Novella

She's the Girl Next Door

Maci Price isn't really into relationships. Having four very protective older brothers has always made having a boyfriend very difficult anyway. But her friend is set on finding her the right guy—and thinks the mysterious Connor Green is the perfect pick.

He's Her Brother's Best Friend

Connor Green is trying to find himself again. He loved, then lost, and it's time for him to pick up the pieces. His brooding is making his friends crazy, but Maci, who has grown up into a gorgeous and incredibly sexy woman, is about to break the spell.

They're Made for Each Other

When Maci starts up old pranks to get Connor out of his slump, an all-out war leads to a night that will break all their rules . . . and a relationship they must keep hidden. Together they're electric. Apart they're safe. And soon they'll each find that they're exactly what the other needs.

DECEIVING LIES

A Forgiving Lies Novel

Rachel is supposed to be planning her wedding to Kash, the love of her life. After the crazy year they've had, she's ready to settle down and live a completely normal life. Well, as normal as it can be. But there's something else waiting—something threatening to tear them apart.

Kash is ready for it all with Rachel, especially if "all" includes having a football team of babies with his future wife. In his line of work, Kash knows how short life can be and doesn't want to waste another minute of their life together. But now his past as an undercover narcotics agent has come back to haunt him . . . and it's the girl he loves who's caught in the middle.

Trent Cruz's orders are clear: take the girl. But there's something about this girl that has him changing the rules and playing a dangerous game to keep her safe. When his time as Rachel's protector runs out, Trent will turn his back on the only life he's known—and risk everything if it means getting her out alive.

CAPTURING PEACE

A Sharing You Prequel Novella

Coen Steele has spent the last five years serving his country. Now that he's back, he's finally ready to leave behind the chaos of the battlefield and pursue his lifelong dream. What he wasn't expecting was the feisty sister of one of his battle buddies—who has made it obvious that she wants nothing to do with him—to intrigue him in a way no woman has before.

Reagan Hudson's life changed in the blink of an eye six years ago when she found out she was pregnant and on her own. Since then, Reagan has vowed never to let another man into her life so that no one can walk out on her, or her son, again. But the more she runs into her brother's hot and mysterious friend, the more he sparks something in her that she promised herself she wouldn't feel again.

Can two people with everything to lose allow themselves to finally capture the love they both deserve?

SHARING YOU

Twenty-three-year-old Kamryn Cunningham has left behind a privileged, turbulent past for the anonymity of small-town life. Busy with her new bakery, she isn't interested in hook-ups or fix-ups. Then she meets the very sexy, very married Brody. Though she can't deny the pull between them, Kamryn isn't a cheater and she's not good at sharing.

Twenty-six-year-old Brody Saco may be married, but he isn't happy. When his girlfriend got pregnant six years ago, he did the right thing . . . and he's been paying for it ever since. Now, his marriage is nothing but a trap filled with hate, manipulation, and blame—the remnants of a tragedy that happened five years earlier. While he's never broken his vows, he can't stop the flood of emotion that meeting Kamryn unlocks.

Brought together by an intense heat that is impossible to resist, Brody and Kamryn share stolen moments and nights that end too soon. But is their love strong enough to bear the weight of Kamryn's guilt? And is Brody strong enough to confront the pain of the past and finally break free of his conniving wife?

LETTING GO

A Thatch Novel

Grey and Ben fell in love at thirteen and believed they'd be together forever. But three days before their wedding, the twenty-
year-old groom-to-be suddenly died from an unknown heart
condition, destroying his would-be-bride's world. If it hadn't
been for their best friend, Jagger, Grey never would have made
it through those last two years to graduation. He's the only one
who understands her pain, the only one who knows what it's
like to force yourself to keep moving when your dreams are shattered. Jagger swears he'll always be there for her, but no one has
ever been able to hold on to him. He's not the kind of guy to
settle down.

It's true that no one has ever been able to keep Jagger—
because he's only ever belonged to Grey. While everyone else
worries over Grey's fragility, he's the only one who sees her
strength. Yet as much as he wants Grey, he knows her heart will
always be with Ben. Still they can't deny the heat that is growing
between them—a passion that soon becomes too hot to handle.
But admitting their feelings for each other means they've got to
face the past. Is being together what Ben would have wanted . . .
or a betrayal of his memory that will eventually destroy them
both?

CHANGING EVERYTHING

A Forgiving Lies Novella

Paisley Morro has been in love with Eli since they were thirteen-years-old. But after twelve years of only being his best friend and wingman, the heartache that comes from watching him with countless other women becomes too much, and Paisley decides its time to lay all her feelings on the table.

Eli Jenkins has a life most guys would kill for: Dream job, countless women, and his best friend, Paisley, to be the girl he can always count on for everything else. But one conversation not only changes everything between them, it threatens to make him lose the only girl who has ever meant anything to him.

When tragedy strikes his family and Eli is forced to reevaluate his life, he realizes a life without Paisley isn't a life at all. Only now, he may be too late.

GET BETWEEN THE COVERS WITH THE HOTTEST NEW ADULT BOOKS

JENNIFER L. ARMENTROUT

WITH YOU SAGA
Wait for You
Trust in Me
Be with Me
Stay with Me
Fall With Me
Forever with You

NOELLE AUGUST

THE BOOMERANG SERIES
Boomerang
Rebound
Bounce

TESSA BAILEY

BROKE AND BEAUTIFUL SERIES
Chase Me
Need Me
Make Me

CORA CARMACK
Losing It
Keeping Her: A Losing It Novella
Faking It
Finding It
Seeking Her: A Finding It Novella

THE RUSK UNIVERSITY SERIES
All Lined Up
All Broke Down
All Played Out

JAY CROWNOVER

THE MARKED MEN SERIES
Rule   Jet
Rome   Nash
Rowdy   Asa

WELCOME TO THE POINT SERIES
Better When He's Bad
Better When He's Bold
Better When He's Brave

RONNIE DOUGLAS
Undaunted

SOPHIE JORDAN

THE IVY CHRONICLES
Foreplay
Tease
Wild

MOLLY MCADAMS
From Ashes
Needing Her: A From Ashes Novella

TAKING CHANCES SERIES
Taking Chances
Stealing Harper: A Taking Chances Novella
Trusting Liam

FORGIVING LIES SERIES
Forgiving Lies
Deceiving Lies
Changing Everything

SHARING YOU SERIES
Capturing Peace
Sharing You

THATCH SERIES
Letting Go
To the Stars

CAISEY QUINN

THE NEON DREAMS SERIES
Leaving Amarillo
Loving Dallas
Missing Dixie

JAMIE SHAW

MAYHEM SERIES
Mayhem
Riot
Chaos

Available in Paperback and eBook Wherever Books are Sold
Visit Facebook.com/NewAdultBooks
Twitter.com/BtwnCoversWM